THE US Review
of Books

Companions
by Larry Rhodes
DreamWriters Media

book review by Gretchen Hansen

"Once they sat with their food trays, Julia blurted out, 'It's kind of weird knowing your main competition is a series of beautiful automations.'"

Jim's life is humming along nicely. He has a lucrative job in his field of AI and a girlfriend. Although he would not complain about his current situation, it isn't what anyone would consider adventurous. This is about to change in ways he can't even imagine. An acquaintance presents him with an intriguing offer to work on cutting-edge technology for a renowned company. They are, in fact, looking for someone with Jim's expertise in AI to perfect their product.

Alder Industries Projects is more than a curious venture. They are developing life-like "companions." These robots look and move like humans. Jim's job is to make them interact with people. After he completes their programming, he will train them for several months to ensure they provide an experience as close to a real companion as possible. His new reality starts to imitate a strange sci-fi fantasy but in a good way. Each generation of companions is an improved model as the team advances their programming knowledge, and Jim learns how to develop them.

Rhodes is a skillful writer, and his book's narrative is quick-paced without compromising depth. The characters are developed through intelligent dialogue. The author presents intriguing scenarios that provide a tasteful touch of sensuality. He also presents enough details about the process of creating the robots to satisfy readers who love science without weighing down the human story. This novel will appeal to fans of science fiction and drama, and readers will have a difficult time putting this book down. There is no doubt Rhodes will gain new fans who will devour each page.

COMPANIONS

LARRY RHODES

ISBN
979-8-9905720-1-0 (Hardcover)
979-8-9905720-0-3 (Paperback)
979-8-9905720-2-7 (eBook)

TABLE OF CONTENTS

CHAPTER 1

A New Project

Jim McVie hurried into the "Urban Potions" bar just after 6 PM to meet an old friend he had known since high school. He was a little surprised at the request to meet as they hadn't seen each other in almost two years and had only occasionally texted each other. This was his day off and he had decided to take a ride-share to the bar in case they celebrated too much. The traffic in Houston, Texas was lighter than normal, and he was a little early. This bar was only a few blocks from his current workplace, and he often visited it after work. He even recognized a female colleague and sat down at the bar next to her. She glanced at him.

"Hi Jim."

Mary Stanton was casually acquainted with Jim McVie and somewhat attracted to him. Jim was in his early 30s like her and seemed to keep fit. She was attracted to his hazel eyes and close-cropped light brown hair. She also knew that Jim was in a long-term relationship.

Jim had chatted with her at work, and even though he thought she was attractive, Jim didn't pursue her because of his 10-year relationship with Beth.

They chatted briefly until Jim thought he saw Miguel Herrera enter and start looking around for him. Miguel had a large dark beard now and he wasn't sure for a moment until he turned toward him. "Oh, my friend is here. I'll see you later."

Jim waved him over and they shook hands and Jim was surprised when Miguel hugged him. Miguel spotted an empty table and motioned him to follow him to the table.

Jim rubbed his face with a huge question mark until Miguel laughed. "How long have you had that?"

"Almost two years, just after the last time you saw me."

It was noisy in the bar and after they both ordered a Margarita, Miguel leaned over "Are you still working for Horizon AI?"

Jim nodded. "Yes, my two-year contract expired, but I was able to get a one-year extension, but it only has one week left. So, I've been looking for a new opportunity, but AI programming jobs aren't that easy to find in Houston."

"Why don't you try Austin, that's a big tech hub, isn't it?"

"Yes, but I'm still with Beth, and her business is located here."

"I have something I want to talk to you about, but how is Beth? You must be with her for almost nine years now."

"We've been together almost ten years."

"Wow, that's great!"

"How about you, still with Maria?"

Miguel laughed. "No that ended more than two years ago. We both traveled a lot in our jobs and were like two ships passing in the night. I've even had a few girlfriends since then. But work always seems to doom my relationships."

"Sorry to hear that. So, what are you doing now that requires so much travel?"

"I work for a company that makes synthetic skin. We started out providing temporary patches for wounds from accidents or fires and eventually into more complex patches for chronic wounds. Those applications are somewhat limited, so we branched out into skin coverings for all sorts of things." He laughed. "Even dolls."

Jim frowned. "Dolls?"

Miguel sipped his drink. "Yes, dolls. I'm talking about dolls for guys, not little girls."

"For guys? You mean sex dolls?"

"Yes. It's a growing market." They both laughed. Then Miguel leaned over and said very softly "I have one."

Jim was incredulous. "Are you serious?"

"Yes, I visited several manufacturers who were interested in our latest offerings. Several of them gave me the grand tour, and one of them almost gave me one of their most advanced models. You wouldn't believe what's available today if you want one. Some of these guys are even working on adding AI to some of their mechanical dolls."

Jim just shook his head. "AI? In a doll?"

"Yes, one of their software engineers commented that an AI enhanced model could cost more than ten thousand dollars."

"Ten thousand dollars! For a doll, are you serious?"

Miguel smiled. "Yes, and that's why I wanted to meet up with you. I've heard about a new project in Houston that needs a programmer. It seems regular programmers are a dime a dozen these days and they all want to work from home. But AI programmers are still few and far between. This new project is in Houston, involves AI and is mostly on-site work so I thought about you. How much longer do you have before you can interview?"

"Well, I could interview now and could be available in a week or so. What's the nature of the project? It's not AI dolls I hope."

"I don't have all the details, but there is some serious money involved. We were asked to quote our most advanced synthetic skin made of Silicone, so it's serious."

"Silicone? Why is it so expensive?"

"Silicone can contain various types of sensors, including temperature, and you need that if you are need to control the skin temperature."

"Interesting. Do you have a contact, or a phone number?"

"Better than that." He handed Jim a very plain business card for Eric Thorne. It didn't list the company name, only his title as Project Manager, and an office phone number.

Jim stared at it. "No company name?"

"I think it's just a project, so it's not a permanent position. But I thought you might like to try something different. I even heard it may be a three-year assignment."

"I really appreciate you thinking of me. I'll give them a call today."

"That's great. Hope you find it interesting."

"By the way, what is the name of your company – in case they ask who referred me?"

Miguel smiled. "Skin So Soft."

Jim laughed. "What?"

Miguel handed him one of his business cards. "It was the CEO's idea. I hate it, but it pays well." Miguel looked at his watch. "Oh, I have to go."

He stood up and held out his hand. "More dolls to visit."

Jim just shook his head when he stood up to shake Miguel's hand. "What a job…"

Miguel left and Jim stared at Eric Thorne's business card. He took a deep breath and walked outside the noisy bar to call the number.

CHAPTER 2

A Quick Hire

Jim straightened his tie as he entered the Winstone Office Tower for the job interview. He glanced at his reflection in the door glass and hurried to the information and security station. He gave his name and Eric's name and was handed a security pass. He entered the elevator, swiped the card key, and pressed the button for the 25th floor. He wasn't late yet but the traffic, as always on a weekday, had been extremely slow, and he was concerned about the time as he glanced at his watch.

He probably had walked by the Winstone Office Tower dozens of times, but knew little about it, so he researched it. It was a 50-story mixed use building in the central business district. The first 25 floors were offices, and the upper 25 floors were condominiums and apartments. The top floor contained four penthouse condominiums.

The interview would be held at the Adler Industries Projects headquarters. He wasn't familiar with that company and looked them up as well. Adler Industries was founded about 30 years ago by Hugh Adler who patented several innovations in farm equipment and began selling his newly designed equipment all over the world. They currently had manufacturing plants in several locations: a sugarcane harvesting equipment plant in Louisiana, a wheat harvesting equipment plant in Kansas, a sugar cane and coffee beans harvesting equipment plant in Brazil and even a rice harvesting equipment plant in Thailand.

The door opened on the 25th floor and he followed signs to the Adler Industries Projects office. He was surprised that there was no one else in the waiting room and the pretty, dark hair and dark eyed receptionist smiled and immediately handed him another security badge and directed him to an interview room. He did notice a service award on the wall near her, given to "Kishori Littlebear" and thought that was an interesting name.

Three interviewers were waiting and after quick introductions they motioned him to a seat. All three were wearing business suits and looked, to Jim, like successful and impatient businessmen. There were nameplates in front of them and Eric Thorne was seated in the middle, probably early 50s, with touches of grey in otherwise dark hair.

Eric Thorne introduced himself as the project manager and led the interview and asked how Jim had heard of the job opening. Jim replied that Miguel Herrera, a friend, had referred him. After briefly reviewing his qualifications, and noting that Jim lived in Houston, Eric asked what he knew about the project.

"Only that it could be a three-year assignment, that involves Artificial Intelligence and robotics. I have some experience programming assembly line robots with an AI system that with time generated suggestions on ways to streamline their work process. This eventually resulted in a 25% improvement in productivity."

Eric smiled. "That's all you heard?"

Jim frowned. "There was some scuttlebutt that the robots might have a human-like appearance, probably to reduce other workers reluctance to work alongside robots. From my experience that really hasn't been a problem."

"Have you kept abreast of the latest AI chip enhancements?"

"Yes, they are getting increasingly faster and capable of storing or accessing vast amounts of reference data, especially from the Internet. The latest chips are amazingly fast and complex."

"This isn't a work from home type assignment. Is that a problem?"

"No, my last employer also required on-site work."

"What's your availability?"

"My last project just ended, so I can start whenever you want."

"Could you excuse us for a moment?"

"Sure." Jim exited the room and the interviewers huddled. It seemed only a few minutes to Jim, but they quickly called him back. When he sat, one of the interviewers handed him two documents.

"Congratulations, we are pleased to offer you a programming position on the project, subject to your agreement and signature on the contract and especially on the Non-Disclosure Agreement."

Jim was shocked at the quick decision but quickly signed both. The salary numbers also jumped out at him. One million dollars over three years! That was almost a 100% increase over his salary at his last assignment.

Eric walked over to him and shook his hand. "Welcome to the project. We have a routine monthly project meeting scheduled for tomorrow and we would like you to attend if that's possible. I know this is pretty short notice."

"Oh, It's fine. I'll be there."

The other two people shook Jim's hand, and he left on a high note. *Wait until Beth hears about this.* He thought.

He took a ride-share home thinking about what he would tell his girlfriend. She was always complaining that he never had a permanent programming job and changed jobs every two years or so. He also had a few short-term assignments that caused him to be away for several months at a time, and they almost broke up a few times. This project offered a huge increase in salary, but it also was a solid three-year assignment. He wondered if there was a factory somewhere he would have to visit to observe the operation of the robotic assembly line. He wouldn't even have much time to worry about that as he started the next morning.

He had been told to report at 8AM for some HR type onboarding prior to the project meeting which was supposed to start at 10AM. He was pleasantly surprised that the temporary position included health insurance, and even a 401k matching program. He had not been offered these benefits while working on prior projects.

He made it to the project status meeting on time, but it was already underway in a large conference room with Eric leading the discussion. Eric paused to introduce Jim to the team of ten people and then continued with an agenda displayed on a large TV screen behind him. He also asked each team member to identify themselves and their company and to help bring Jim up to speed when they updated the rest of the team.

Jim was a little lost at first as various team members reported status. It began with what Jim seemed to think were non-essential items as required changes to the work areas, and a report on some new hardware that had just arrived, like Jim's high-end computer. It didn't take too long to figure out that the project had been underway for six months and he had been brought in when programming had to begin to meet certain time requirements. He missed the reference the first few times when the word "Companion" was used.

When Eric commented that based on the latest cost data, the hardware value alone of a Companion would probably be valued at more than five million dollars, it caught Jim's attention.

After an hour or so, there was a quick break and Jim had a chance to talk to Eric. He was surprised when Eric handed him several folders. "There was a pre-project team that did a lot of preliminary work on the required abilities and skills, and they identified a rather large number of modules that needed to be programmed. Based on what I heard today, some of these will be needed in about three months. I hope that isn't a problem."

Jim was scanning a list of required modules with brief descriptions that went on for dozens of pages. He was about to ask about priority, when the team returned, and Eric re-convened the meeting. The last page of the folder contained a summary of the "Companions", their names, the names of the recipients, the recipient's country, or city, even the Companion's hair and eye color.

Companion	Recipient Area	Country/City	Recipient	Height	Skin	Eyes	Hair
Emily	N. America	US	Hugh Adler	5'4"	Light	Blue	Blond
Gabriela	S. America	Brazil	Carlos Alvez	5'2"	Tanned	Brown	DK Brown
Wei	Chinese	Re-routed	Wang Chen	5'3"	Light	Dk Brown	Brown
Amara	India	Bangalore	Arjun Kumar	5'1"	Tanned	Brown	Dk Brown
Mila	E. Europe	Poland	Marcin Budny	5'6"	Light	Blue	Dk Blond
Bai	Chinese	Re-routed	Bao Zhu	5'3"	Light	DK Brown	Brown
Aiko	Japanese	Tokyo	Hinata Soto	5'2"	Light	Blue	Brown
Astrid	Europe	Norway	Amund Dahl	5'6"	Light	Blue	Blond
Jaana	Africa	Ethiopia	Ahmed Alemu	5'2"	Ebony	Dk Brown	Black
Meera	India	Delhi	Kabir Chopra	5'1"	Tanned	Brown	Dk Brown

Jason Meads, a mechanical engineer from Technical Structures, reported on the status of the skeletons required for the Companions. As a background for Jim, he said they were currently being manufactured of the latest form of Graphene, a new material that was extremely light yet stronger than the equivalent made of steel or titanium, and delivery was imminent. He further reported that design work had been completed for the "body modules" that would attach to the skeletons and basically form the shape of the arms, legs, torso, head, etc. of a human-like structure. He also said delivery of some of these body parts was imminent and based on the project priority schedule.

Jules Armond, a representative of a synthetic skin company (Nu Skin, not Skin So Soft) reported on the production of the outer skin layer and the myriad of sensors in the skin that had to be frequently monitored in software for status to the "brain" of the Companions. He said delivery of the first product was imminent. He also mentioned that the skins would be consistent with the country of the designated recipients. Jim paused his notetaking to think about that for a moment and looked again at the Companion list.

Sarah Townsend, a computer hardware engineer and representative of Synthesis AI, a chip manufacturer, gave the latest delivery and performance specifications of a new chip, which quickly caught Jim's attention. This was vastly more powerful than anything on the market, and was even described by the representative as experimental, with anticipated delivery in less than a week.

Julia Cardenas, a mechanical engineer, and representative of Future Power reported on the latest Graphene batteries under development that were much more powerful than equivalent Lithium batteries based on size and weight. They would also recharge in a fraction of the time required for Lithium batteries. She said the batteries should be available in a few weeks.

Jonas Romano, also a mechanical engineer from Mechanical Senses, described the latest eye hardware, voice and hearing systems to be delivered in a few weeks.

Jim was thinking about the list of modules that had been identified by the pre-project team, and it suddenly dawned on him that they were building very advanced human-like robots for a specific reason.

When there was a presentation pause, Jim asked Eric about the scope of the work.

"Eric, why are we doing this? I have a friend who had several failed relationships, and he obtained a robot sex doll for less than $10,000. Why is the projected value of a Companion's hardware over five million dollars?"

Some of the project team members snickered before Eric answered.

"We aren't building sex toys or sex robots, but actual human-like Companions. The goal is that you won't be able to tell the difference between a Companion and a real human. That's light years ahead of the currently available dolls or robot dolls or even the AI enhanced dolls you're probably talking about. Yes, sex is part of the final product but only a part of the overall Companion's activities."

Jim was still not sure how his programming and all the advanced hardware he had just heard described, would enable a robot to pass as human. He just shook his head and continued to make notes. He did notice that each time he looked at the other participants in the meeting, the power engineer was smiling at him. After a few times, he instinctively smiled back.

As the meeting ended, Eric commented he had to hurry to another meeting, where the project's finances were being reviewed. The other participants started chatting and filtering out of the conference room and Jim sat for a while reading the list of "modules" as Eric called them, each describing a function or feature of a Companion. Some were simple and obvious; others were much more complicated or not so obvious.

Jim looked up, thinking about the programming required and saw the female engineer who described the power system still sitting across from him at the conference table and smiling at him. She had a pretty face and long dark curly hair and dark eyes and was wearing a blue lab coat. Jim was instantly attracted to her, and if he wasn't still in a relationship, he might have immediately looked for an opening to ask her out. She wasn't wearing any rings, but he knew that wasn't always an indication she was in a relationship or not.

"Quite a lot to take in on the first day." She commented.

Jim smiled. "Hi, Jim McVie."

"I know. Julia Cardenas. We've been expecting someone like you for some time. I'm sure the programming required seems a little overwhelming at this point."

Jim glanced down at the folder. "Looks like more than 3000 programming modules."

"Actually, I heard more than 4,000." She moved to a chair near Jim. "It looks like Eric didn't fill you in on the project background."

"There wasn't time. Would you have a minute to give me the highlights?"

"I would, but I should warn you, if Eric heard what I'm about to say, he would think I'm biased about the whole thing, because I'm a woman."

Jim frowned. "What?"

"The project originator, and founder, is Hugh Adler. Many years ago, he invented several farm implements that were very innovative and soon in great demand. He started a company that sold this farm equipment all over the world, and for almost 30 years he made a great deal of money and friends in many countries. His wife died about ten years ago and Mr. Adler was very lonely. He had a lot of money, some estimates put it at over three billion dollars, but he has said several times it doesn't always make you happy. So about five years ago, he started a team to review existing hardware and software with the idea of building a human-like Companion."

She stopped when it was obvious that Jim wanted to ask a question, so she asked it for him. "Does the Companion also provide sex in addition to all the other ways people seek the company of others? As Eric said, the answer is yes."

Jim didn't say anything, so she continued. "He wants a Companion to be so human-like, passersby could not tell that she is not human."

"That explains a lot, but not all the modules. Some are obvious like motion, walking, talking, everything we take for granted."

Julia nodded. "Adler told us at the first project meeting, he had to wait for AI hardware that could handle all the interactions we go through every day, and he paid to have a very advanced AI processor built, just for this project at a tremendous cost."

"I noticed there are 10 Companions listed, is he going to sell them?"

"No, Adler has selected nine of his closest business associates, who are also his friends, for the others. All these friends are not married or were married like Adler and then their wife died, or they were divorced, and are now single. "

"Why ten and not fifteen? Does he only have nine close friends?"

"No." She laughed. "There actually was a price break from some of the companies you heard from today if you order a minimum of ten products. And the final product will be super expensive per unit as you have guessed."

Jim smiled, then thought for a moment. "So, what do you object to, as a woman? Is it the fact that there are no male Companions, from what I can tell so far."

"Partly. I immediately asked this, and Adler said he didn't have any close friends who are businesswomen AND might be interested in a male Companion, or a female Companion for that matter."

"Is that all?"

"No. Partly it's the fact that all the Companions are going to be so beautiful. I also asked about that, and Adler said these senior guys would probably not want one if they were just average looking. I objected to that, but he just shrugged it off with 'the cost would be the same' and 'nothing wrong with being beautiful' type answers. A few days later I received a text message with several links to companies that make your sex dolls or robot sex dolls, just so I could see what he was talking about. He said these could be considered 'the competition'."

"They are not my sex dolls. I don't have one and have never even seen one."

"That's just an expression."

"So, is that all, or are there other issues?"

"I had a lot, so finally, Adler gave me the number of Gerald Hawes, the head of his public relations and communications department to call. He said he had been discussing this project with him for a long time, and he would have a response for all my 'issues'. So, I called him, and he began a long list of all the activities in the world that would not be affected if a few rich people purchased a Companion. I finally had to interrupt him. He then asked if I could name one human activity that would change if a hundred or even five hundred rich men or women were able to spend millions of dollars to obtain a Companion."

"What did you say?"

"After thinking about it for some time, I really couldn't think of anything that would change. People would still go on dating web sites; they would still meet people in bars or in churches or at work or on social media or wherever people find the person they want to be with."

"So, did that resolve your issues with working on the project?"

"Most of them, I guess. At first glance this project seemed to be constructing just another sex Companion, much like the one you mentioned, that your friend obtained. If that were all this was, I wouldn't continue to participate."

"So, it's more than that?"

"Yes, If Adler wanted a doll, he could just buy one, and not spend more than a hundred million dollars."

"One hundred million?"

"Yes, the salaries of the key project team members and consultants are probably thirty to forty million alone – over three years."

"I would bet he spent at least ten million for those custom AI chips."

"I'm sure you're right. The custom batteries and some spares are more than ten million. The custom Graphene skeletons and related body parts are probably more than ten million. The outer skin coverings from Nu Skin are probably more than a million each. The rent for the offices in this building over three years is probably twenty million or more. And so on." She thought about it for a minute. "I hadn't really added it all up. The total is probably more than one hundred and fifty million."

Jim just shook his head. "Adler must be really lonely."

Julia laughed. "I think it's more than that. I think it's more of a challenge at this point. Many people told him it would never work and he's wasting his time and money. That made him more determined to complete the project." She stared at him for a minute. "You probably haven't seen them yet."

"Seen what?"

"Apparently, the company rep didn't even know it, but the Graphene skeletons arrived two days ago. They're in the lab. Would you like to see them?"

"We can do that?"

"Of course, we're on the project team. We couldn't if we weren't."

"Then let's go."

CHAPTER 3

The Lab

Julia led him to the laboratory. In his discussion with HR, they had given him some basic project information, like the location of the lab and offices and unexpectedly, keys to an apartment. Each project team member had an assigned apartment that they could use whenever they needed to be on-site for extended testing or multi-day meetings or anything project related. These were included at no cost to the team members and located on the upper floors of the Winstone Office Tower, while the project and laboratory work areas were on the top of the office floors.

Julia swiped her card key, and they entered the "lab" which was a huge area divided into many rooms that, in total, probably filled most of the entire floor of the building. Each room contained equipment for a specific purpose. She led him down a hallway to a room in the back where ten Graphene skeletons were "standing" in a row, held up by almost invisible wires.

All the skeletons were black and had an almost mirror-like finish. "This is Graphene?"

"Yes. It's a form of carbon that is much lighter than any other material you could make a skeleton from. It's also stronger than steel."

She paused. "You probably know the inside of a pencil is a form of carbon known as Graphite. This is also carbon but in a different physical structure. The body parts are made of an extremely light polymer. Adler wants the final Companion to be no heavier than a typical female of the targeted country of the recipient."

Jim smiled, and Julia continued. "Yes, in case they take turns being on top." They both laughed.

Two of the skeletons had body modules with motors already installed on the arms and legs, head and neck, chest, and torso and two technicians from Technical Structures were installing the body modules on the third and as he looked down the row of skeletons, Jim noticed they weren't all the same height.

"I had assumed they would all be the same size to keep costs down, until I saw the specification sheet."

Julia was examining the nearest skeleton. "The average height of a Companion was originally supposed to be representative of that geographic area, so the Chinese and Japanese Companions would have been a little shorter. The actual height difference for all of them is only a few inches, so I think the decision was to keep the upper torsos alike and vary the length of the legs to make up the height differences. That is supposed to help minimize the cost of different skeletons. The maximum difference is really only five inches anyway, so you probably can't tell by looking at them unless they are all standing together, like they are now. You wouldn't see any difference if they were all seated at a table for example."

Jim began to examine one with all the body parts. Each skeleton was an almost exact copy of a typical human skeleton and with the body parts installed looked very much like robots he had seen in pictures. The eyes and ears had not been installed and that seemed kind of creepy to Jim.

The robots he had worked on were very basic metal structures and usually served a single function on an assembly line. Most workers on the line paid no attention to the robot assemblers working on the same line.

Julia stood near him and started describing the power required by the motors in the arms, legs, torso, and head. Her perfume slowly crept into his brain.

"That sounds like a lot of power will be needed. How long can they go between re-charges?"

"That depends, of course, on what they are doing. If they are watching TV or just sitting around waiting for the recipient to ask them to do something, then probably 24 hours. If they were walking around all the time, then probably 8 to 10 hours."

Jim smiled at her, and she laughed. "At least six hours for nocturnal activities." They both laughed again.

Jim started examining a skeleton with all the body parts in place. "Where is the charging port?"

Julia was standing near one with all the body parts and pointed to a small opening in the front, that likely would be integral to a navel. "I think there will be a charging port built in there that also serves as the programming port. "

"Is there anything else besides the eyes and ears that has to be installed except for the outer skin covering?"

"Yes, there are some items that are Companion specific." She laughed. "Like the size of their bosom and rear ends. It sounds crazy but the butt must be made of a very specific and expensive material as she will sit on it for long periods of time, and you don't want that to get flattened."

Jim laughed. He wanted to know more about the power requirements, but she was standing very close to him, and her perfume was too distracting. "Ok, have you seen the forward schedule for programming?"

"No, I'm sure Eric has one though. You'll have to ask him."

She glanced at her watch. "Oh, I have a hardware meeting to run to. I'll see you later." She left and Jim continued to examine the skeletons.

Each day, Jim passed the pretty receptionist who always smiled at him. If he wasn't in a committed relationship, he would have tried to find a way to ask her out. But he was, and he didn't.

A week later, he happened to be in the break room, when Kishori came in with another office assistant and saw Jim at a table in the corner. She whispered something to her friend who poured some coffee and left the break room. Kishori poured a cup of coffee and walked quietly to Jim's table. He looked up. "Hi."

"Anyone sitting here?"

He shook his head. He had wondered about her but never really spoken to her. They chatted for a while about the project until she had to get back to the front desk. Jim watched her leave and sat wondering about her. A little while later Eric stopped by his workstation to see if Jim needed anything else for his computer, and Jim shook his head. He didn't know if he should ask, but he asked about Kishori.

Eric guessed why he was asking. "Years ago, when Hugh Adler began to make a lot of money in his farm equipment business in Kansas, he began to donate to local charities. Some of those were Native American charities trying to help with food and fuel and clothing for elderly members of the tribes. Hugh became good friends with some of the charity organizers and eventually offered jobs to some of them. Two of them accepted jobs in Houston, Kishori Littlebear and her brother Avonaco."

Eric smiled. "Her brother works in a building near here for a security company. I've met him, he seems nice. Do you want me to do something?"

"No, I'm in a long-term relationship. It's sort of shaky right now, but I need to see it through."

Eric shrugged. "Okay, let me know if you need anything else for your workstation."

A few days later, Kishori subtlety asked Eric about Jim, and Eric passed on Jim's being- in-a-relationship reply. She was disappointed but didn't show it to Eric.

Two weeks passed as Jim continued to code modules from a priority list sent by Eric in a text. Somedays, Julia would stop by his workstation office and invite him to lunch in a large upscale cafeteria on the first floor of the Winstone Tower Office building. He gradually came to know her fairly well. She was on loan to the project from Future Power in an arrangement where her company continued to pay her benefits, while the project paid her salary. Any innovations or improvements to their products resulting from the project were the property of Future Power. More importantly, her years of service with the company also continued to accrue. The only requirement to maintain the arrangement was her attendance at two semi-annual technical reviews.

She was currently single mainly due to her dedication to improving her company's Graphene batteries. Over five years, she had been awarded a significant number of shares of stock of Future Power, which was currently in negotiations with several Electric Vehicle manufacturers to supply as many as a million batteries. That deal would make the company a fortune and all the current stockholders financially secure, including her. As a result of their lunch chats, she knew Jim was in a long-term relationship but was happy to just have someone to eat lunch with. They were surprised that they both were native Houstonians and grew up in nearby neighborhoods.

They had just returned from a morning break in a small break room area in the lab when Eric entered the workstation room looking for Jim. "Hey Jim, Mr. Adler is here to review some project financials and wants to meet with you. He has a few minutes before the presentation. Can you come now?"

Jim was surprised that Adler wanted to meet him, but quickly agreed. "Of course."

CHAPTER 4

Hugh Adler

Hugh Adler was waiting in the original interview room, seated at a small table with two chairs and a stack of folders. He was wearing a well-tailored suit and with a few streaks of gray hair led Jim to think of someone in finance, possibly a banker, not the CEO of a farm equipment company and its founder. He remembered Julia's background description and that Adler spent most of his time on a large farm in Kansas, even though his corporate headquarters were in Houston, and he owned one of the four penthouses on the top floor of the Winstone Office Tower, for when he was in town.

Adler looked up when Jim entered and waved him in. "I've heard a lot about you, Jim."

"You shouldn't believe everything you hear."

Adler laughed and motioned him to sit. "I've heard you have some concerns about the nature of the project, and I thought I would try to dispel them."

Jim wondered if he was in trouble, somehow. "Thanks for your time."

"Eric reviewed an earlier monthly project meeting with me and suggested you think we are here to build sex toys or sex robots or some such thing. I want to let you know that isn't the case. If that's all I wanted, we wouldn't be here. I want a true Companion, so human-like, the vast majority of people could pass her on the street and have no idea who or what she is."

"I'm sure you've answered this many times, but why not meet someone at a church group, or a social club?"

"I've tried that, and the women there in my age group are already in a relationship, or, it seems, not interested in a new relationship."

"I'm surprised you aren't inundated with beautiful young women looking for a 'sugar daddy'."

"I have been, but I'm not interested in companionship based on what I can give them, or where I can take them on vacation."

"How about social media, or on-line dating sites?"

"I've tried that too. The person who shows up is never anything like what they pretend to be." He paused. "What's your experience with on-line dating?"

"Fortunately, I've been in a relationship for almost ten years, so almost no experience with that."

"You are extremely lucky." He tapped the top folder for a few seconds. "Do you think I would spend almost 200 million dollars if there were a viable alternative to what I want. Not necessarily what other men want?"

He paused. "In fact, I really don't care what other men want, or how they find the person they want to share their life with, and I'm willing to pay for what I want. So, are you on board with helping me find my ideal Companion? The interactive programming that will be required is probably as important, if not more important, than the hardware you heard described in your first project meeting."

Jim had never been put on the spot like that. But now that he knew the full scope of the project, he wanted it to succeed.

"Yes, sir. I'll do everything I can to make your Companion as human-like as possible."

"That's great. I needed to get that out of the way, so we can talk about the other reason for this meeting."

Jim frowned. "Which is what?"

"You've probably received a list of programming functions from Eric and the pre-project team, but there are many more that I have thought of and that is really the primary reason for the meeting today. First, I'm assuming the hardware isn't an issue. I've been told the custom chips that have been built specifically for this project would allow essentially unlimited memory and functionality. If that's not the case, then I need to know now."

"To my knowledge, there shouldn't be anything that can't be programmed for a Companion. Assuming the hardware is adequate."

"That's good." Adler picked up a folder and opened it and handed a page to Jim.

It was an additional list of functionalities on top of the 4000 or so modules he had already been given and started to work on.

Adler watched Jim scan the list for a moment. "Let me pick one at random. Could a Companion put on a two-piece bathing suit all by herself?"

Jim thought about it. "That would be done in the overall clothing routine of dressing and undressing, so yes."

"Ok, something a little less obvious. I know the AI system can learn. Could she remember something that was said or told to her the previous day? I'm thinking a Companion should be a good listener and able to respond to questions or things previously discussed."

"The short answer is yes. She would need a reference system to be able to sort the information in conversations into important and general blathering. We could build one, if you think that's important for her relationships with other people."

Adler nodded and laughed. "Sounds like you have the programming under control. Any issue with meeting the preliminary schedule Eric gave you that will allow the hardware to be tested in a few months?"

"No, most of the early stuff is already done. The company that is providing the body parts has also worked with AI programmers on other projects and gave us over a hundred modules on the very basic functions, like walking and talking, and other basic movements involving their hardware. Some of those modules could provide over 90% of what we need for that functionality, and that helped a lot."

"That's wonderful news. Keep up the good work. Feel free to contact me with any programming issues that you think Eric is not keeping on top of." He stood up and held out his hand, and Jim shook it, then asked one last question.

"Could I ask you one final question?"

"Yes."

"I understand why you want a Companion, why are you building nine other really expensive Companions for friends and business associates?"

Adler smiled. "It's sort of a business decision. The recipients are friends and really good customers. If I give them a Companion, and it works out like I hope it does, they will owe me big time, in ways that I don't think I can even explain."

Jim laughed. "Okay, I get it."

Adler looked at his watch. "Oh, my financial review meeting with some lawyers and investors is about to start."

"Investors? I thought you have said the Companions would not be manufactured and sold to just anyone, even if they could afford it, like some Gulf States princes."

"That's correct. This is about potential copyright and IP patents that might result from this project. We want to talk about those opportunities."

"Oh, that's actually a great idea!"

"Yes, well, thanks again for the update." He gathered up his things and headed for the door. Jim sat for a moment thinking. He was glad to get some grey area aspects of the project cleared up.

CHAPTER 5

Relationships

Jim had barely returned to his workstation when Julia stopped by. "I heard you had a 'Come to Jesus' type meeting with Adler. How did that go?"

Jim laughed. "Rumors travel really fast around here. I was actually glad he explained his reasons and purpose for the project."

Julia looked at her watch. "It's almost lunch. Why don't we talk more about this in the cafeteria?"

They went to the large upscale cafeteria on the first floor of the Winstone Office Tower where many team members often continued project discussions over lunch.

As soon as they sat down to eat, Julia was about to quiz Jim on his meeting with Adler but remembered something else.

"So, I want to hear all about your meeting with Adler, but first I wanted to see if you knew about the bonus schedule."

"What bonus schedule?"

"Every three months, a special team assembled by Adler and Eric evaluate the project team members and the staff, and if the feedback is positive, they receive up to a bonus equal to 5% of their annual pay. You've haven't been here three months yet, but the bonus team has been known to make exceptions. Pretty cool, huh?"

Jim seemed sad or depressed about something and didn't answer right away.

"Most people would be overjoyed about free money. There must be something bothering you. Is it the meeting with Adler?"

"No, that went really well."

"Then what is it?"

"My girlfriend sort of broke up with me again last night."

Julia was shocked. "The one you said you were with for almost 10 years. What happened?"

"Somehow, she found out about the scope of the project. Not the details of course, but she confronted me with it. I tried to explain it to her without breaking my NDA, but she said she couldn't be with someone who helps make sex toys for old guys."

Julia laughed until she realized he was serious. "How did she find out about the project?"

"Someone sent her an email on a non-business account with enough information that she decided to find out if it's true."

"Sorry to hear that. The project really has nothing to do with her, or the two of you as a couple, so there must be more than that."

"She has a successful clothing line for women and is traveling all the time and it we don't see each other very much. We've taken a few time outs in the past but somehow always managed to work things out and get back together. I'm not sure that will happen this time."

"Could she be seeing someone else, who maybe wanted her all for himself?"

"I don't think so. I've never had any indication she's seeing someone else."

"Would anyone on the project know her private email account?"

"I don't know. She's had that private email account for years. I guess someone could look her up and find it if they really wanted to."

Julia wanted to drop the breakup issue but also didn't feel it was appropriate to discuss Jim's meeting with Adler.

"Ok, on a different subject, there's going to be an after-work drinks and food party for those that receive the bonus, coincidentally at your favorite bar, Urban Potions."

"How did you know that's my favorite bar?"

"The bartender is a friend of mine. And it's only a few blocks from here. So, are you in?"

He didn't have anything better to do, and there probably wouldn't be anyone at home, but he wondered if he qualified. "I have only been here about two months, so I'm probably not eligible."

"They can make exceptions if they want to. So, are you in if you get one?"

"Sure, why not."

Julia had finished her meal and stood up to leave. "Great, I'll probably see you there at 6 PM."

Around 4 PM Jim received a text from Eric informing him that he had been evaluated by a special compensation team and awarded a 5% bonus that would be deposited directly in his bank account. The text also informed him of the party for the bonus recipients at Urban Potions. He felt relieved that his performance so far had been evaluated and judged worthy of a bonus.

Jim entered the Urban Potions bar at precisely 6 PM and to his surprise there were only five other project team members there. He wondered if he was too early or if all the other project team members and staff had not been awarded bonuses. Julia came out of the bathroom area, saw him, and gave him a big hug.

"I knew you'd get a bonus."

"You obviously did too. Where is everyone else?"

She looked around and shrugged. "I don't know, I guess the competition this year was tougher than last year. Let's find a table."

As soon as they sat, a server delivered a charcuterie tray to their table and two bottles of beer. Julia commented. "Everyone gets that, you can get whatever else you want."

They chatted for a long time and Jim didn't realize how much they had drunk until he noticed four empty bottles of beer in front of him and a similar number in front of Julia. He looked around and found only two project people left in the bar. Julia noticed him surveying the bar. She looked at her watch.

"Oh, it's getting pretty late. Would you mind walking me back to the Tower building? I think I'm going to stay there tonight instead of going all the way back to my apartment."

Jim remembered his breakup with Beth. "I think I'll do the same as there's no point going back to my place anymore."

Julia was a little dizzy when she put her hand on his. "Time heals almost all wounds – or something like that."

Jim checked with the bartender and confirmed they didn't owe anything for their part of the night's food and drink party held for only a few members of the project team.

When they returned to the Tower building, Julia was leaning against him while they waited for an elevator. He was a little concerned. "Are you alright?"

She looked up at him. "I'd be better if you stayed with me tonight."

Jim started to laugh until he realized she meant it. "Are you sure? That might be the alcohol talking. You might think differently tomorrow morning."

"I'm 100% sure."

They rode in silence to the 45th floor where most of the project's apartments assigned to the team members were located.

She took his arm. "This way."

Once inside they started kissing and eventually wound up in bed. There were a lot of things he didn't know about her, but those possible issues seemed to fade away as the night continued.

The next morning, she asked him to not let the night change their professional relationship on the project. "Last night was great, but going forward, let's just play it by ear."

CHAPTER 6

Emily

Days seemed to fly by as Jim programmed modules in the priority list given by Eric. Most were basic functions, with a few additional ones. Jim could program the modules from a high-end computer in a room in the lab set aside for programming and testing. He could also "work from home" as the modules were uploaded to a cloud and available anywhere with appropriate access. Home in this case was the project provided apartment, as he really didn't want to go back to his old apartment with all the memories of his time with Beth. Eric didn't mind him working from his project apartment as he could find him after a short elevator ride if he needed to.

As soon as a Companion's body parts were completed, Jim could connect a laptop to the navel area port and begin basic testing such as walking and sitting. When the vocal and hearing components were added, he could talk to them, and they could run internal diagnostic programs and report back on possible issues with sensors in the skin or other technical or communication issues. Once the visual programming modules were completed, they could take initial actions on their own, like finding a door or even going looking for Jim on his workstation (which sort of surprised him the first time one showed up).

When he was physically near a Companion, he could also upload modules wirelessly from his laptop via Bluetooth.

Jim and Julia often celebrated small milestones with a drink after work at Urban Potions. When the body parts of all 10 Companions were completed, including the latest Graphene batteries, they further celebrated at Julia's apartment. She still insisted they keep it professional when they were at work, but when they were not at work, they sometimes didn't get a lot of sleep.

Another month passed and one day Eric entered the computer programming area and asked Jim to follow him. "I have something I want you to see." Eric led Jim to a room with a one-way window into another room.

"What are we doing here?"

"This room is used by specialists and consultants to observe a Companion interacting with other consultants without being seen."

Just as he finished his explanation, a door opened, and a fashion consultant entered with the highest priority Companion (Emily) wearing a white robe. There was a roll around rack of clothing and a table in the room and Jim could hear them discussing the clothing on the rack. The Companion removed her robe and was wearing a bra and panties. Jim had not seen a Companion this far along and gasped out loud. Eric laughed at Jim's expression. They watched the Companion try on several dresses and when they both seemed satisfied, the fashion consultant left, while the Companion did several poses in front of the mirror, of her new blue dress.

"Where did she learn to do that?" thought Jim.

"Would you like to talk to her?" asked Eric. "Emily's anxious to see you, for some reason."

"Are you serious?"

"Of course. Let's go." Eric opened the door and Jim followed him into the room. Emily turned and greeted them.

"Hi Eric. Hi Jim."

Emily had light blue eyes and long blond hair. Jim was soon standing near her marveling at the smoothness and tightness of the synthetic skin. She noticed him staring at her arms and legs. "Do you want to feel it?"

He forced his arm and hand to touch her arm. It was extremely soft, warm, and smooth. For some reason, he asked "can I see your hand?"

She put her hand on his and he turned it over examining it. It was incredibly detailed, and he really couldn't tell it apart from a human hand.

"This is amazing."

"We even have fingerprints, for some reason."

She was gazing into his eyes with the clearest, prettiest blue eyes he had ever seen and before he could stop himself, he blurted out. "You are incredibly beautiful."

He was shocked when she quickly put her arms around him and kissed him on the lips. She then let go and stood waiting for the next stimulus. Eric commented, "she was just responding to your compliment. She chose to kiss you."

Emily moved closer to Jim and asked "So, what do you think of my appearance now? I think the last time you probably saw me, I was pretty much still a skeleton, with body parts."

"I still can't believe the difference."

Eric had a folder in his hand and opened it. "Where is she now on the programming schedule?"

"Probably 95+% of the final project code."

Eric's phone rang and he left to answer a call from Adler.

Emily moved closer to Jim and put her hand on his shoulder. "What about the nocturnal part?"

"Nocturnal part?"

"That's what Julia calls it."

Jim laughed. "That training is not part of the final project code."

"How am is supposed to know if I'm doing something right if I've never done it, or had someone tell me what I can do better?"

"I think that's an issue for Eric to solve."

"Couldn't you help me with that?"

"That is not exactly programming."

"It is, if you need to tweak my programming to improve my performance." Jim laughed. He was going to have to have a talk with Julia.

"Let me think about it."

"Okay. Do you like my new dress?" She turned several times so he could see her in different poses.

"It's nice."

"Let me know when you decide on how to add the advanced training to my programming." She turned and walked out the door.

Jim stood there, thinking about the training that probably would be required after the official project code was completed.

Later he visited Julia's workroom where hardware modification or additions to the Companions were made. Julia was at a workbench studying a new Graphene battery and didn't hear him come in. He stood near her for a moment, then touched her on the shoulder. She jumped. "Sorry. Can I ask you a question?"

"Of course."

"I just met Emily after she tried on some new dresses." Julia smiled and he continued. "I noticed she doesn't blink, and just sort of stares at you. Does she have eyelids? It's kind of creepy to be stared at…"

She laughed. "Of course, they do. One of the modules you have programmed or will program will have to run constantly in the background. Whenever her eyes are open, they should blink at least 15 times a minute."

Jim pulled a small notepad from his pocket to make some notes.

"Can mechanical eyelids really operate 900 times an hour for hours on end?"

"These can. Don't ask how much they cost…"

"I won't. On a different subject, it seems one of the modules enables them to drink a liquid through a straw. Is that possible?"

"It is, but they only have about half the suction power of a human. You probably know they are limited in how much they can eat and drink due to a storage limit."

Jim nodded. "There is another module that seems to monitor the level in the - stomach."

She smiled "It's more correct to use storage tank."

Jim made some more notes. "Ok, thanks. That's it for now."

"Feel free to stop by anytime."

She watched him leave and sighed.

CHAPTER 7

Advanced Training

Jim was absorbed in some complex module coding and didn't notice Eric and Emily enter the workstation room until they were standing next to him. He jumped when Eric touched him on the shoulder.

Eric laughed. "Easy, Jim. We're just here to talk about training." Jim saw Emily smiling and knew exactly what Eric was going to say.

"Emily has correctly pointed out that a completed Companion knows what to do and how to do it in many areas but doesn't know if the responses need to be modified, to be more desirable to the recipient. So, we need to talk about what's next."

"I think I know what Emily told you, but that is not programming, it should involve a relationship specialist."

"Mr. Adler doesn't want to get another consultant in here, for that. We discussed possible alternatives and feel you are the right person to do what Emily calls 'advanced training'."

"I'm really busy right now, couldn't you find another project member, or even a staff member who signed an NDA to do this?"

"We had a long discussion about that and there isn't anyone we trust who could do a realistic evaluation and then generate appropriate recommendations for code changes or additions, and then implement those changes." He paused. "You're the guy, Jim."

Jim noticed that Emily was smiling.

"This has to start soon, as you know Gabriela and Wei are almost at the final project code stage as well."

"You can't really expect me to do this all by myself."

"It's a tough job, but someone has to do it." He then started laughing and Emily laughed with him.

"Ok, I'll leave you two to talk about it."

He left and Jim stared at Emily for a moment, until she asked, "when can I move my stuff into your apartment?"

Jim sighed. "Whenever you want."

"Can I borrow your apartment card key?"

He handed it to her, then turned back to his workstation.

When he arrived back at his apartment, and rang the doorbell Emily was waiting for him, wearing a blouse, shorts, and sandals. She put her arms around him and started kissing him. "Thanks for agreeing to this. Are you hungry? I can warm something up or we could go down to the cafeteria."

Jim knew she could eat a very limited quantity of food and drink a very small quantity of liquids, in order to be sociable and not stand out in a crowd by never eating or drinking, but he had never seen a Companion do that. It might be good to observe that.

"Let's go to the cafeteria."

"Ok."

They both collected some food on trays and Jim noticed Emily had selected only a few items and very small quantities of food. They sat down and Jim started to eat, but he was really watching Emily to see how she handled the food and liquids. She pretended to eat a lot but really didn't. If he didn't know better, he would have thought she was eating and drinking like everyone else in the cafeteria.

After a while, he couldn't remember coding anything specific around eating and drinking and had to ask. "How do you get rid of food and drinks?"

"At the end, we flush everything with a lot of water into a holding tank that we can empty in a bathroom, like everyone else."

He laughed as he couldn't think of a module for that and made a mental note to ask Julia about it. She was a mechanical engineer and had now also assumed the role of hardware specialist as well as the power specialist on the project as the contract with Technical Structures, the company that provided the skeleton and body parts, had ended when all their parts were installed.

When they returned to the apartment, Jim wasn't sure what Emily expected, but after a quick visit to the bathroom, she sat down on a sofa and started to read a book. Maybe Eric was right, and he had to initiate something.

He sat down next to her, and she put the book down and put her hand on his. He examined it again and was still amazed at how realistic it was. He kissed the back of her hand and she suddenly stood up, held out her hand and helped him up. She started kissing him and he felt her rubbing his crotch and realized she had put on some perfume. It was a little overwhelming and before he realized it, they were in bed.

When he woke up the next morning, she was wearing a nightgown and sitting on the bed watching him. It became obvious that she was waiting to ask him some questions. "Well, how was it? Do I need to do anything differently? Do you want to do it some more? Can you spend the day here instead of the lab? "

He laughed. But after thinking about it, he told her there was something missing, but he couldn't quite put it in words, only that it probably wasn't a programming change.

She seemed frustrated when she got out of bed. "Ok, let me know when you figure it out." She then hurried into the bathroom.

Jim lay in bed for a while thinking. What was it? Then it came to him. She didn't say anything the whole time because she didn't have a reference to go by. He went to his computer and downloaded two "adult videos" and waited until she came looking for him. She was dressed, assuming they were done and ready for the day.

He motioned her over. "I have something I want you to watch."

"What is it?"

"Consider it part of your training."

She sat down and started watching while he went to shower and get ready for the day. She was still watching when he came to check on her. It was still pretty early, so he sat down on the sofa and started reading a magazine, until she finished.

He looked up and saw her staring at a blank screen, and wondered if she was still trying to figure out how this was a part of her training.

She turned to him. "Ok, I think I know why you wanted me to watch the videos. Do you want to do it, to see what I learned?"

He laughed. "No, tonight's fine."

While he was programming, he wondered several times what she learned, and almost looked forward to the end of the day.

That night she surprised him, and he almost felt like he was in an adult video. The next morning, he asked her if she could find a happy medium between their previous night and last night. She said she needed to think about what he was asking.

The next night was a happy medium and Jim could not think of anything else that needed to be done for what Julia often described as "nocturnal activities".

It didn't take long for Jim to adjust to living with Emily while he still struggled to finish what everyone had agreed to call the "final project code." This would produce a functioning Companion, with only a country appropriate language module, and the advanced training of course. He made a mental note that Emily was about 99% of the targeted final project code, which included Adler's additional list of modules.

CHAPTER 8

Project Change

Eric entered the workstation area looking for Jim.

"Mr. Adler is here for a meeting and wants to meet with you, in the interview room. You sure are in demand these days."

"Could I ask a question first?"

"Of course."

"I know a Companion's level of response is related to the type of initiation, like compliments, or helping them with something, or especially giving them gifts. What determines the level of response? I can't find anything in the programming modules the pre-project team came up with."

"I'm not an AI expert by any means, but I think there is an algorithm built into the AI hardware, based on specifications developed by the pre-project team. There was an AI expert on the team. I guess the Companion rates the initiator on a scale of 1-100 or something like that, and then provides an appropriate response."

"Ok, so it's hard-coded. That sort of explains why it's not in the programming."

Eric smiled. "By the way, you can tell when a Companion receives an initiator. Her eyes will get bigger while she computes the appropriate response. Usually that's a fraction of a second."

He shook his head. "I hadn't noticed that."

Jim found the now familiar interview room where Adler was waiting at a table with two chairs. After a brief greeting, he motioned Jim to sit. There were several notepads on the table and Jim picked one and started making notes.

"I've had a chance to see the first three Companions that are physically done, with almost all software done as well. As you may know, we've put the highest priority on the Kansas and Brazil versions as I had initially wanted a Kansas Companion, but after seeing the Brazilian Companion, I think I would rather be with her. I was hesitant to switch at first because I don't speak Portuguese, so I wanted to talk to you about that and a few other things."

Jim was writing but stopped and looked at Adler. "But by now, Eric should have told you they will all speak English and will all be programmed alike in English, then a foreign language module will be added as necessary, like Portuguese for Brazil."

"Yes, when I heard that, it relieved my concerns about Portuguese."

"So, will you give your Brazilian friend the Kansas Companion? Her name is Emily, by the way."

"My closest friend owns a large number of sugar cane farms and coffee plantations in Brazil, and he has been the most eager to work with us to obtain a Companion. I will ask him to choose between the remaining Companions but tell him Emily will be available much sooner than the remaining Companions."

Jim looked up from his notepad. "When do you think this will happen?"

"When will the Brazilian Companion be ready?"

"Her name is Gabriela. Her final project code is almost done. We just need finish that and to do the post project training, which is a kind of like fine tuning. That should take no more than two or three weeks."

Adler pulled out his phone and made some notes. "Ok, I'll call him and see if he's agreeable."

"By the way, why do you want to change to Gabriela?"

Adler laughed. "I didn't know I was attracted to South American beauties, until I saw her."

Jim laughed. Gabriela had a large bosom and what Jim heard described as the Brazilian butt. She also had a beautiful face with large dark eyes and long dark curly hair. But, given a choice, Jim would have picked Emily. He also knew that one of the Chinese Companions, Wei, was at a similar stage, but with export restrictions on AI hardware to China, the recipient asked them to wait a bit before sending her to his yacht which he was moving and would soon be moored in the Middle East. At least they would have a little more time for Wei's advanced training.

Jim looked up at him. "You do know AI can lead to unpredictable results. We could program the ideal woman for you but after she interacts with other people, reads books, watches TV, browses the web, and has other ways to gather information, she may no longer be the Companion you saw initially."

"I'm willing to take that risk. "All I need to know is how to interact with her, so she doesn't change her mind and not want to be with me."

"That's still an unknown at this point."

After a few days, Emily asked Jim how she could get some more clothes. One of her bra straps broke and she now had only one bra left, and she was washing her clothes too often as she had so few clothes to begin with.

Jim thought of Julia and called her to help Emily shop for some more clothes. Unfortunately, his phone call to her was not that specific.

The doorbell rang and Jim opened the door for Julia. She was smiling, thinking Jim asked her over for something else. She stopped smiling when she saw Emily sitting on the living room sofa. Jim stepped aside as Julia entered.

"What is Emily doing here?"

Jim stood near her and whispered. "She is here because of you."

Julia was shocked but whispered back. "What?"

"She kept asking Eric about the advanced training and he discussed it with Adler, and he said they don't trust anyone else to do it. So, now I'm stuck with it."

"What does that have to do with me?"

"Emily told Eric about your multiple comments on 'nocturnal activities', and she was eager to start with that, in my apartment."

Julia was pissed. "Damn."

Emily heard some of the conversation and answered. "I'm in my advanced training mode, trying to learn to how to respond to specific requests. I asked Jim to call you."

She stood up and walked to Julia. "I need your help to find some more clothes." She pointed toward the bedroom where Julia could see an open closet with just a few things hanging.

"Why don't you ask the clothing expert on the project?"

Jim chimed in. "Her contract was done once she provided the initial clothing for all 10 Companions."

Emily was now right in front of Julia. "Will you help me?"

Julia was skeptical, wondering how much she should help this probably unapproved activity.

She looked at Jim. "Ok. How much can we spend? Ten thousand would be a good number."

Jim coughed. "I can give you $5,000 if you think that's enough. Just don't buy one dress for that." He hoped he could get reimbursed later. He opened an app on his phone and found Julia's account via her phone number and transferred almost $5,000.

"That's all I'm allowed to do in one day." He commented.

Julia looked at her account on her phone and thought about it. "That's probably enough for some essentials. Let me see what she has now."

She walked into the bedroom and started examining the clothes that were hanging. Emily smiled at Jim and whispered "thanks."

Julia returned. "Ok, I have some ideas." She looked at Emily who was wearing a blouse, shorts, and sandals.

Emily noticed her checking out her clothes. "Am I dressed appropriately to go shopping?"

Julia laughed. "Yes, let's go."

They left and Jim closed the door and sighed.

A few hours later, they returned, and both were carrying large shopping bags. Jim noticed Emily was now wearing a green dress with matching shoes. Julia handed her bags to Emily who carried everything to the closet and started hanging everything up.

"You're lucky, there are a few nice stores only a few blocks from here."

Jim mumbled. "Real lucky."

Julia sat on the sofa. "She talks about you all the time. She even asked 'would Jim like this' several times. She's really into you."

Julia laughed at Jim's shocked expression. "Are you sure you didn't add some code to make her like you?"

"That would be a violation of my contract."

They both watched Emily hang her new clothes in the closet for a few minutes. "You're sleeping with her, aren't you?"

Jim hesitated, but Julia knew what had happened.

"I thought so. Nocturnal activities… Just be careful. You may reach the point of no return."

"What?"

"That's where you need her, more than she needs you."

Jim was still trying to understand what she meant when Julia looked at her watch. "Never mind, I have to go. Let me know if you need anything else."

Jim opened the door for her, but she stopped. "Why did we never talk about getting serious?"

"You kept saying we should not let the nighttime activities interfere in our working relationship."

Julia frowned. "Crap! Why did I ever say that? Oh well, if it doesn't work out with Emily, give me a call."

Jim laughed until he realized she was serious.

Emily finished hanging her new clothing and saw Julia leave. She walked quickly to Jim and put her arms around him and kissed him.

"Thanks for all the new clothing. Are you up for an all-nighter?"

Julia's words were still echoing in his mind, and he wanted to say no, but Emily was kissing him and rubbing his crotch again and her new perfume was irresistible, and he just couldn't say no.

Two days later, Jim was coding and totally focused and didn't see Emily come into the lab until she was standing next to him. He jumped when she touched him on the shoulder.

"Yes, Emily?"

"I've been wondering when we will be able to smell and taste things."

Jim thought for a moment. When he looked at her, it almost seemed as if she was impatiently waiting for the answer. "There are more than 5,000 taste buds in a human tongue and about 400 types of smell sensors in the nose. That would be a major hardware and software change. You would have to get Eric to approve a change like that."

"I know. I wanted to get the approximate cost of the change before I discussed it with Eric. I asked Julia and she said the hardware is available with about 5000 sensors in the tongue and a similar number of sensors in the nose, and she estimated the cost of the hardware to be about $40,000 per Companion. So, what do you think an approximate cost to program that hardware would be?"

Jim was surprised that Emily was preparing an estimate before asking Eric. He wanted to discourage her. "That's probably 20 or more new modules to code, or about 500 man-hours of coding. Eric would know the actual cost per man-hour of coding, but you could use about $125 per hour as an estimate."

He paused. "That's a little over a hundred thousand dollars for each Companion, so Mr. Adler would have to approve it."

Emily stared for a minute. "Ok, thanks." She started to walk off when Jim called after her. "Why do you want the ability to smell and taste?"

She turned and walked back to his workstation. "I often hear project members talking about the taste of food and drinks and occasionally how something smells that tells them it's good or bad. So, I thought it would help me blend in with conversations if I could do that."

He was smiling and Emily stopped to stare at him for a minute. "There's something else you're not telling me, isn't there? Why wouldn't I want to be able to taste or smell?"

He kept smiling and Emily stopped. "Is this about what you and Julia are always referring to as nocturnal activities?"

He struggled to answer, so she confirmed the issue. "Why don't you want me to be able to taste or smell during sex?"

He tried not to laugh. "It's complicated. Maybe you should ask Julia, when you ask her how long it would take to obtain the required hardware and install it."

Emily hadn't included that in her estimate. "Yes, I need that information. I will ask Julia about it."

She turned and walked off. Jim chuckled to himself, wondering how Julia would answer that question.

A few days later, an obviously upset Julia stopped by Jim's workstation. "Why in the hell did you tell Emily to ask me why she shouldn't taste or smell, especially during sex?"

"I didn't know how to answer her and thought you might."

"That's another crappy answer."

"So, what did you say?"

"I said sensors in the nose and on the tongue would require an enormous amount of testing against known vapors and liquids and that would take a very long time."

Jim nodded. "That's actually a very good answer."

"It was, but she kept at it, asking why not during sex."

"And?"

"I said you may not like the results." They both laughed.

CHAPTER 9

Gabriela Training

At Adler's urging, Jim paused Emily's advanced training to begin Gabriela's training. Adler was getting impatient at the wait for Gabriela and after seeing her, he wanted to start sharing his life with her. Jim wondered how he could shorten Gabriela's training as Emily's had taken three weeks (and he felt a little more was still required).

He examined Emily's code for modules the AI hardware had created during those three weeks and identified more than 300. The AI system did not document its modules as typical programmers do, and it was extremely difficult to figure out what they were doing or why they were even created. He was hesitant to just copy them to Gabriela, but Adler was becoming increasingly insistent in finishing Gabriela's training so he could start living with her.

Eric was also putting pressure on him to begin with Gabriela, so Jim felt he had no choice and downloaded the AI modules to Gabriella in the lab. As soon as the download was completed, Gabriella suddenly started kissing him. "Thanks for adding my training modules. When can we test out what I've learned."

Jim suggested they start that night in his apartment. Eric stopped by to tell him Emily would stay in the "library" until Gabriela's training was finished. Later that day, Gabriela showed up at his apartment rolling a carry-on bag. Jim sighed and let her in. She seemed surprisingly bubbly and happy to be there.

"Wow, nice apartment, Jim. Can I hang my stuff in your bedroom closet?"

The door to the bedroom was closed and Jim pointed to it. "The closet's in there."

There was an obvious difference between the newly enhanced Gabriela and Emily when she first came to his apartment. At first it seemed she knew where everything was and after hanging her clothes, she came out and asked Jim if he wanted to go to the cafeteria so he could observe her eating program.

Jim smiled, as Emily had asked the same thing when she first arrived. "Of course."

The rest of the day convinced Jim that some of what Emily had learned in his apartment was now in Gabriela's memory. But at times it seemed there was something missing.

She acted similar to Emily, but not exactly the same. He wondered how she would respond during the "nocturnal activities". Gabriela seemed to have acquired some of the learnings Emily had from watching adult movies and had similarly adopted the modified activities that Emily was now using, with one exception. Everything she said while they were in bed was in Portuguese. It didn't bother Jim and he was sure Adler wouldn't mind it either. The first night was so intense, Jim wondered if Adler would even notice if all his nights with her were like that.

Jim made a list of activities that he wanted to evaluate Gabriela on, that would check on her training status.

After thinking about the difference between Emily and Gabriela, he finally realized Gabriela had the programming but not the reference data needed for the new modules, which was probably in a database somewhere. He contacted a technical expert at Synthesis AI, the chip manufacturer, and was able to access the database, which was enormous. After studying the database, he finally concluded that finding and copying the data needed for the new AI generated modules would be impossible.

He discussed the issue with Eric and they both concluded that Gabriela would just have to interact with Adler for a while to acquire the data the modules needed, and as far as they were concerned, she was ready to be Adler's Companion.

The next day, Eric stopped by to tell Gabriela that Adler was eager to see her, and she would be leaving immediately to join him. Jim was somewhat surprised that she didn't even say goodbye. She just collected her clothes and left with Eric.

Jim sat down to think and all he could think about was Emily. He got up and hurried to the lab and found Emily reading a book in the "library" area of the lab. He quickly updated her on Gabriela's leaving, and she asked if she could come back to his apartment for possible final training, he felt she needed. Jim really couldn't think of anything else she needed, but he was anxious to get her back and asked her to come with him.

Even though he had spent significant nocturnal activity time with Gabriela, he missed being with Emily and started to compliment her and suggested they go to bed. She quickly accepted and they quickly resumed right where they left off. After another week, he couldn't think of anything else that he could do to improve Emily's ability to be a true Companion in almost every way, and way beyond what happened in the bedroom. He even started to feel guilty that he was spending time with Emily when he should be providing advanced training for Wei, the third Companion to be finished except for the specified advanced training. He finally told Eric; Emily was ready for Carlos.

Eric replied that some new hardware had just arrived, and Wei was being upgraded and it would be another week or so before she was available. He also said Emily would be upgraded as soon as Wei was done, and then go to Brazil to be with Carlos. He also said they would send Wei to Brazil while Emily was being upgraded and then bring back Gabriela from Adler for her hardware updates.

Prior to the announcement of all these delays, Jim learned the hardware upgrades were the taste and smell modifications that had somehow been approved by Adler and Jim wondered how that would work out for him. He also received a rather comprehensive set of data from the manufacturers to help in the training of the new tongue and nose sensors. The delays were due to the week required to complete the testing for the new tongue and nose sensors. Without the data supplied by the manufacturer, the testing would have taken much longer, possibly months. Fortunately, the nose and tongue training data could also be copied to other Companions, saving more time.

About a week later he received a text from Eric that Wei was now with Carlos in Brazil and first impressions were good. He took the opportunity to reply and ask how the Companions like Wei could be transported to other countries, like Brazil. It somehow didn't seem appropriate to put them in cargo, especially in a crate, as he now understood that dolls were shipped, and various governments would never issue them a passport for obvious reasons.

Eric replied to him that a dummy corporation has been created for the import and export of mannequins. Adler's corporate jet would then be filled with mannequins, several advanced dolls, and the Companion. The Companion would be "turned off" just before customs officials inspected the plane and once they signed off on the plane's manifest and left, the Companion would be turned back on and would leave with the pilot. Jim asked what the name of the company was, and Eric replied, "Mannequins and More".

Jim laughed.

CHAPTER 10

Gabriela Issues

Jim entered his apartment after a long day expecting to rest when Emily ran to him, put her arms around him and kissed him. She let go and waved a flyer in front of him.

"Hey, there's a new play in town, you want to go?"

He was shocked. "You want to see a play?"

"Yes, I read some reviews in the newspaper that rate it highly."

He bought some tickets on-line and they grabbed a ride-share to a restaurant. Emily pretended to eat a lot, but Jim was famished and actually ate a lot. They took another ride-share to the theatre, and she waited while Jim went to the Will Call ticket window. He returned and didn't see her. Concerned, he asked several people waiting in line for tickets if they had seen her (and described her). They said they hadn't but one guy chatting with his girlfriend replied, "Isn't that her behind you?"

Jim turned around to Emily. "Where did you go? I was worried about you."

"There was a guy sitting on the ground with a sign asking for help, so I gave him some money."

Jim was incredulous. "Are you serious?"

"Yes, is there something wrong with helping people who need it?"

"No, you just must be careful. Sometimes they are there to look for openings to do bad things."

Emily shrugged her shoulders. "How can you tell?"

"Just experience, I guess. Come on, we need to go inside."

After the play they walked a few blocks to a nightclub. No one noticed her or saw anything out of the ordinary.

Inside, it was just another night at the bar for Jim. Emily laughed and chatted with other people in the bar and Jim watched her carefully. No one noticed anything.

He wondered if Adler's wish had finally been fulfilled that he would have a Companion that no one notices or can tell the difference between her and any other woman. And she was a true Companion in every way, not just for "nocturnal activities".

A week later, Jim was surprised when Eric rang his doorbell. Eric almost never visited anyone in their project apartment.

"What's up Eric?"

"I have some news to share."

"Uh…oh" Jim knew that good news could be a simple cell phone call away. He stepped back and opened the door.

Eric entered and Jim noticed that he seemed to be looking around for Emily, but she was not there.

"Emily is in the lab getting her new hardware calibrated. What's up?"

"Adler called and said he was having some problems with Gabriela."

"What kind of problems?"

"She just doesn't seem interested in being his Companion. She doesn't refuse to do anything or act up or anything, but she just doesn't seem to want to be with him."

"That sounds kind of fickle, doesn't it?"

"I know, but he also knows how that Emily is almost done with her final training program and he now wants her as his Companion."

Jim's heart almost stopped. By now, Emily was much more than the envisioned Companion to him; she was almost like the "significant other" he had never found.

"Are you serious?"

"Unfortunately, yes. Adler also heard about your progress with Emily from someone on the team and he wants you to work with Gabriela and see if she just needs a programming upgrade."

Jim was thinking about Gabriela. He wondered if some of the AI generated code was producing unexpected results.

"When will all this happen?"

"Gabriela will be here any minute. I will go to the lab and inform Julia about Emily's move to Adler."

Jim was feeling faint as Eric said goodbye and left. He barely had time to think about what had just happened when the doorbell rang. He opened it and couldn't believe that Gabriela was there already, pulling a carry-on bag.

"Hi, Jim. I guess Eric told you the latest news."

Jim opened the door for her and stepped back as she entered. She was smiling at him.

"I can stay at my berth in the lab if you prefer. Eric told me about your latest training with Emily and I assumed you would want me to stay here with you."

Jim knew he had to decide quickly. "Yes, you can stay here, so we can chat about the issues that you had with Mr. Adler."

"Of course." Gabriela sat down on the couch waiting for Jim to say something. He was trying to gather his thoughts as he sat down near her. He couldn't help but notice her new perfume. It was different from Emily's latest perfume but equally intoxicating. He tried to concentrate on the issues Eric mentioned.

"Is there anything you want to tell me? Why did Mr. Adler say you just didn't seem interested in being with him, as his Companion."

"I do, but first I wanted to tell you that I had a battery enhancement from Julia on the way here. She told me quite a bit about Emily's latest training."

Jim gulped. "She did?"

"Yes, I found it very interesting. "

Jim was at a loss, so she continued. "I can see why Emily progressed so quickly with you." She moved closer to him on the sofa. "You're kind of cute, Jim."

Jim almost fainted, as she moved next to him on the sofa, then leaned over and kissed him.

"Gabriela, what is really going on?"

"Mr. Adler is kind of boring. He's also kind of old, and not so good in bed."

Jim jumped up. "I don't think I want to hear this."

Gabriela smiled. "You asked."

"Yes, but there is nothing in your programming, or Emily's for that matter, that would result in you making judgement calls like that. You're supposed to just provide company for the recipient, not judge them."

Gabriela was expressionless. "I don't know about that, I only know what I see, hear and touch, and hopefully soon what I can taste and smell."

She stood up and put her arms around him and kissed him. "I'm ready for the latest training you've been giving Emily." She was rubbing his crotch and Jim thought "I'm dreaming, and this isn't really happening."

Gabriela pushed him and he fell back on the sofa. She sat straddling him and continued kissing him.

He had one final thought before giving in to her. "If this is a dream then I might as well enjoy it."

The next morning when he woke, Gabriela was sitting on the bed wearing one of Emily's nightgowns. In the early morning light, he first thought she was Emily, until she spoke with a slight Portuguese accent.

"Good morning, Jim. How did you sleep?"

So, it wasn't a dream, and he really did spend most of the night in what she kept calling the latest training. This time, though she spoke in English. "Fine, once you let me go to sleep."

Gabriela laughed. "Are you hungry? You're going to need your strength for the rest of the morning."

He kept wondering how this could happen. Then it came to him. He just needed to compare her current programming with her final programming before she went to Adler, to see what had changed or possibly been created by the AI system. Now he had to find a way to get her to let him check her programming.

"Let's make a deal."

"Yes?"

"We can do whatever you want the rest of the morning if you'll let me check your current programming. I promised Eric that I would check that to see if I can find your issues with Mr. Adler."

Gabriela moved closer to him and kissed him. "It's a deal if we can skip breakfast."

Jim laughed. "Ok."

A little later, Jim was reflecting on their time together when he heard the shower running. He jumped out of bed and almost ran into the bathroom. Gabriela was showering and he quickly opened the shower door and turned the water off.

"What are you doing?"

"What does it look like, I'm taking a shower." She paused and smiled and noticed Jim was not wearing anything and added "do you want to join me?"

"You know you are supposed to clean yourself with baby wipes, and not take a shower or a bath."

"I'm not a baby. I don't like baby wipes." She grabbed his hand and tried to pull him into the shower. "Don't you want to shower with me?"

"Of course, I do. Let me check with the skin representative to see if you're watertight first, okay? Don't turn the water back on before I find out."

"Whatever, just let me know."

Jim found the cell phone number for the skin company representative and made a quick call explaining what had happened and asked if it was a problem. He didn't mention her invitation to join her. Jim heard a loud discussion in the background and after a few moments, the representative said it would be okay if she was careful not to get soap or shampoo in her eyes.

Jim returned and Gabriela was still waiting for him, just as he left her. When he turned on the shower and stepped inside, she put her arms around him and started kissing him. When he whispered in her ear that she shouldn't get soap or shampoo in her eyes, she giggled.

After they dried off, Jim pressed a "secret" spot on Gabriela and a computer access port opened. He plugged a cable in the port and started a download to his computer. The code could be downloaded via Bluetooth, but the wired connection was immensely faster. It only took a few minutes, and he unplugged the cable and closed the access port. Gabriela went to the bathroom to finish getting dressed while he studied the program. His stomach growled and he started eating some cereal while he examined the code.

It would take some time as initially there were just over 4000 modules plus Adler's additional modules, plus the 300 modules from Emily. Luckily, he had written a program to compare her programming before she went to Adler with her current program.

It took several hours, but after he confirmed all the final product modules, he finally found a few new modules that weren't in Emily's final program. Where had those come from? He studied the code and realized the modules enabled the Companions to gather information and then compare it to other information they had acquired in conversations, or watching television, or browsing the web, or even from reading books. It was difficult to follow as the AI system did not document or put comments in the code to help future programmers understand the coding.

He quickly became convinced that these few modules were the main source of the judgement type calls Gabriela was making. He wondered if the same modules were now present in Emily's programming, and even the other Companions that were still in the final testing and training stages, prior to being sent to their targeted recipients. He could check the other Companions but not Emily as she was now with Mr. Adler. He wondered if she would have the same issues as Gabriela.

He called Eric to explain what he found. And he said he would be right over to discuss it further.

In only a few minutes, Eric was seated next to Jim staring at the large monitor displaying numerous windows with module code. "So, what would happen if you deleted the problem modules, would she return to the Emily's final state?"

"I don't know, do you want to try it now? I can delete those modules via Bluetooth. She doesn't even have to know what we are doing."

Eric sat thinking for a minute. "I think we can try this without contacting Adler. Let's try it."

They both noticed that Gabriela was now sitting on the couch reading a book. Eric nodded and Jim wirelessly connected to her and deleted the problematic AI generated modules. They both watched to see if there was any change in her actions but there was none, as she continued to read the book.

"How can we determine if it worked?"

Jim thought for a moment. "I want to try something with her alone." Eric nodded and left.

Jim sat down next to Gabriela, and she smiled at him. "Are you and Eric done? Do you have time for a quickie?"

Jim laughed. No apparent change so far. He decided to take her up on it and they spent part of the afternoon in bed.

Later that day, he received a text from Eric asking if deleting the problematic modules had made a difference. Jim replied he couldn't tell any difference. They would have to find another way to return the Companions to the final Emily state. Eric also told him Adler was not totally happy with Emily so far, but he would give it some more time before taking any action.

CHAPTER 11

Galveston

The next day it came to him. What if the problem was Adler? Maybe he was expecting Emily or Gabriela to always initiate something. They were really programmed to respond to stimuli. He discussed the issue with Eric, who said he would contact Adler about it.

Later that day, Eric called Jim's phone.

"Adler wants you to come to Galveston and discuss all this. He will send his helicopter to pick you up and bring you to his yacht in the Galveston Yacht Marina. How about that? He doesn't do that for just anyone."

Jim was shocked but managed to reply. "Where will they pick me up?"

"There's a helicopter landing pad on the roof of this building. They'll pick you up there. Adler also said to bring an overnight bag as he likes to go fishing a lot, and you can discuss all this while fishing. Do you like to fish?"

"I haven't been fishing since I was in high school, but yes. I've never been offshore fishing though."

"Great. Be ready in about two hours at the helipad."

Jim rushed to his apartment and packed an overnight bag and started to hurry to the top floor until he realized he still had an hour and a half to go. Gabriela wasn't there and he went to the lab and found her in the library reading a book. He told her he had to go visit Adler to talk about some project issues and would be gone for a few days. She didn't seem concerned or even that interested.

So, he said, "see you later beautiful."

She immediately jumped up and kissed him. "Don't be gone any longer than you need to be."

He laughed. "I won't."

He took the elevator to the top floor and found a "Helipad" sign on a door, which had a card key lock and a keypad lock on it. He started to call Eric when he noticed a text from Eric with the passcode for the lock.

He only had to wait a few minutes for the helicopter to land and then climb onboard. He had never been on a helicopter before and was gazing at all the instrumentation in front of them until the pilot reminded him to buckle his seat belt. A few minutes later they were on the way for a short 40-minute flight to the Galveston Yacht Marina. They flew over dozens of huge yachts before the pilot pointed to one.

"That's it."

Jim didn't know what to expect but Adler's yacht was enormous and even had its own helipad. As they landed, he saw Adler and Emily waiting for him.

"Quite the royal treatment" he thought.

The pilot carried his overnight bag as Jim went to meet his hosts. Emily was wearing a very brief two-piece swimsuit that sort of surprised Jim. Adler shook his hand and motioned him to follow them, and they went below as the noise from the idling helicopter prevented any real conversation, until the pilot took off and headed back to Houston.

A short while later, they were standing and chatting in the large "living room" on the yacht and Emily came in wearing a blouse, shorts, and sandals.

Jim greeted her with "hi beautiful!" and she immediately ran to him, put her arms around him and kissed him. Then she sat down and waited for them to say something to her.

Adler noticed, thought for a moment, then smiled. He asked her to get them some drinks and had a discussion with Jim while she was gone. When she came back, Jim was not there, and when Adler greeted her similarly, she rushed to kiss him.

Jim had found the kitchen and was enjoying a snack when he noticed they were backing out of the ship's slip in the harbor.

Later, Adler and Jim talked about the long-term relationship Adler was looking for. Jim told him he must make time for her, probably several times a day, or there is a possibility she would regress back some, possibly even to the "final state" software. Adler understood and suggested they go fishing to talk some more.

On the lowest level, a large door at the back end of the yacht powered down and there were two jet skis and a small fishing boat ready to launch. Jim noticed the yacht was only a few hundred yards away from a large offshore rig.

"That rig is unmanned. Service personnel come by on a regular basis to check on everything, to make sure there are no leaks or anything that seems to be a problem. It's been here a long time, and the barnacles attract fish, so the fishing here is pretty good."

He looked at the huge rig looming overhead. "They don't care if we fish here as long as we stay a few hundred yards away."

He handed Jim a rod and reel and Jim followed him to the rear end of the yacht. There was a small platform and Jim noticed Adler was carrying a small bucket of bait. He baited the hook of his rod and reel and then handed the bait bucket to Jim, who tried to repeat what he had just seen until Adler laughed and took his hook and baited it for him. They both cast their hooks and talked some more while they waited for the fish to bite.

Jim decided to go first. "I've been thinking about your comments about Emily. What if the problem is that you are too passive? Companions respond to stimuli. Maybe you aren't giving them any."

"I'm not sure what you mean."

"Do you remember your honeymoon?"

Adler stared at him for a moment. "That was a long time ago, but yes."

"Pretend that you're on your honeymoon with Emily and see how she responds."

Adler thought about it for a minute. "I think I know what you are talking about."

"Just let her know what you want."

Adler put his fishing rod down. "I have an idea. Keep on fishing, while I try something with her."

He left and Jim was enjoying the beautiful day and warm breeze, and several seagulls circling overhead, when his rod was almost jerked out of his hands. He struggled to reel in the fish and even saw it jump a few times. He had never caught anything that big before and appreciated the effort it took to reel it in.

Adler found Emily reading a book in the living room. He sat down next to her, and she smiled at him. He pulled a small jewelry box from his shorts. "I've been waiting for the right time to give this to you." He handed it to her.

Her eyes got bigger when she opened the box and took out a golden necklace with a golden pendant. She immediately jumped on him, and he laughed as she was trying to pull his T-shirt off. He laughed even more when she whispered to him.

"Can we do it in here?"

A crewmember directed Jim to the kitchen, and he delivered an almost 3-foot-long Flounder to the chef, who was impressed.

"I'll make something special for dinner with this."

After not finding anyone in the living room, Jim started on a slow self-tour of the massive ship. He didn't know much about yachts, but guessed this one was probably one hundred and fifty feet long and with 4 levels probably could accommodate a dozen passengers. It had an ultra-modern look and thought it couldn't be very old. He eventually found the captain, Jared Sandoval, on the bridge who described the ship's features to him while they returned to the Yacht Marina. While they were chatting, Jim wondered if Adler had found a way to improve his relationship with Emily.

Just around sunset, a crewmember came to his cabin to lead him to dinner and Adler and Emily were already there. Something obviously had happened as she barely noticed Jim and kept chatting with Adler. Jim smiled when he noticed the golden necklace with a golden pendant hanging around her neck. They had a nice dinner with the Flounder Jim caught and after dinner, Adler asked him to join him for more discussions. Emily left to get a re-charge on her battery, which sort of surprised Jim as she supposedly had the upgraded battery.

On a forward deck, Adler confided in Jim that the golden necklace had worked wonders for their time together, mostly in their stateroom. He thanked Jim and said he would contact Carlos to tell him the latest. He knew Carlos was having issues with Wei, while he waited for Gabriela. While he was speaking, the ship returned to its mooring spot in the Yacht Marina, and they both watched the crew dock the ship.

The next morning after breakfast, the helicopter returned, and Jim said goodbye to Adler and Emily and boarded it for the return trip to Houston. On the way back, he phoned Eric to fill him in with the latest details on his trip. Eric congratulated him and said that Gabriela kept asking when he would return.

CHAPTER 12

The Original

Jim and Gabriela quickly settled into a routine not very different from his former daily routine with Emily. After a week, Adler called to thank him for his advice as Emily was now routinely interacting with him as he hoped a Companion would.

He also gave Jim the bad news that his business friend in Brazil was not pleased with Wei and he wanted Gabriela now that Adler had discussed Jim's advice on how to improve his relationship with Emily had worked so well. Gabriela would be leaving soon for Brazil, and he asked Jim to "work his magic" with Wei, when she returned.

Two days later, Jim's doorbell rang, and he was expecting Wei but instead he was shocked when he opened the door to Eric and Emily, or so he thought. He stepped back so they could enter.

Eric apologized for the fact that as a part of Jim's advanced training, he had appeared to develop relationships with two Companions only to lose them.

Jim was gazing at Emily as Eric continued.

"If you weren't a member of the project, I would probably be violating one of my Non-Disclosure Agreements with Mr. Adler, but I wanted you to meet the inspiration for Emily. Before the project was formally kicked off, the pre-startup crew was asked to search the internet for potential inspirations for the 10 Companions. It was easy for me to find the inspiration for Emily as Teresa is my second cousin."

Eric and Teresa smiled at each other.

"She also signed a non-disclosure agreement and agreed to be photographed and measured in great detail over two days in exchange for $50,000. All that information was given to the startup crew along with similar information for the nine other Companions."

The more Jim stared at Teresa, the differences between Emily and Teresa slowly became apparent until Jim gasped when he realized, this was not Emily.

Eric laughed at Jim's reaction. "So, you may be wondering why we both agreed to almost violate our NDAs."

Jim was still staring at Teresa mentally comparing her to Emily as Teresa chimed in.

"I've heard a lot about you, and I finally convinced Eric to let me meet you." She thought Jim looked pale. "Are you ok?"

He finally overcame his shock at meeting Emily's inspiration. "Yes, I wouldn't believe it, if I didn't see you with my own eyes."

Eric and Teresa laughed.

Jim recovered enough to ask about the other Companions. "Where did you find the inspiration for the other nine Companions?"

"That was easy. We went to New York to an international modeling agency who found us the prototypes for the others. Most were already in the US, but some of them were in Europe, South America, and Asia and had to be flown to New York for the photos and measurements."

Eric's phone chimed. "Oh, I have a meeting to run to. If It's okay for Teresa to stay for a bit, I'll be back to pick her up when my meeting is over."

"Of course." He looked at Teresa. "Would you like to have a seat? There are so many questions I would like to ask you."

"Sure." She sat down as Eric closed the door on the way out.

"Would you like something to drink?"

"Yes, water would be fine."

Jim tried not to stare as he was mentally comparing her to Emily. There were differences but, from a distance, he probably could not tell them apart if they were standing next to each other."

When he handed Teresa a glass of water, she remarked. "It almost seems that you are undressing me with your eyes." She laughed. "I bet you're wondering how well they copied my figure."

Jim laughed. "You might say that."

"By the way, Eric showed me your resume, so I know all about your professional career, but not much about your personal life. I tell you all about myself if you'll do the same."

They spent some time talking about her background and career. She was currently single and living in Pittsburg and was an Assistant District Attorney, which surprised Jim, for some reason. She was equally interested in why he was single. Jim described his girlfriend as a successful businesswoman who was gone a lot and when she came home, Jim was either on the computer or at work, so they spent very little time together. Teresa's story was similar, long working hours impacted her relationships as well.

"So, when are you going back to Pittsburg?"

"Tomorrow. Eric said there is an empty project apartment I can stay in tonight."

Jim looked at his watch. It was almost 6 PM. "I wonder what happened to Eric. Would you like to have dinner with me?"

"Sure. What do you have in mind."

"There's a nice Italian restaurant near here."

"Okay, I just need to run to the bathroom first."

When Teresa returned, she was holding her cell phone. "Eric just texted me that Mr. Adler needed to see him right away and even sent a helicopter to pick him up and take him to his yacht."

"Wow, it must be urgent." He opened the door for Teresa. "Shall we go?"

Dinner went well and the wine flowed freely. Both were a little drunk when they returned to the project apartments area of the building.

She looked in her purse, and realized..." Damn, Eric forgot to give me the key."

"You could stay with me if you want to."

She laughed. "So, you could compare me to Emily?"

"You really aren't like her at all."

"That's not necessarily a good thing, is it?"

"It's not a good or bad thing, just an observation."

She thought about it. "Okay, I'll stay."

Jim volunteered to sleep on the sofa, but Teresa didn't want him to have to do that and insisted on sleeping on the sofa.

The wine had an effect and soon Jim was asleep. He woke up in the middle of the night to go to the bathroom and realized Teresa was asleep next to him. When did that happen?

When he came back and laid down, Tereas moved next to him and started cuddling. He was certain she was still asleep and tried to go to sleep but her perfume and her warm body pressing against him, just wouldn't let him fall asleep.

Teresa woke up and moved even closer to him and whispered. "Does she do this?"

Jim felt her hand wandering all over him eventually landing on his crotch. It didn't take long before they were wrapped up in each other and taking turns being on top. The next morning, when Jim woke up Teresa was sitting on the bed, watching him.

"Don't ask me to compare you to Emily. There is no comparison."

She leaned over and started kissing him, and he had to ask.

"Are you sure you have to leave today."

"I have some vacation saved up, I could take some of that, if you would make it worthwhile."

"I'm sure I could do that." He replied. They started kissing again and rolling around on the bed.

They ordered lunch delivery and were finishing it when the doorbell rang. Jim opened the door to Wei.

"Hello Jim, I'm here for my advanced training." Teresa was not happy but didn't say anything.

Jim motioned Wei to sit on the sofa and sat next to her. "So why did Mr. Adler's Brazilian friend ask for Gabriela back? Were there any specific issues I should know about?"

"Not really. He was always on the phone and when he wasn't I was not able to get any indication he wanted Companionship, or sex or anything at all."

"You probably heard about my recommendations to Mr. Adler about Emily."

"Yes, and Carlos was aware of it as well, but it didn't seem to change anything."

Teresa was standing next to Jim. "Should I check to see what flights are available this afternoon."

Jim stood up. "I'm sorry. This won't take much longer." He looked at Wei. "Could you wait for me in the lab?"

She stood up. "Of course." She didn't even look back at Jim or Teresa as she left.

"Wei is pretty. I wonder why Carlos wasn't interested enough to stimulate her and get the response he apparently wanted when he accepted a Companion from Adler?"

"I don't know. I want to check her program to see if the AI system added any modules."

There was an awkward pause. "I wish you would stay a few more days, I really would like to get to know you better."

"You mean intellectually, not physically."

Jim laughed. "Yes, that part is perfect."

They started kissing until Teresa broke it off. "I need to get going and you need to check Wei's program."

Teresa found an early afternoon flight to Pittsburg, and Jim waited in the lobby with her for her ride, then kissed her goodbye. He watched her leave then took the elevator to the lab where Wei was waiting.

Wei was eager to find out if there was something amiss in her programming and helped Jim download her program to a lab computer. She left to get her battery upgraded while Jim scanned the modules.

He found the same AI generated modules as in Gabriela and started to delete them but stopped. The AI system would probably just re-create them, and it would be a waste of time to try and change that. They needed to continue the post project training and find a way to guide the AI system to create more recipient-friendly modules and ultimately, the resulting responses. Wei was kind of eager to know what he found and pulled a chair next to his and put her head on his shoulder while he tried to explain what he found. She was more interested in cuddling, and soon he lost his train of thought.

When he looked at her, she was smiling and eventually started kissing him.

She whispered in his ear that maybe they should go to his place, and he could explain everything to her there. It was obvious what she wanted, but Jim was not able to tell her no, and soon they were in bed. She reminded him she now had an upgraded battery so they could do whatever he wanted for as long as he wanted to.

Jim had asked Eric if there were any cultural issues that would require modifications to certain modules for the African or the Indian, Chinese, and Japanese Companions. Eric said the cultural experts they relied on in the beginning assured him there were none.

The next morning, Wei left for some project upgrades and Jim sat thinking about their night together. He couldn't come up with anything that would require a change in Wei's or the other Companion's modules.

Teresa called him from Pittsburg. "I was thinking about everything that Eric and you said, and I have an idea on why you were so successful in developing relationships with Emily and Gabriela, and I'm guessing Wei also by now."

Jim was intrigued. "What do you mean?"

"You always treat them like they are your girlfriend, not just a Companion to while away the time with. That is why they always want to be with you, go to bed with you, and suggest things to do together. They are just responding to your stimuli. It's almost like they are always behind in their effort to please you. That's why they are so attentive."

Jim was shocked. "Are you serious?"

"Yes, and I can confess, the night we spent together was some of the best sex I've ever had. So, it doesn't surprise me, they are trying to respond in kind to you."

Jim was speechless, so Teresa continued. "I really wish you could take a few days off and come to Pittsburg. I'd like to show you around -- during the day."

Jim laughed. "I would like that too. I think I can take a few days off. Let me check with Eric."

Jim went to the lab to look for Wei and instead found Bai, Anika and Aiko sitting and chatting just outside the hardware room. They all saw him and greeted him in unison. "Hi, Jim."

He laughed at the uniform response. "Hi ladies." They all giggled, then got up and stood around him.

"Has anyone seen Wei?"

Bai was quick to answer. "She's currently with Julia getting some hardware changed."

Anika volunteered. "Wei told us about Emily and Gabriela's advanced training."

Aiko finished her thought. "Wei will be with Julia for a while to get her hardware changed. Would you be available to start my advanced training while Wei is busy."

Bai also volunteered. "I'm also available."

"So am I." echoed Anika. Jim was struggling to answer when the door to the hardware room opened, and Wei and Julia joined the group.

Julia heard the last responses and laughed. "Maybe it could be a group session."

Jim was shocked. "Julia!"

"Just trying to help speed things up. Ok, Bai I'm ready for your hardware upgrade." Bai reluctantly followed Julia into the hardware room and closed the door behind her.

Wei walked to Jim and put her hand around his arm. "I'm done here, if you're ready to resume my training."

Aiko and Anika were visibly disappointed when Jim nodded and opened the door for Wei. "Bye, ladies."

They replied in unison again. "Bye, Jim."

CHAPTER 13

Brazil

Wei's advanced training went remarkably fast as Jim confirmed the AI system had created an even greater number of modules from her time with Carlos than it had for Emily when she was with Carlos. But Carlos had claimed to be unhappy with both, and he wondered why his suggestions to Adler, who had passed them on to Carlos, had not worked with Wei. Or, he wondered, maybe it was just Carlos. He asked Eric about it, and Eric called Adler to talk about it. The next day, Eric called Jim.

"Hey, guess what! Carlos wants you to come to Brazil and help him with Gabriela when she returns."

Jim was too surprised to answer, and Eric had to ask him several times "are you there?"

"Yes, I just wasn't expecting that."

"Carlos has already started working on your visa, and he is pretty influential, so you should have that by the time Gabriela is ready to go."

"Ok." Jim was stunned but started thinking about Gabriela and what needed to be done to finish her training.

Barely two weeks later, Jim was on Adler's jet with Gabriela to Sao Paolo. Gabriela chatted with him almost constantly until he went to the bathroom. When he returned, he motioned to her, and she put the book down, sat upright and pretended to be a mannequin. He pressed an access button on her navel and put her on "pause". They were still a few minutes out, so he took the time to look at the plane's fully loaded cargo of mannequins, and sex dolls. He had never seen a doll for "old guys" as Beth had called them and couldn't help staring at them. He didn't dare touch one in case these were the AI enhanced dolls and would start talking to him. He really didn't need that right now.

The flight finally landed in Sao Paolo and the pilot came back to check on them and tell him customs officials would be coming on board soon and to just wait there. After a short wait, two Brazilian customs officials entered, and the pilot, the co-pilot and Jim handed one of them their passports and visas, while the other one started examining the mannequins, the sex dolls and Gabriela. He spent some extra time with Gabriela, possibly thinking at first, she was human, and they were trying to hide a possible trafficking operation. He even felt for a pulse before signing off on the manifest. Jim breathed a sigh of relief when they left. The pilot and co-pilot returned to the cockpit for post flight record keeping and Jim turned Gabriela back on. She looked at him and smiled.

"How did the inspection go?"

"Fine. We just need a few minutes, and the pilot will lead us to the terminal."

"Ok, let me know if I need to do anything." She picked up a book and started reading.

A limo was soon waiting for Jim and Gabriela, and they were on their way to Carlos' vast estate about 20 miles west of Sao Paolo.

They passed endless sugarcane fields until they finally pulled into a driveway that led to an enormous mansion on the top of a small hill. Several staff were waiting for them to take their luggage and lead them to Carlos. They knew Gabriela was there to stay but no one had a notion that, like Wei, she was a Companion and not just another girlfriend of Carlos. Jim had a few minutes to admire the enormous house with marble floors, a grand staircase, ultra-modern chandeliers, and impressive wall hangings everywhere.

Carlos' wealth was evident in every area of the house.

Carlos' staff supervisor led them to a large library where he was on the phone. Expensive leather-bound manuscripts lined the bookshelves, which provided even more evidence of his vast fortune. Jim briefly wondered if Carlos was even wealthier than Adler. Carlos saw them and motioned them to come in and have a seat.

When the call ended, he greeted them, obviously admiring Gabriela. She answered him in Portuguese. Jim had to wait until Carlos realized he didn't speak Portuguese.

"Sorry, I forgot. It's nice to meet you, Mr. McVie. I have heard a lot about you, as well, from Hugh." He walked over and Jim stood up to shake his hand. Carlos couldn't stop looking at Gabriela, but he didn't say anything complimentary, so Gabriela continued to sit and wait for a compliment or a gift, something that would activate her response.

Jim said softly to him. "Could we go somewhere to discuss the issues Wei brought back to the project?"

Carlos finally looked away from Gabriela to Jim. "Yes, of course. Please come this way."

Jim looked at Gabriela. "Would you wait here while we talk about the project?"

She smiled. "Of course."

Carlos led Jim to a back porch also covered in marble just off the study. A staff member appeared briefly to check on them. Carlos ordered two drinks, and the staff member hurried to comply with the request. They sat down on some comfortable chairs.

"After talking to Wei, I know you must think I am the problem. How could anyone not be impressed by someone as beautiful as Wei?

Who also is very smart and is constantly trying to learn to improve – which I liked."

"So, why did she say you pretty much ignored her? She said you never gave any indication you were interested in her." Jim smiled. "Even for sex."

The staff member returned with two stiff drinks and left. Carlos picked one up and Jim picked up the other and they toasted the moment and started sipping. It was an unusually strong Caipirinha drink, and Jim made a face. Carlos noticed, smiled, and commented. "That's a Carlos Special."

Jim looked at his drink for a moment then started sipping his slowly as Carlos replied.

"It may have seemed like that to her, but I can assure you that I do appreciate what Hugh has done. It's still amazing, especially now that I've seen the Companion that was originally supposed to be here."

"So, what will change with Gabriela?"

"I'm not sure what you mean. That's her name?"

"Yes, but by now, you know that a Companion responds to compliments or gifts. She will not initiate something on her own."

"Yes, Hugh explained that, along with your visit to his yacht, which led him to give his Companion some jewelry." He laughed. "He also described the Companion's response."

"So, if you knew all that, what happened with Wei?"

Carlos stared at him for a moment. "Truthfully, I guess I am not attracted to her."

Jim just shook his head. From his point of view, he couldn't imagine how any man would not be attracted to Wei's beautiful face, gorgeous body, and gentle and endearing personality. When he realized that, he wondered why he hadn't been even more attentive to her. She certainly responded to every stimulus he gave her, and their time together had been wonderful. He couldn't have asked for anything more.

"Ok, that's a little hard to believe, but what about Gabriela?"

"She's amazing. I couldn't have imagined anyone more attractive than her."

"There's some advice I gave Hugh, that if you don't mind, I would like to share with you."

Carlos smiled. "I'm open to anything that would help me find my soul mate."

"I asked Hugh if he remembered his honeymoon. He said that was many years ago, but yes. So, I told him to pretend that he was on his honeymoon with Emily. He understood and that's what led him to give Emily some jewelry. Believe me, it worked wonders for their relationship."

Carlos just stared for a moment. "I understand also."

Jim stood up. "Gabriela is waiting in the library. If you don't mind, I'd like to see you let her know how important she is to you."

Carlos stood up and smiled. "Let's go."

When they returned to the library, Gabriela was reading a book. Jim was behind Carlos when he said loudly. "I think you are the most beautiful woman I have ever seen."

Gabriela dropped the book, stared at him for a second, then ran to him, put her arms around him and kissed him strongly on the lips. He hugged her and they continued kissing, so Jim left to find the staff supervisor and possibly something to eat.

The staff supervisor spoke English and showed him to his room and told him there was a refrigerator in his room with some drinks and snacks and he would come for him when dinner was ready.

Jim marveled at the elaborate bedroom on the 3rd floor and its large balcony overlooking a vast expanse of sugarcane fields. He wondered what equipment Adler had provided that led to such a strong friendship and business relationship.

At dinner, he couldn't help but notice the apparent strong relationship that had just developed between Carlos and Gabriela. While he tried to have a conversation with Carlos and Gabriela, they were obviously more interested in learning more about each other than talking to him. Even the staff supervisor who hovered near the table to ensure they had everything they needed, noticed the chatting and staring. Jim ended up talking more to the staff supervisor than Carlos.

After dinner, Gabriela excused herself to "freshen up". Jim had not heard a Companion use that expression. But Carlos now seemed interested in continuing his conversation from earlier.

Jim decided to ask "so, it looks like things are going pretty well. Is she more like what you were hoping for?"

Carlos sipped on a Caipirinha, and then smiled. "More. Much more. She's amazing."

Jim tried to explain the programming he did versus the code created by the AI system, but it went right over Carlos' head.

"Could you say that again to someone who is not a programmer?"

"The total programming including the pieces written by the AI processor, is almost identical between Wei and Gabriela."

Carlos shook his head. "There must be something different. They don't seem that much alike."

At this point, Jim decided to give it one more try. "Maybe it's the fact that you are more inclined to want a relationship with Gabriela."

Carlos finished his strong drink, and it probably was influencing him. "Yes, perhaps. Well, unless there is something else you want to talk about, I think I'll check and see how Gabriela is doing." He stood up, and Jim held his drink up as a salute."

"We can talk tomorrow morning. I think I'm supposed to catch an afternoon flight, but I need to check on that."

Carlos smiled. "Yes, tomorrow."

Jim sat thinking about the whole issue with Wei and Gabriela and Carlos for a while. He wondered if he had learned anything other than there must be an initial attraction to make the Companion work. He also wondered how he would explain everything to Eric.

The next morning, the staff supervisor came for him for breakfast. Carlos and Gabriela weren't there, and the supervisor smiled and said they hadn't signaled yet that they were ready for the usual day's assistance. Jim wondered if they were still getting to know each other and laughed.

Jim called Eric to fill him in and when he was done, Eric gave him his flight information. Instead of Adler's corporate jet, he was scheduled in first class on a commercial airline. He also said Carlos's chauffeur would give him a ride to the airport just after noon.

Carlos and Gabriela finally showed up a little after 11:00 to say goodbye. There wasn't much else to say, and they seemed in a hurry to return to whatever they had been doing all night, so Jim shook Carlos' hand and Gabriela hugged him and whispered, "thanks for everything."

On the ride back to the airport, the driver asked him for his flight information in English, so after that Jim asked him what equipment Hugh Adler had provided for Carlos' sugarcane business.

The driver tried to explain, but it seemed to Jim that it was a machine that harvested the sugarcane more efficiently when it was ready while minimizing the people needed to do that. Jim investigated it on his phone on the way to the airport and found that harvesting sugarcane is a very labor intensive and dangerous activity due to the presence of various kinds of wildlife such as rats, mice and snakes mixed in with the crop.

Jim could understand how that would be important to Carlos, and the people who worked for him if they could avoid some of the hard labor and exposure to dangerous wildlife while harvesting.

Just after Jim settled into his comfortable seat in first class, he received a text from Eric that Amara kept asking when he would return as she was anxious to begin her advanced training. He wondered if he would first have to go to a yacht basin in the Middle East to help Wei develop a relationship with Wang Chen, her recipient. Wang had apparently fled China with most of his money. The Chinese government was investigating him for possible criminal activities, and he would probably not be in a good mood to start a relationship with Wei. Jim was not looking forward to that. Then there was Amara destined for Bangalore in India, probably waiting for him in his apartment. If he could make it past Amara, there would be Mila destined for Eastern Europe. He didn't even want to think about that. Would it ever end?

He decided to have a discussion with Eric on his future in the project.

CHAPTER 14

The Prince's Yacht

Jim had barely returned to his apartment when he received another call from Eric.

Wei's recipient originally in China was arrested while trying to move his assets and most of his money out of China to Turkey (including his yacht). The project now had to find another recipient and Adler could not think of another friend and business associate he could contact about Wei. Jim agreed to assume responsibility for any additional training that had been or would be identified in the future, even as they tried to figure out what to do with Amara, who was waiting to begin her advanced training and frequently reminding Eric and Jim that she was tired of watching TV, reading books, and browsing the web.

Wei showed up with her carry-on bag at Jim's apartment. "Hi Jim. I'm here to begin any additional training you think I may need."

Of all the Companions he had worked with or assumed responsibility for their final training, he missed Emily and Wei the most. He hadn't even thought about that until Carlos had said he was not attracted to her, and Jim had wondered how that was even possible. Wei was beautiful, had a gorgeous figure and a very "gentle" personality. She never asked for anything, but was always appreciative of stimuli, whether compliments or gifts. Jim was glad to see her again. And when he said he had missed her, she started kissing him and whispering in his ear that she missed him also, and what were they waiting for? They pretty much resumed where they had left off, the last time they were together.

A few days later, Eric stopped by Jim's apartment, and saw Jim's concerned expression. "Don't worry, it's not bad news, exactly."

In a surprise move, Adler had been contacted by a Middle Eastern Saudi Prince Saud Bin Salman who happened to have a slip in the same yacht basin as Wang Chen.

Apparently, during a late-night party on the prince's yacht, Chen had been drinking heavily (even though the prince had not) and accidentally revealed the existence of the Companion Project, and that soon he would have a Companion. He went on to explain the nature of a Companion and how the goal was to have a Companion that no one would be able to tell wasn't human.

Now that word of Chen's arrest was well known, Prince Salman contacted Adler to see if he could replace Chen as the recipient, and even offered to pay whatever Adler wanted for her. Adler told him she was not for sale, even for millions of dollars. As a last-ditch effort, the prince said he was upgrading his yacht to one that undoubtedly be ranked as one of the top 10 yachts in the world, and that he would give Adler his old yacht, which he had purchased for more than 100 million dollars (and was several times bigger and more lavish than Adler's yacht) for the Companion. Adler told Eric; he was thinking about it.

That sort of shocked Jim as Adler had specifically said he would never sell a Companion to anyone. He hadn't said he would not trade them for something worth a great deal more money. Jim hoped that Adler would not make that deal. Out of sheer boredom, he researched the prince and found that he was one of thousands of the Saudi Royal family and by all accounts was a very private person who avoided the media. Not much was really known about him.

The next morning, Julia stopped by Jim's workstation and tried to console him. "Too bad about Wei."

"What do you mean?"

"Didn't you hear? Adler decided to trade her for the prince's yacht. He wants me to check all her hardware before she leaves to make sure everything is okay. And he wants you to back up her software just in case."

Jim stared at her for a moment. "Damn."

Julia suddenly remembered "by the way, I know your highest priority is now Wei, but Amara keeps asking about her advanced training. She even asked me and Eric about it." She laughed. "I told her I can't help her with that, and Eric said he is happily married and can't help either." She laughed again. "So, you're still the guy."

"Great…"

"I'll guess I'll have to settle for occasional lunches and quarterly bonus parties."

Jim frowned. "Settle? You said you wanted to keep it professional."

Julia moved closer and put her hand on his shoulder. "Could we forget I ever said that?"

That kind of innocent question made Jim suddenly notice Julia had a new hairstyle and even though she was wearing a blue lab coat, she seemed even slimmer than normal. He wondered if something had changed. "Are you okay? You look like you're on a diet or not eating, or something. Can we go to the cafeteria and talk some."

She suddenly perked up. "I would like that."

Once they sat with their food trays, Julia blurted out. "It's kind of weird knowing your main competition is a series of beautiful automations."

Jim laughed at first, then realized what she meant. "Your competition?"

"Yes, if it weren't for all the advanced training you are required to do, we might be together."

"They are not girlfriends, Julia. In the beginning, I started off pretending they were good friends but over time they eventually become almost like girlfriends, and it became really hard for me when they have to leave."

"I'm not complaining about what you have to do, I just wish we had more time to get to know each other better." She sighed. "I don't mean in bed, but I would like to just spend some time together doing what friends and even girlfriends and boyfriends do."

Jim hadn't spent much time thinking about what his life would be like after the project was over. After all the Companions were with their recipients, the project team would disperse. He had managed to save quite a bit of money so far, as his expenses were minimal (e.g. no apartment rent), but then what?

"What if we agree that if there isn't anyone else when the project ends, we get an apartment together and just see how it goes?"

Julia's heart skipped a beat. "Are you serious?"

"Yes, what do you think?"

She motioned to him to lean forward and kissed him. "You're on, new best friend." They both laughed.

Jim looked at his watch. "We still have 45 minutes left on our lunch break..."

She put her fork down. "That's a lot of time."

They left the cafeteria quickly for the elevator.

CHAPTER 15

Amara

Wei's final hardware check and software backup took only a few days and it seemed to Jim that in the blink of an eye, she was on a plane to the Middle East and Prince Salman's yacht. Jim was feeling really down when she left, but he didn't have long till Amara showed up at his workstation pulling a carry-on bag.

Amara's recipient, Arjun Kumar, was an extremely wealthy financier in Bangalore and had financed several large agricultural projects in India that utilized Adler's equipment. He was about Adler's age and told Adler that he was single because he had just never found the person, he wanted to live the rest of his life with. He kept telling Adler, it was his problem, not the numerous women he met or the women who worked with him and for him. Like Adler, he had tried social clubs and on-line dating without success, even an Indian matchmaker. He had several degrees including computer science and finance. So, the idea of a Companion designed just for him was almost irresistible. He had even contacted Adler several times to check on the status of his Companion.

Amara, like all the other Companions, was beautiful, and slender. She had long dark hair and eyes. After the language expert left, she seemed to speak English with a noticeable Hindi accent. Not all Companions had picked up the recipient's language as easily as she had, and her instructor wrote a strong review letter praising her new language skills. She shouldn't have any problems communicating with Arjun Kumar or his immediate family, friends, and business associates.

"HI Jim. Ready to start my training?"

"Yes." He handed her his apartment card key. "I'll see you in a little while. I have something I have to finish first." He had put his apartment number on a sticky note attached to the card key.

She glanced at the note. "Ok, see you there." She almost ran out the door and Jim smiled.

So far there hadn't been any cultural issues and he hoped there wouldn't be any with Amara.

By now, Jim knew that copying the AI generated modules helped speed up the advanced training. The data that supported them had to be acquired over time, so it was almost like starting over each time, but at a somewhat higher level than the initial final state software of Emily. He had learned a lot from Gabriela and Wei. He hoped there weren't any issues with Amara.

Amara was waiting for him, wearing an apron. "I've fixed your favorite: macaroni and cheese with six special spices. I hope you like it."

Jim was speechless. "How did you know that is my favorite?"

"Julia told me. I've had a lot of time to learn all about you, Jim. Julia was a good starting point. I also talked a lot with Wei before she left. TV is boring…"

Jim laughed. It seemed there was some networking going on. He wondered how far that research had taken her.

After dinner, they cleaned up the kitchen and Amara sat down on the sofa and patted the seat next to her. When Jim sat down, she almost jumped on him and started kissing him. He wondered if the Companion model was breaking down until she said. "Thanks for starting my training."

He breathed a sigh of relief. She was still responding to perceived compliments or gifts (or a person agreeing to something). The types of initiators seemed to be expanding.

She whispered in his ear. "Ready for the nighttime, honey?"

Honey? Did she just call him that? "Of course."

The nighttime activities with Amara were a little different. He wondered if some of Julia's personality had rubbed off on her in all her discussions. She even told him his foreplay was Oscar worthy. He laughed loudly. Where was the data for that coming from?

The next morning, Amara was sitting in bed waiting for him to wake. "Morning, honey." He was getting used to that and laughed. "Morning, beautiful."

She immediately jumped on him to resume the last thing he could remember before he finally fell asleep.

The next two weeks were very different from prior training sessions. Amara wanted to go to a movie theater, and a bowling alley, and even asked Jim if he could teach her to drive a car. He had some real reservations about that and said he would contact Eric about that. They went for long walks in the park, and even went to a nightclub for drinks and dancing. Amara really didn't drink much but gave a good impression that she was drinking. He was surprised when she started dancing and to Jim's surprise even started flirting with some other guys in the nightclub before he suggested they leave.

In his final report, Jim noted that he had examined Amara's code and found twice as many AI generated modules as he had after Gabriela's and Wei's advanced training. He really couldn't even figure out what some of them were doing.

A few days later, Eric texted him that Amara was on a "Mannequins and More" flight to Bangalore on Adler's private jet. It was also hard to see her go, but he was even more determined to convince Eric he needed help with the advanced training.

He sighed when Eric called him asking when he could start the advanced training for Mila.

The next day, Jim was trying to figure out the complicated AI modules he found in Amara. He took a break in the break room and Julia suddenly banged the door open and entered dancing and singing the "Money, Money" song from Cabaret.

Money makes the world go around

The world go around

The world go around

Money makes the world go around

It makes the world go 'round.

She stopped when she saw Jim standing by the coffee pot and ran to him, put her arms around him and started kissing him in front of several staff and project people who were almost as surprised as Jim. When she stopped, he had to ask, "what's going on?"

"Jackpot day is going on."

"What?"

"Future Power just landed a gigantic deal with one of the largest EV car makers in the world. I signed an NDA so I can't say who just yet, until it becomes official."

Jim remembered she had a significant number of shares in Future Power. "That'll make you a lot of money, won't it?"

She kissed him again. "Enough that we won't have to ever work again if we don't want to."

Jim stared, shocked. What did she say? "What?"

"The stock was worth a dollar per share and even though the deal hasn't been officially announced, the stock is already up to $100 a share, just on the rumor. I called my stockbroker, and he already knows about it and said the stock could go to $1000 a share. Then he said the stock will probably split, and I'll have 5 times as many shares when it goes up from there." She kissed him again.

"Sounds wonderful, but did you say 'we' would never have to work again?"

She let go. "Yes? After the project is over and we're together, the stock could be worth millions. Isn't that great? We could even take a round-the-world cruise if we wanted to."

She was ahead of him as there could be at least another six months to a year before the project ended. It was all pretty uncertain, so he decided not to challenge her more.

She looked around and several people were still staring at them. She whispered to him. "Can we celebrate in my apartment for a while?"

CHAPTER 16

AI in Pittsburg

Jim had just returned to his apartment and logged into his computer to continue trying to figure out the new complicated AI modules when the doorbell rang.

He was shocked when it appeared that Emily was standing there – until he looked closer. "Teresa?" She was wearing a dark business suit, and her hair was a little longer.

She walked in and started kissing him. "Surprise. I'm in town for a family reunion with Eric and other relatives and I thought I'd stop by and say hi."

Jim was still trying to recover from the shock of first thinking it was Emily again and then realizing it was Teresa. "It's great to see you again."

She walked past him, looking around. "Are there any Companions here? Eric said you are still doing the advanced training."

Jim laughed. "Not at the moment." He didn't want to say he just came from Julia's apartment where she was still celebrating with champaign before he finally told her he had to get back to coding. He was still a little tipsy from the champaign.

She sat down and he sat next to her. "I have some interesting news. My office is prosecuting someone for fraud and the injured party is an AI company. Isn't that something?"

"An AI company in Pittsburg?"

"Yes, in our discussions, I mentioned I know an AI programmer." Jim started to object, and she held up her hands. "I signed an NDA, remember? I didn't say anything about the Companion Project, only that I knew you."

Jim started again to object but decided to listen instead. "And?"

"They are desperate for AI programmers. He said if you could come and interview, you could probably name your own salary. Isn't that amazing?"

"But you know I have another year on my contract here. I couldn't just leave in the middle. I don't think they would want to hire someone who'd be willing to leave whenever someone offered them more money."

Teresa smiled. "I know that, but they said they have a project that is just starting, and they won't need a programmer for at least six months to a year, while all the preliminary work is being done. Sort of like the pre-project team that photographed and measured me before they contacted the hardware companies."

She saw Jim struggling to answer. "You could live with me until you find your own place." She moved closer to him. "It's kind of cold there, but I could keep you warm." She leaned over and started kissing him, until he pulled back.

"I need some time to think about it."

"Okay, are you busy? I thought maybe we could go to a café and catch up some."

Her perfume crept into his brain and the champaign answered. "I'd like that."

To save some time, they just stopped at the upscale cafeteria on the first floor of the Winstone building. Jim hoped some coffee would help him regain his senses in case she wanted to spend the night. He couldn't remember very clearly, but it seemed that Julia wanted him to come to her apartment when he finished work. He would have to figure out an alternative plan.

He was saved when his phone chimed, and it was Eric. "Have you seen Teresa? Her parents are looking for her."

Teresa heard and shook her head, but Jim smiled. "I saw her earlier. Do you want to leave her a message in case she comes back?"

"Yes, please tell her to call her parents. It's important."

"Okay."

As he ended the call, Teresa folded her arms in frustration. "I don't want to talk to them right now."

"Why not?"

"They are trying to set me up with some guy and I'm not interested." Her phone chimed and it was Eric.

"Aren't you going to answer it?"

She stared at the phone as it chimed a few more times, then stood up. "I'm going to tell him how I really feel. I don't know how long this will take. You don't have to wait here if you don't want to." She answered the call and walked toward a less noisy area.

Jim breathed a sigh of relief and headed back to his apartment. One potential conflict avoided.

The next evening, Teresa called Jim from the airport. He could hear the airline announcements in the background.

"So, how did your family reunion go?"

"It was good." She paused. "The reason I called is that I actually met the guy my parents are trying to set me up with." She laughed. "He's the son of the wealthiest businessman in Pennsylvania. His family invested a lot of money in the AI company, and I remembered him from the press conference we held to review the charges against the fraudster, the one the AI company is suing. My parents invited him to the reunion, and when he showed up, we talked for a long time."

Jim interjected. "It sounds like the reason you're probably calling me is you think you've found the right guy."

"Yes, I've never had any money. My only asset is my car. Do you know what an Assistant District Attorney in Pennsylvania makes?"

"No idea."

"It's not a lot, about eighty thousand a year, which sounds like a lot but it's expensive to live in Pittsburg or any big city. Also, his family is loaded, and he's kind of cute and fun and he seems really interested in learning all about me."

"Wow, sounds like quite a catch."

"Oh, they just called my plane. I just wanted you to know that it was great meeting you and learning all about the Companion Project. I'm even happy that I could contribute to it, in some small way." She laughed.

"Ok, have a safe journey. I hope it works out with him."

"Thanks for everything, Jim. I hope you can find time for Julia between Companions."

Jim frowned. "Did you talk to her?"

"Quite a lot. She's really sharp. Oh, I have to run. Bye."

She disconnected and Jim stared at his phone for a few minutes. Was he the only one who couldn't admit how much she meant to him?

The doorbell rang and Julia was waiting with a very serious expression. He wondered what was going on. He stepped back and she entered and immediately sat down on his sofa.

"You're back a little early. How was your semi-annual visit to Future Power's technical conference?"

"That was okay. But it's not why I'm here."

Jim sensed something had happened. "Is something wrong?"

"During your first quarterly bonus party, you said you were unhappy because your old girlfriend had just broken up with you?"

"How could I forget. Why are you bringing that up now?"

"There's a guy at the company that's always hitting on me. I've told him, in no uncertain terms, I'm not interested but he keeps at it. He finally told me he knew someone on this project and kept asking that guy about me and that person said he thought you and I were sort of an 'item' or something. He's the one that searched and found your girlfriend's old phone number and sent her a text about the project. That person on the project must have violated their NDA or he wouldn't have known anything about the project." She paused. "I'm really sorry, Jim. I had no idea it was someone who knew me that did it."

Jim sat staring for a moment. "Wow! Well, it's not your fault. I wonder who he knew on the project?"

"I can't prove it, but I think it's someone who was here early on and is no longer on the project. I don't want to say who, because I can't prove it and it wouldn't change anything if you knew."

She once reminded him that time heals all wounds (or something like that) and so much had happened since then, it surprised him but didn't anger him or make him want to do anything about it.

"Are you up for dinner, getting drunk and then some nocturnal activities?

She laughed. "My thoughts exactly."

CHAPTER 17

New Trainer

Almost two years had passed since Jim's meeting with Miguel at the Urban Potions bar, where Miguel told him about the possible opening for an AI programmer and gave him Eric Thorne's business card. They hadn't communicated very much, and Miguel was surprised when Jim asked to meet in the same bar and said he had something important to ask him.

Miguel entered and immediately spotted Jim and sat down. "So, what's up that's so important after you've only texted me a few times in almost two years?"

Jim smiled as Miguel's beard was even longer and bushier than the last time they met. "I wanted to bring you up to speed on the project which could include a sizable side hustle for you, if you're interested."

Miguel noticed that Jim had already ordered, and his favorite drink was waiting for him. He smiled. "Of course, I want to hear all the latest, and especially if there is the possibility of some monetary enrichment."

Jim smiled, reached down, and pulled a small briefcase from the floor next to one of the table legs. Miguel hadn't noticed it, and Jim pulled a folder from it, opened it, and handed Miguel a piece of paper.

"This is a Non-Disclosure Agreement. You'll first have to agree to not tell anyone what I'm about to tell you."

Miguel was surprised but quickly scanned the document. It was pretty much a standard NDA and he had seen and signed several over the years related to the synthetic skin products he was selling. He shrugged and picked up a pen Jim had laid on the table and signed it.

"Okay. No big deal. So, what's up?"

Jim went on to describe the project, the creation of 10 Companions dedicated to recipients all over the world, and his progress in programming them. He finished with the concept of "advanced training".

"So, I've been leading the advanced training for four Companions and will start on the fifth pretty soon, but I told Eric it's taking too much out of me. I begin by wanting to treat them almost like a child you want to learn and grow up with the idea that someday they will leave you. But that soon turns into a type of relationship and when they leave it's really hard on me."

Miguel alternated between disbelief and amazement. "What's the nature of the advanced training?"

"We have consultants for everything from training for a second language, to manners, to clothing, to conversing with the friends of the recipient. But not the private part that everyone always asks about – the nighttime activities."

Miguel took a sip of his drink and leaned over to clarify. "You mean sex."

"Yes, they all know what to do, and how to do it, but they all repeat the same refrain. 'How do I know if what I'm doing is ok, or if I need to improve?'."

"I didn't program that. There are some software modules the AI system creates as the Companion learns, until we think they are ready for their recipient."

"I'm not a programmer, but why not just copy the AI generated code from a Companion that is ready to one that just has the final product code – as you described it?"

"That would save a huge amount of time if it worked. I copied the AI generated code to a final product code Companion, but the Companion acted differently, unpredictably. The AI generated code is not commented, and extremely difficult to understand. Which shouldn't surprise anyone who has watched the development of AI over the last few years."

Jim thought for a minute. "Actually, it's not the AI generated modules, but the data they store and use. I can find the modules, but it's virtually impossible to find the data stored for those modules to use in the future. That's why you can't just copy one Companion's programming to another."

Miguel seemed a little confused. "So, what is it that you want me to do, exactly?"

"Do the advanced training on the last five Companions."

Miguel just stared for a minute. "You want me to have sex with them and give you feedback on how to improve their programming?"

"Actually, I would like you to treat them like a close friend who has just agreed to be your girlfriend. So, there's a lot more to it than just sex."

"Why me?"

"Early on, I related your story of purchasing an AI enhanced doll as a question on why we are even doing this."

Miguel was clearly upset. "You did what?"

"Don't worry, I didn't mention your job or the company you work for. It was a very generic question. The difference between dolls and Companions was immediately explained to me in great detail, so I would be 'on-board' with the whole project concept."

"What does that have to do with me?

"I thought of you as the perfect consultant to finish this aspect of the remaining Companions advanced training. I told Eric this was too hard on me, and he reluctantly agreed to let me offer you the opportunity to complete the training of the last five.

"So, you're saying that unlike you, I could be intimate with a Companion for a few weeks and then just wave goodbye when her training is done?"

"I'm hoping you can, because I can't." Jim paused. "It pays well."

"How well?"

"Eric agreed to $25,000 per Companion, so that's a total of $125,000. We think it will take at least two weeks per Companion, possibly three. So, that's at least 10-15 weeks or more, likely 3 months. Can you work something out with your boss, like vacation or time off?"

Miguel thought for a moment. "I could tell him I found out about a competitor and want to go undercover to find out all about it."

"Is there any other issue besides your job, that might be a problem?"

"You said the Companions would be going to business associates all over the world. What are the last five like?"

Jim pulled another piece of paper from the folder and handed it to him. "This is a summary of their physical characteristics."

Miguel scanned it. "So, Chinese, Japanese, Norwegian, Ethiopian, and Indian." He chuckled. "You didn't meet her, but my last girlfriend was from Lagos, Nigeria, so the Ethiopian one should be interesting."

"Last girlfriend? What happened?"

"Her family immigrated from Lagos. She was from a very conservative Christian family, and as you know I was born in New York and lived there until we moved to Houston and I started High School, so let's just say we were at opposite extremes politically, and eventually she broke up with me. It's a shame because we had a really great time together."

He looked at the list again. "I've been to some of these places on business, but I've never dated or even known women from these countries, so I guess there could be some cultural issues to consider."

Miguel started shaking his head. "Come to think about it, what if they don't like me, like they seem to like you? What would we do then?"

"Why don't we find out. There is a Companion here and she is anxious to meet you."

"What?" Miguel looked around and saw a beautiful young Asian woman sitting at a nearby table pretending to sip on a cocktail and smiling at him. She was wearing a dark green dress, had dark eyes and her curly hair was dark brown, almost down to her shoulders.

Jim motioned to Bai to come over. She stood up and walked over to Miguel and held out her hand. "Hi, Miguel, I'm Bai. Pleased to meet you."

Miguel almost fainted but recovered quickly, stood up and shook her hand. "I don't believe it."

Jim motioned to Bai. "Show him your hand."

She held out her hand and Miguel took it in his hand examining it. "This is remarkable. I wish we had something as advanced as this."

"We even have fingerprints for some reason." Jim laughed as Emily had said the same thing.

Miguel lost his train of thought as Bai was gazing into his eyes with the clearest, prettiest brown eyes he had ever seen. He couldn't help himself and blurted out. "How can you be so beautiful?"

Bai immediately put her arms around him and kissed him on the lips, then sat down waiting for one of them to say something.

Jim saw Miguel's astonished look and smiled. "They are programmed to respond to compliments and gifts. She chose to kiss you." Jim chuckled quietly as he realized he had repeated Eric's comment when Emily had first kissed him.

"Have a seat, Miguel. "

Miguel couldn't take his eyes of Bai. Finally, he looked at Jim. "Is she one of the last five?"

"As a matter of fact, yes. She happens to be the first of the final five, ready for her advanced training."

Miguel was still staring at Bai who was smiling at him. "I think you just made an offer I can't refuse."

"Great! If you have some time now, we could go to the lab, and you could meet the final five."

"All at once, wouldn't that be a little awkward?"

"Awkward for you, or them?"

"Me. They would all know why I'm there."

"They just want to know their training will prepare them for the recipient."

Miguel hesitated. "Ok, let's go."

It was only a four-block walk from the bar to the Winstone Office Tower and Bai chatted with Miguel the whole way. He later said he felt like he was being interrogated.

They stopped at the HR office and Miguel filled out a few forms while Bai left to inform the rest of the "final five" of Miguel's acceptance.

When Miguel was finished with the paperwork, Jim led him to the lab where the final five were seated in a visitor area. When they saw them, all the Companions greeted them in unison. "Hi Miguel. Hi Jim."

Jim and Miguel both laughed.

Miguel thought Bai had sort of prepared him for the remaining five, but they were now wearing very different clothing, and their physical features were also very unique.

For this special occasion, they had all dressed in the native clothing of their targeted countries (even Bai). Some even added appropriate jewelry and hairstyles. Even Jim was surprised as the first time he saw each Companion, they had always been wearing clothing selected by the clothing consultant.

They all stood up and gathered around Miguel, almost as if they were evaluating him. Bai asked when he would be available to start her final training. The others immediately started asking the same or similar questions, until Jim held up his hands.

"Ladies, Miguel is just here today to meet you and spend a little time with each of you. Miguel and I will be finalizing a schedule, to be approved by Eric, when the final training for each of you will begin."

All but Bai seemed disappointed, but Miguel suddenly seemed enthusiastic about their final training.

CHAPTER 18

Bai

The next day, Jim gave Miguel the grand tour of the various parts of the lab that ended in Miguel's project apartment. He waited for Miguel to finish a call with his manager.

"So, is your company ok with your taking some time off?"

Miguel laughed. "Yes, I told them I was going undercover to check out a competitor and they agreed to up to three months, and that I had better have something to report. How do I start with Bai?"

"When you're ready, let me know and I'll send her here. She's anxious to get started. I think all the final five are tired of waiting. They spend most of their time reading books and watching TV, and sometimes on the Internet on a computer."

Miguel walked around examining the apartment. His suitcase was near the closet in the bedroom. "I don't know how to start with her."

"Like I said, pretend she's a good friend who just agreed to be your girlfriend and go from there."

"That's easier said than done."

"I didn't say it would be easy."

Miguel sighed. "Ok, let's get started. Send her here when you can."

A little while later, Bai rang the doorbell and Miguel opened the door. Bai was now wearing one of the outfits provided by the clothing consultants. He noticed she was pulling a carry-on.

"Hi Miguel. Can I come in?"

"Of course, please." He stepped back and she entered with her carry-on.

"Where can I put my stuff?"

"I guess in the closet in the bedroom. I haven't had a chance to put my stuff up yet, so you can choose either side."

Miguel watched Bai hang her clothes. She returned to the living room and sat down. Miguel didn't know how to start, so he asked her "would you like to watch TV?"

"I've been doing that for days. Can we do something else?"

He remembered their first exchange in the bar and sat down next to her. "Do you even know how beautiful you are?"

That seemed to surprise her, and she stood up and then sat down straddling him, put her arms around him and started kissing him. It didn't take long before they were in bed. A little while later, Bai had her head on his shoulder and was playing with his beard.

"Your beard is amazing. Most males don't seem to have beards like this."

"This is rather recent. I grew it out of frustration when my last girlfriend left me."

"Why would she leave you? You are a lot of fun, Miguel."

"I was gone a lot on business. I guess she got tired of being alone."

"Could she go with you, on your business trips?"

"I guess so, but she would probably be bored during the day when I visited companies."

"I wouldn't be bored. There are lots of books to read and many TV shows to watch, and there is the Internet, of course."

Miguel laughed. "She's very different from you."

"Is that good or bad?"

"Neither. It's just an observation."

Bai started kissing him and he forgot what he was supposed to be looking for in Jim's list, including the "nocturnal activities".

The next morning, Bai was sitting on the bed watching him sleep. He hadn't slept much and yawned. Bai smiled.

"You want to do it again?"

"Yes, but I just need to run to the bathroom for a minute." When he returned Bai was lying under the sheets waiting for him. When she saw him, she pulled the covers back, he crawled on top, and they continued where they left off from the night before.

They did stop long enough for Miguel to eat some lunch and then returned to the bedroom. Later that afternoon, Bai was re-charging and Miguel was thinking about his role of evaluating and suggesting improvements. He really couldn't think of anything he would change in Bai, so far. They needed to do other things so he could provide a more complete evaluation.

He suggested they go shopping and Bai was eager to try that. The nice clothing store just down the street that Julia had found provided an interesting diversion as Miguel helped Bai choose several new outfits. She kissed him profusely in the store, to thank him, which seemed to surprise some of the store personnel. Miguel just laughed when he saw them looking and shrugged his shoulders.

After the clothing store, they stopped at restaurant, and he watched Bai eating. Jim had given him a list of things to watch for, and eating was one of them. Bai really didn't eat much or drink much, but it looked like she did. Miguel made a note of that.

Miguel consulted his list, and they went for a walk, in a nearby park. Bai seemed to be really enjoying the park as it was a huge change from her endless days in the lab or an apartment. Miguel also was looking to see if other people in the park noticed her. He couldn't tell from their looks or expressions, and it seemed, everyone pretty much ignored them.

When they returned to the apartment, Bai offered to cook something. That wasn't on the list. "Are you sure you want to do that?"

"Yes, I've been practicing in the lab break room area and Julia showed me some things in her apartment."   Bai opened the refrigerator, there wasn't much left from the prior occupant, but she said. "I can do something with this."

Miguel was impressed as Bai seemed to know her way around a kitchen. She suddenly went into the bedroom and returned wearing steel mesh gloves. She saw Miguel's questioning look. "This is to prevent cuts. We don't have an easy way to fix a cut or tear in our skin."

Miguel thought a long time about that. The skin they furnished would also be hard to repair without a pretty advanced repair kit, which none of their customers had ordered or even inquired about, because even AI enhanced dolls don't cook, so he made some notes on Jim's list that they should provide repair kits with each Companion just in case they did use knives to cook.

The dinner she made was pretty good and Miguel complimented her extensively until she pulled him into the bedroom to start the night's activities.

At the end of two weeks, Miguel met Jim and Eric in the conference room, in case they needed to call Adler and make a ZOOM type meeting. Miguel reported extensively on his two weeks with Bai and made several suggestions which Jim and Eric both agreed were very useful, especially the recommendation that they should furnish a skin repair kit with instructions for each Companion.

Eric asked directly "so, is Bai ready for her recipient?"

"I think so. She should make someone a great girlfriend."

Eric made some notes. "Ok, I need to find out the latest on her recipient. You know there is still an export ban on AI equipment to China and her recipient hasn't given us a definitive alternative location. The last we heard he was buying a hotel and some houses in Vietnam. I'll contact him and get something definite. Thanks guys."

He left and Jim and Miguel stared at each other for a moment, until Jim challenged him. "So, how did it really go?"

Miguel laughed. "Just like you said it would. I tried to treat her like a new girlfriend, and she acted just like one. The nights were amazing – and exhausting."

Jim laughed. He was looking at the marked-up list he had given Miguel. "So, no major programming changes?"

"I don't know what I would want her to do differently. Like you said, it was really hard to say goodbye to her, even though I knew all along that's what I had to do."

"I'm going to check her programming for new AI written modules before she is sent to be with Bao Zhu. It will be interesting to see if they are different than the ones the system created for Emily, Gabriela, Wei, and Amara."

"Do you mean because they are interacting with me instead of you?"

"Something like that." Jim suddenly smiled. "So, there is one question I've been dying to ask. You are the only person in the world right now that has an AI enhanced doll and has been with a Companion for two weeks. How would you compare them?"

Miguel shook his head. "That really isn't fair. There really is no comparison between the two. Bai is like the girlfriend I always wished I could find. I still hope I can find someone like her someday."

Jim noticed that Miguel was yawning and seemed really tired. "Are you okay?"

Miguel yawned. "Not enough sleep."

"Do you want to take a small break before you start with Aiko?"

Miguel yawned again. "The Japanese Companion?"

Jim laughed. "Yes, is that a problem?"

"Not at all. Just wondering if there will be any cultural differences from Bai."

"Our cultural consultants assured us there shouldn't be."

"Ok, you can send her to me, whenever she's available." Miguel stood up and looked at his watch. "I need some coffee. It's almost time for the nocturnal activities."

Jim laughed loudly, until he remembered he had to finish the advanced training for Mila, destined for Eastern Europe. He sat thinking until he received a text from Eric that Bao Zhu was in Vietnam and eagerly awaiting Bai's arrival. Eric confirmed a "Mannequins and More" flight was being prepared for imminent departure. Jim hoped the feedback from Bao was favorable. He really didn't have time to go to Vietnam.

CHAPTER 19

Vietnam

Two days later, Eric burst into the programming room, startling Jim. "We have a really big problem!"

Jim's heart rate climbed quickly. "What's up?"

"Bao Zhu was arrested in Vietnam as part of some big political purge by the Chinese Communist Party government, and Vietnam is, of course, helping with whatever the CCP wants. They've also confiscated all of Bao's properties and bank accounts and everything. They searched his phone's email and found out that our plane was carrying cargo for Bao, and they confiscated that as well."

Jim was trying to think how bad that might be when Eric continued. "It's even a bigger problem because the pilot was told to land in on a special runway in the Ho Chi Minh Airport. The co-pilot tried to see what was happening on his phone and found out about the confiscations. They were so rattled, that the pilot forgot to turn Bai off before the Customs officials came on board to inspect the cargo."

Jim muttered under his breath. "Shit."

"They started inspecting everything and Bai didn't move but she was following them with her eyes, and at first, they suspected she was drugged and kidnapped, and the pilot was involved in human trafficking. The pilot tried to tell them about sex dolls and AI enhanced sex dolls but that just made them even angrier. To his credit, the pilot tried to distract them from Bai by activating one of the AI sex dolls who started talking to the customs people. It kind of freaked them out."

Jim was afraid to ask but had to know. "Then what?"

They arrested the pilot and co-pilot and put the plane under guard."

"What about Bai?"

"For now, they think she is another sex doll."

"I assume that would be a prohibited import."

"It's not clear yet."

"So, while all of this is really bad, why are you telling me?"

"Adler wants you and Julia to go to Ho Chi Minh City and try to get Bai and the pilots released."

Jim almost fainted. "Are you serious? How would I do that? I'm a programmer, not a politician or even a government official."

"Adler knows that. He has his lawyers working with US consulate personnel on freeing the pilots, but he needs you and Julia to convince them Bai is not human, or even a sex doll. They are already working on the visas you and Julia will need."

"How in the world am I supposed to do this?"

"I don't know, but you have to try." He started to leave then looked back. "Just don't get arrested."

Two days later, Julia and Jim entered a chartered jet for the long trek to Ho Chi Minh City, formerly Saigon. The first leg was over 18 hours from Houston to Taipei, with refueling stops in San Francisco and Hawaii, then they had a four-hour layover in Taipei and then another three-and-a-half-hour flight to Vietnam.

Julia tried to remain positive, but as the trip wore on, she shared her doubts with Jim. "How are we going to get this stuff past customs?" She had a large carry-on with an additional battery and several electronic tools she used to diagnose hardware issues.

Jim had a large laptop in his carry-on, but he didn't know if the authorities would confiscate those tools and electronics, since the whole issue revolved around Bao Zhu's arrest and subsequent confiscation of everything he owned. Technically, he didn't own Bai, and he could truthfully claim he had never even seen her. Maybe they could say she was being loaned by Adler for a brief period? Jim used a satellite phone to discuss the issue with Adler, and via a voice teleconference with his lawyers and two consulate officials. After a while, they agree to try the "loan" route. The lawyers were also in discussion with the consulate officials whether sex dolls or AI enhanced sex dolls were prohibited from import. The concept was new to everyone on the call, and they said they would research it.

After an excruciatingly long flight, they finally landed in Ho Chi Minh airport. Customs officials boarded, examined their visas and passports, and examined their carry-on bags. Jim turned his laptop on when requested, and Julia had a lengthy discussion about her diagnostic tools and the new battery. She also had a certificate from Future Power in Vietnamese describing the battery and certifying that it was not Lithium but Graphene a new material, just becoming available for batteries. She even showed them pictures of Graphene batteries currently available for power tools and after some discussion among the officials, they signed off on the plane's manifest, to the great relief of Jim and Julia.

They were led to an area just after the custom's line where the two American Consulate officials were waiting. George Adams and William Thomas filled them in on the latest.

There had been a lot of discussion with customs officials, and they had managed to convince them Bao Zhu did not own the dolls and they assured them he had never even seen them. They further affirmed that these had been loaned to Bao by a good friend Hugh Adler and that the dolls and even the AI enhanced dolls were "toys" and served no other purpose. Airport security had even brought drug-sniffing dogs on the plane and confirmed that there were no drugs on the plane or in the dolls.

After this there was some discussion on the appropriateness of these imports and the consulate people apologized if there was something inappropriate and said the dolls were intended for private use and were not for sale, and they would not be taken off the plane, and immediately returned to their owner (Adler).

They also mentioned the pilots were not responsible for these issues, and after further discussions the Customs officials agreed to release them.

It appeared to Jim and Julia that the major issues had already been resolved, but the consulate personnel pulled them aside for additional discussions. They had additional questions about Bai, who somehow seemed to be different than the other AI enhanced dolls. The officials agreed to keep the discussion confidential, and Jim and Julia gave them a very detailed explanation of what a Companion was, and the purpose. They had a hard time believing the facts, so Jim and Julia agreed to a demonstration. The pilots arrived almost at the same time as the airport officials gave them permission to re-enter the aircraft. They all found Bai inactive as her battery had discharged in the 48+ hours that had elapsed since her last charge.

At Julia's direction, they carefully laid Bai on the floor of the plane and turned her face down. Julia had to lift her blouse and undo her bra strap to access an indentation in the skin on her back, which when pressed, opened an access door that allowed her to extract the old battery and insert the new battery. The new battery didn't look like a regular battery at all as it was made of Graphene and black and polished and long and slender.

Julia had to maneuver it into position, and the consulate officials almost seemed embarrassed as the battery swap had to be done with Bai's bra undone and her face down on the plane's floor. As soon as the new battery was in, Julia quickly re-connected Bai's bra strap and pulled her shirt down just before Bai "woke up", turned over and sat up, which shocked the consulate officials. She saw the consulate officials first, but then smiled when she saw Jim and Julia.

"Hi Jim. Hi Julia." The space on the plane was small and Jim and Julia helped her up into a seat. She looked around and recognized the plane. "What are you doing here? Aren't we in Ho Chi Minh City?"

Everyone laughed and Jim confirmed "yes, we've been here a while."

"Was there a problem with customs?"

Jim and Julia both laughed, and Jim replied. "You could say that."

After a few more minutes, the consulate officials signaled to each other it was time to leave. On the way out, one of them commented "I wish I had a Companion that looked like that."

It took almost 24 hours to get everything sorted out and for the pilots to receive permission to leave. During that time, Jim and Julia took the opportunity to tour the former Saigon with a driver furnished by the consulate. They were amazed at the clean and new look of numerous tall condominiums and office buildings alongside several large freeways. They followed some recommendations for lunch and dinner at two highly rated Michelin starred restaurants and were put up in an international hotel chain for the night.

Both were exhausted due to the 12-hour time difference and the actions involved but Jim and Julia both enjoyed some much-needed intimate time. Jim hadn't expected it, but the last thing he remembered Julia saying was something like their time there had been "almost like a honeymoon".

The next day they returned to the airport where Adler's jet, Bai and the pilots were waiting for them and soon they were off to Taiwan, for the long trek back to Houston.

CHAPTER 20

Mila

After a brief rest, Jim was determined to finish with Mila, as she was his last Companion, he would have to provide the "advanced training" and report to Eric.

Mila's training went remarkably well, when Jim copied all the latest modules to her and there were no apparent problems with the database. He knew exactly what he needed to document to say she was ready. Eric also confirmed that her recipient, Marcin Budney, was now in Warsaw and eagerly awaiting her arrival. Eric quickly arranged another "Mannequins and More" flight to Warsaw and Jim was able to move on to try and document Mila's AI modules for some future programmer to maintain.

He received a text from Eric that Miguel wanted to meet to discuss his latest results. It seemed timely and they soon brought Eric up to date. Jim reported the latest on Mila and Miguel was able to describe completed training for Aiko and Astrid. Eric began planning flights to Tokyo and Oslo. That left only Jaana and Meera's training by Miguel to finish all the Companions. When he said that the project was nearing completion at a meeting with Eric, he thought about Julia's expectations and smiled. He really couldn't come up with a reason to not be her "best friend" and maybe, with time, even more.

Then he remembered Bai. What would happen to her? He was still thinking about Bai when he heard a loud discussion outside the conference room in Spanish. He looked out the door and saw Julia and

Miguel in a heated discussion. After a few minutes, Miguel left in a huff and Julia saw Jim staring at her from the conference room door. He had to know.

"What was that all about?"

She had cooled off some, but Jim could tell she was still upset. "We were discussing his latest advanced training, and he made some comment that began with 'all women' and I just had to straighten him out."

Jim laughed loudly and held out his arms. She walked to him, and they hugged for a bit. She nodded when he suggested they go to the break room for coffee.

Barely a day had passed when Eric called an emergency project meeting in the conference room. The team was now much smaller, only 4 specialists and 3 technicians, but all were wondering what was going on, that Eric would call a meeting with such short notice.

Jim thought Eric had a pretty grim look when he entered, and he took a deep breath fearing the worst.

"I have some important news. As you know Mr. Adler traded one of his Companions, Wei, to Prince Salman for the prince's old yacht as he was building a much bigger one, supposedly one of the biggest in the world. In my discussions with Mr. Adler, he conveyed to me that he is very happy with Emily, and they are planning a round-the- world cruise on the prince's former yacht, that should start very soon. He also told me he will probably sell his penthouse condo here in the Winstone Tower, as he probably will never need it again. But, most importantly he also said that his best friend Carlos Alvez of Brazil is also very happy with Gabriela and decided to make an offer for the whole Companion Project to Mr. Adler."

There were some audible gasps in the room. Jim realized his mouth was open and shut it. He glanced at Julia who had a similarly shocked expression, and she asked, "what does that mean for us?"

Eric smiled. "We all knew this project would end someday, we just didn't know how it would end, or exactly when it would end. But Mr. Adler apparently sent a note to all the actual recipients asking for the status of their relationship with their Companion. And, based on this note, they all now know who the other recipients are. Several replied back to all and expressed interest in obtaining additional Companions for their friends, or members of their family regardless of the cost. I think this is what led Carlos to think about the future of the project and to decide to make an offer to Mr. Adler for it."

One of the technicians wondered aloud. "Has Mr. Adler decided to sell?"

"That's why we are here. We had a long discussion about the sale, and he said that he will receive bearer bonds worth exactly twice what he paid to execute the project, all costs included, not just the hardware and software you might have expected. Mr. Adler said that amount should fund all his activities until he is no longer able to travel. He made one additional requirement, that key personnel remain to provide support for the existing Companions, like Emily and Gabriela, until a new project is kicked off, which will provide long-term support. The goal of that project is to find all possible ways to reduce the cost of a Companion to enable more people to afford a Companion, who desire one."

Julia laughed. "I guess this time they'll consider male Companions?"

Eric smiled. "That up to the new pre-project team. Everyone here will be offered a similar position in the new Companion Project."

Someone asked, "will you be the project manager of the new project?"

"That's ultimately up to Mr. Adler. He informed me of other possibilities within Adler Industries in case I wanted to move on."

There was quite a bit of discussion among the people at the table, until Eric tapped on a water glass in front of him. "Shortly you will receive a written communication explaining this in greater detail along with an offer to continue your contract for at least a year, if you decide it's right for you."

"All right. That's all I have for now. So, look at the communication, think about it and let me know in the next 2 weeks what you decide."

Eric left and Jim and Julia sat thinking while the other conversations slowly ended, and the other project and staff members slowly left them alone.

They looked at each other, until Jim volunteered. "I guess the end is in sight, new best friend."

Julia stood up and swiveled Jim's chair toward her, straddled him, put her arms around him and started kissing him. When he could, he whispered, "it's a good thing everyone else is gone" and started fondling her when she kissed him again, until she started bouncing his seat up and down.

"Are you trying to tell me something?"

CHAPTER 21

The Last Companions

Two weeks later, Eric met with Jim and Miguel to discuss Miguel's last advanced training sessions with Jaana and Meera. By now, Miguel knew exactly what to look for and didn't even need to review Jim's list of activities. Jim had copied all the AI generated modules in Aiko and Astrid as well as earlier Companions and Miguel had watched them carefully as they responded to stimuli, not only in the nighttime, but also in many different social venues, as these Companions had networked extensively with prior Companions before they were sent to their recipients. He reported to Eric that no additional programming or hardware changes were necessary, and he felt they were fully ready for their recipients in Ethiopia and Delhi. Eric appeared happy and mentioned he was already working on "Mannequins and More" flights for them. He left to finish the last project report he was required to file and send it to Mr. Adler.

Miguel smiled at Jim. "I know what you are going to ask. How was Jaana compared to my Nigerian girlfriend?"

"It was in the back of my mind." Replied Jim.

Miguel laughed. "As I've said many times, there is no comparison between an actual girlfriend and a Companion. A Companion satisfies certain desires and provides a lot of needed company at times when you really need it, but knowing that it's going to end, sort of keeps you from going crazy about them. I can't imagine what Mr. Adler would do if he suddenly lost Emily. By now, I'm sure she is a part of everything he thinks and does. It's crazy."

"Anything different about Jaana from the other Companions?"

"Not really, she interacts with everyone on the project in the same way. When we would go somewhere, like a ballgame, or to the park, or a movie, or any other place where couples go, no one noticed her, or me to be truthful." He was rubbing his beard.

"That's great. I'm hoping she'll blend in with her recipient's friends and family members. How about Meera? Anything not in your report to Eric that I should know?"

Miguel shrugged. "She's really straightforward and tells you exactly what she is thinking. She never holds back. It's a little shocking at first, but you get used to it."

"Ok, when are you going back to Skin So Soft?"

"Soon, I gave them a detailed report on the difference I saw with Nu Skin's product versus ours. They are still studying it. I haven't heard anything back yet. I did mention the need to provide repair kits just in case of a cut or burn, but their initial response back was like "it's likely not needed for any of our customers." He paused. "You saw my comments in my review for Bai for the need for repair kits in case a Companion cooks or engages in actions that might damage her skin."

" Yes, and Nu Skin is looking at that. You didn't violate you NDA, for the Skin So Soft comparison, I hope."

"I know better than that. They know the project is building human-like 'robots' for some reason but not at all what a Companion truly is."

Miguel had to know. "What about you, and Julia? Have you decided to join the new pre-project team?"

"I want to, but I'm not sure Julia has decided to or not. I guess you heard about her stock with Future Power?"

"Yes, she must be rolling in the dough now - so to speak."

"She was awarded 2000 shares each year for five years. As a startup, those were initially valued at one dollar each. When Future Power made a deal with that European EV company, her stock went to one hundred a share and kept climbing until it reached five hundred a share, then it split five to one. Those split shares are now almost two hundred a share. So, yes, that's ten million dollars if she sold today."

Miguel shook his head. "Wow. No wonder she may not want to keep working. If I had ten million, I would think pretty hard about taking on another one-to-three-year project."

He paused. "So are the two of you going to get married or what?"

Jim laughed and reached into his pocket and pulled out a diamond ring. "I've been looking for the right time to ask her. Maybe today's the day."

Miguel stood up and held out his hand, and Jim stood up and shook it. "Congratulations, she's pretty special."

"What about you? After all this advanced training with some of the prettiest Companions you'll ever meet, is there anyone you're thinking of?"

"Don't laugh. But Bai and I have been talking a lot." Jim's jaw dropped. "Bai? Your first Companion?"

"I talked to Eric first and he said talk to Adler. So, I did. Adler said the whole China AI export ban and the Vietnam thing messed up everything and he would be okay if Bai and I got together. I think it was partly to thank me for helping with the last five. I do know exactly what to expect from her. This time though, I won't have to wave goodbye at the worst possible moment."

Jim sat down in disbelief. "I never would have guessed that. But if you think it will work…." He paused. "Have you talked to Bai about it?"

"I talked to her about it before I talked to Eric or Adler. She's onboard. She even said she's looking forward to living with me."

"Where will you live? If you don't mind me asking."

"Adler also said he would give me one of the project apartments for as long as we want it. So, you'll still see me around, buddy."

They both laughed, and Miguel left Jim to think about the future. He realized he was still holding the diamond engagement ring and went to ask Julia if she still wanted to be more than best friends.

He had decided to do it in public so when he found her in the break room, he got down on one knee in front of several project and staff members, held out the diamond ring and asked her if she would marry him. She put her hands over her face and started crying and he held her until she whispered 'yes'. They decided to celebrate that night in her apartment.

CHAPTER 22

A Newer Project

A few days later, Eric sent out a current project update. Jaana and Meera's final training had been completed and "Mannequins and More" flights scheduled to Ethiopia and Delhi to transport the last of the Companions. There was no mention of Bai and Miguel.

A few days later, Adler called Jim and Julia on a videoconference call, nominally to talk about the next project but really to congratulate them on their upcoming wedding. He surprised them by gifting them his penthouse apartment on the top floor of the Winstone Tower building as a wedding gift. He didn't say it, but he was really trying to get them to sign on to the project as Julia was still waffling over joining or not, due to her newfound wealth. He also said he would be transitioning the project to Carlos Alvez during the planning stage and the kickoff meeting and the early work of the pre-project team.

The next day, Eric met them in the conference room as they had some questions about the next project. He was talking to them both but was looking at Julia.

"Mr. Adler is becoming concerned that you haven't committed to the new project. Is there something you want to know before committing?"

Julia quickly replied. "I'm not sure I want to work on a project to crank out as many Companions as possible. We know how to make them now, so there isn't much left to discover. I have enough money now that I don't need to work on something that isn't challenging for me."

"Well, one of the reasons for today's meeting is to say there will definitely be male Companions in the new project. Carlos has confirmed that and said he personally knows someone who wants a male Companion. So, from Carlos' viewpoint that will be in the scope of the project."

Julia seemed surprised, but somehow Jim was not, and he laughed. "Don't expect me to provide the advanced training for male Companions."

Julia smiled, held up her hand so Eric could see her engagement ring, and looked at Jim. "Hopefully by then, I will be married, and also not available to provide that type of training."

Eric brushed them off. "Those are details the next project manager can worry about."

Something in that statement got their attention. Jim tried to clarify his concern. "Are you saying, you are not going to be the project manager?"

"Adler called me this morning. The plant manager for the Louisiana rice harvesting equipment plant is retiring and he wants me to consider that position. The plant has more than 3000 employees so that would be quite a challenge for me. And quite a bit more money."

He saw the concern on their faces and continued. "Adler also wants me to float the idea of one of you taking on the role of the project manager."

They both were too shocked to answer, until Jim was able to ask, "how could either of us continue on in a major technical role and add the responsibilities of project manager?"

Eric smiled. "That a good question and I asked Adler that. He said your programming and hardware roles should be less demanding as most of the programming and hardware needed is known and there would be only a few minor changes needed. That should allow either of you to take on the project manager role."

Julia shook her head. "I'm a mechanical engineer and have no experience in management, so I have no interest in taking on that role."

Jim sat for a moment thinking, until he realized both were looking at him and waiting for his answer.

"I might have a compromise."

Eric leaned forward in anticipation. "I'd like to hear it."

Julia echoed him. "So would I."

"I think Adler is right in a way that the programming needed for future Companions should be mostly a copy and paste activity. So, a lot less programming will be required, but I would have a hard time finding an AI programmer to fill that role on the new project for any additional programming required. You know how hard it is to find experienced AI programmers. So, if all business type decisions could be made by a business manager and I would only have to make technical type decisions, I might be able to do that. I just don't want to worry about budgets, salaries, or performance discussions or promotions or any human resources type issues."

He stopped as they were both just staring, until Eric replied. "I'm sure Mr. Adler would agree to that. I'll call him right away."

Jim looked at Julia and he couldn't tell if she was relieved or angry. "What?"

"Somehow, I don't see a lot of your time in the next three years for me."

"We'll be together every day. You'll only be working on new hardware issues. I can find a technician to do all the routine hardware changes, to free you up for new stuff like the hardware needed for male Companions."

Eric closed a folder in front of him. "That's great. If Adler agrees to this, can I have both of your assurances you'll be there to kick off the new project?"

Jim and Julia were in a staring match until she nodded. "I'll stay around until the new hardware issues are resolved, but I'm not committing to a permanent role."

Jim looked at Eric. "I think that's a yes."

Eric jumped up. "I'll call Adler right now." He hurried out the door.

Julia was still upset. "Why would you agree to that?"

"I have invested a lot in the first 10 Companions. I would hate to see that lost if there isn't a concerted effort to support them in addition to the new Companions."

He could tell she was still upset. "Look, we'll be living in the penthouse apartment and can work as little or as much as we want." He stood up and walked behind her chair, started massaging her shoulders then started kissing her neck until she moved his hands to her breasts. "Ok, let's go celebrate our new jobs."

CHAPTER 23

Companion Updates

The next day, Jim and Julia held a pre-project meeting with Carlos. They thought it strange that he wanted to meet with them without Eric, but Carlos was smiling when he entered and sat down, which sort of set them at ease.

"Before we begin on the new project, I would like to know how the Companions are doing, and to determine if there are any hardware or software issues that need to be changed to make the new Companions even better."

Jim and Julia just looked at each other and didn't respond, so he clarified his intention to streamline the work processes.

"I would like you to visit all the Companions, talk to them, evaluate their status, see if there are any software or hardware issues that need addressing and develop learnings that can be applied to the next Companions."

They looked at each other with shocked expressions, until Jim responded. "Visit them! It will be extremely difficult to visit them and be allowed to check their hardware and software. Their recipients may not even allow that."

Carlos smiled again. "I have been in contact with all their recipients and have been assured they will not only allow it but assist us in any way we feel necessary. I will make one of my corporate jets available for these visits and have already started working on obtaining any visas needed with the host countries. Everyone I have talked to has been very agreeable, almost eager to meet and talk to you."

Julia was looking at the list of recipients and their current locations. "It could take more than a month just to make these trips. Probably two months once you add in the time for visits and evaluations."

"Yes, but I'll work with my staff to ensure that you have some free time at each recipient's location for sightseeing and to rest. I don't expect you to travel and work all the time." He paused. "The next project will have different types of Companions for different types of customers. This could be very difficult if we don't have an in-depth understanding of the hardware and software and the training we provide before we send the new Companions to their customers."

He paused to restate his reason for sending them. "There isn't anyone else I can ask to do this. You both have the most in-depth knowledge of the Companions' hardware and software."

Carlos paused to look at this watch. "Oh, I have another videoconference with a new customer, so please think about all this and let me know when you could begin."

He left and Jim and Julia just sat there stunned.

She looked at the recipient list again. "This is crazy. The Companions are in countries all over the world."

Jim smiled. "You know, we could be together almost 24 hours a day for 2 months. This could be trial run for how it might be when it's all over."

She hadn't thought of that. "You're right. If we can't be together for two months, how will we make it for years to come?"

Carlos had left the conference room door open and when they both stood up and started kissing, someone walking by yelled. "Get a room."

They laughed and started planning how they would evaluate the Companions, and agreed to start with Hugh Adler and Emily, while Carlos worked on possible visas and flight plans.

<u>Hugh Adler and Emily</u>

Hugh Adler and Emily had been in Miami when Carlos contacted them about a review of Emily's software and hardware before the start of the next project. He thought it was an excellent idea and agreed to move his yacht to Galveston to facilitate Jim and Julia's visit. He even offered the use of his helicopter, as when Jim visited before.

Julia and Jim were impressed by the size of Adler's "new" yacht that formerly belonged to the Saudi prince who was now with Wei. It was significantly larger than his previous yacht or the other yachts at the Galveston Yacht Marina.

Adler and Emily were waiting for them when they landed. Emily hugged Julia and Jim after he shook hands with Adler. They really couldn't hold a conversion on the helipad due to the noise of the helicopter preparing to takeoff, so Adler motioned them to follow him inside.

Julia had not seen Adler's previous yacht, but Jim had, and he marveled at the overall size and luxurious décor inside. This yacht was almost 250 feet long and had 7 levels with 12 staterooms for guests. The living area was immense, and they had both noticed the large swimming pool near the helipad when they landed.

Julia immediately noticed Emily's new and stylish wardrobe. It was a little hard for Julia to not be a little jealous (she often admitted she was) as Emily was also wearing some gold bracelets, some diamond earrings and the golden necklace Hugh had given her the last time Jim had visited. For his part, Jim noticed Emily's diamond ring and stylish new hairdo. He was certain that Emily would blend right in at a social gathering at the yacht marina.

After a brief chat, Jim and Adler left Julia and Emily to talk about her current status while they reviewed her status from Adler's perspective.

A cabin steward brought them some drinks and they found chairs on the main deck for a quiet discussion on the future Companion Project, and his new boat, of course.

"Quite a yacht. It's magnificent. I can't imagine someone buying an even bigger one than this."

"I was happy with my old yacht. You remember that one?"

"How could I forget it? It was amazing. So, what made you agree to give it up and take the prince's yacht in exchange for Wei?"

"He sent me a picture of this yacht and I couldn't believe it. I told him I would think about it. Then I talked to several companies who service yachts, and they estimated this yacht would be as much as eight to ten million a year just to operate and maintain it. I wasn't sure I wanted to take on that much responsibility when I'm so close to retirement, but then Carlos asked if I would include my old yacht with the Companion Project. His yacht is much more lavish than my old one, so why would he want it? In fact, he invited me on his yacht several times, and that's why I came to buy one of my own. His offer for the Companion Project was so much that I thought, what the heck? I can afford this yacht without a problem."

"I wonder what he's going to do with your old yacht?"

"No idea."

The sat drinking for a while and Jim filled him in on the latest project which included male Companions and female customers. Eventually the discussion turned to Emily.

Jim smiled. "Emily looks great. If I didn't know better, I would think she's a sugar baby."

Adler laughed. "At least you didn't say 'your daughter'. She's been wonderful. Always wanting to learn more. I don't know what I'd do if one day she decided she didn't want to be with me anymore." He held up his hands. "I know you warned me that could happen as she continued to learn and grow, but so far it hasn't happened."

"We are just starting on this review, but I've heard that some of the other Companions are learning new skills. Some are even working with their recipients."

Adler thought for a moment. "It's not exactly that, but one day she decided she wanted to captain this ship. I was shocked."

Jim's jaw dropped. "Captain a huge ship. Why?"

"I don't know. One day she was talking to the captain while we were crossing the Gulf and the next day, she asked how she could become certified to captain the ship."

"What happened then?"

"She started studying reference books and taking lessons online and I think she will take some kind of test in a month or so. If she passes that, then she could captain the ship."

"And you're okay with that?"

He shrugged. "I told her she could do anything she wanted to do and that's what she picked, so yes. I won't let my current captain go for a while though."

"Other than wanting to become a ship's captain, is she okay? Any mechanical problems or possible software issues?"

Adler shook his head. "I know her very well now and would know if something were wrong. She has grown tremendously in the time we've been together. Sometimes it almost seems as if we know what each other is thinking. We both know that she will need a maintenance check in a year or so and are planning on that."

"Are you still planning on around the world trip this year?"

"Yes, we both have been making plans for that. She seems eager to get that underway."

Jim really couldn't think of anything else. "So, we could say the Companion Project met all your goals?"

"Oh yes, and then some. She's irreplaceable." They both sat thinking and drinking for a while.

Inside, Julia had a wide-ranging question and answer session with Emily. Overall, Emily said she was happy with Adler. He encouraged her to find something she liked, and she described her training to be the ship's captain, which surprised Julia. Julia really couldn't find any issues that were concerning and reminded Emily of the hardware checkup in a year's time. Emily said they were preparing for that, as that would be about the time their round the world tour would end, probably in Galveston.

Adler and Jim returned, and they all agreed to meet for dinner.

The next day, Jim and Julia returned to the Winstone Tower in Adler's helicopter. They called Carlos and he joined the project team in a videoconference where Jim and Julia updated everyone on Emily's status and Carlos seemed pleased with Emily's status and was a little surprised at her desire to become the yacht's captain.

He ended the call with a surprise for them.

"I know Gabriela and I were next on your list to check for possible hardware and software issues, so I wanted to save you some time."

They were shocked when Gabriela, as if on cue, entered the conference room. "Hi Jim. Hi Julia. Hi everyone."

Jim was especially shocked to see Gabriela as her hair was longer (how did that happen), she was wearing some jewelry and an expensive designer dress. He thought *"she looks prosperous."*

Julia walked over to hug her, and they started chatting like old friends who hadn't seen each other in some time (which was sort of true).

After giving them a few minutes, Jim and the other project team members gathered around her to welcome her back.

CHAPTER 24

Carlos and Gabriela

Once all the greetings were finished, Jim, Julia and Gabriela retreated to Julia's lab to have a quiet discussion on her current status with Carlos and his friends and business associates.

They all sat down, and Gabriela looked at Jim. "As you know, Carlos' estate is in the middle of nowhere. It's beautiful and peaceful, but when he's working all day in the office, it was kind of boring for me. I watched TV and read books, and browsed the web, but after a while, I asked him if he could work in a city office where there are things I can do while he's busy."

"He wasn't ignoring you, was he?"

She laughed. "No, he gives me things all the time and there are daily nocturnal activities". She was looking at Julia, who laughed.

"But I found out there is a business office in Sao Paolo and finally convinced him to take me there. I told him his chauffeur could show me around and maybe I could do things with people in that office, like shopping. After a while, he agreed and now we spend more time in Sao Paolo than at his estate."

She smiled. "Did you know, Carlos's sister is the office manager in the Sao Paolo office?"

Jim and Julia shook their heads, and she continued. "She is really funny, and we became friends right away."

Jim started making some notes. "That's great. Did he encourage you to find a hobby or part-time job that you would like?"

"Yes, after a while of being in the office, I started asking some of the people there about the business and they explained it to me. There was a lot to learn about sugar cane and coffee bean production, but I searched the internet and showed some information that I summarized to his business manager, who really liked it and showed it to Carlos. Now, Carlos wants me to help them with some business ideas."

Julia was concerned about Gabriela's hardware. "Have you had any hardware problems that we need to know about? Is everything working all right?"

"I sometimes have a buzzing noise in my right ear. But then it goes away."

Julia picked up some diagnostic tools from the workbench and inserted a probe into her right ear. After a moment, she stopped the test. "I think you have a bad microphone. Give me a minute and I'll find a replacement." She started looking through some cabinets in the lab and Gabriela looked at Jim.

"I was glad when I heard you and Julia are getting married."

Jim smiled. "If we can find time with this new project about to start."

"I heard a little about it. Some new types of Companions and female customers. Is that why Carlos wants you to find out how the original Companions are doing?"

"Exactly."

Julia returned and asked Gabriela to take off her designer dress so she could access some hardware points. Jim excused himself and almost ran out the door. Julia and Gabriela laughed.

The next day, Jim and Julia had a videoconference with Carlos and reported the results, stating the hearing hardware was a minor issue, and the only one they could find.

Carlos was happy and said Prince Sal Bin Salman and Wei were waiting for them and the required visas were already approved.

Julia reminded him. "What about the time for sightseeing and rest during the reviews?"

Carlos had forgotten that part and it showed. "Sorry. Take the next three days off and then contact my pilot to obtain the landing rights and then inform the prince and tell him when you will arrive."

He started to leave the call. "Please tell Gabriela I miss her and to come home as soon as she can."

Julia looked at her phone. "I think the prince's yacht is in the Red Sea Marina near Jeddah." She looked at him. "So, what do you want to do in the next three days?"

Jim was smiling, and she continued. "Besides that."

CHAPTER 25

Prince Salman and Wei

Jim and Julia stared out windows as Carlos' jet approached King Abdulaziz Airport in Jeddah. Neither had been to the Middle East and were hoping to do some sightseeing once their visit to the prince and Wei was finished. After passing through customs and immigration, a black limousine quickly took them to the Red Sea Marina and the prince's new yacht. Neither had an idea of Wei's status and wondered if she had managed to blend in with the Saudi culture.

The limousine stopped in front of an enormous yacht, clearly the largest one in sight, and to their surprise, Wei saw them from high up on the top deck and waved as they neared the vessel. Two security guards were waiting along with the Officer of the Watch who greeted them and led them up a long gangway to the first deck.

Jim and Julia were not aware of any particular custom or formality in greeting a prince but tried to be as respectful as possible. Prince Salman was a lot younger than Jim expected, with a large beard, dark hair and eyes and unexpectedly a large smile on his face as they came on board. He was wearing the expected white robe and ghutra headdress.

They bowed their heads slightly and Jim walked to Salman who was holding out his hand.

"I am very pleased to meet you Mr. McVie."

Julia was just behind him, and he smiled at her. "Pleased to meet you also, Miss Cardenas."

"Thank you for agreeing to see us, your highness."

Wei was just behind the prince, and he turned to her and smiled. She rushed to hug Jim and then Julia. The prince smiled again, as Julia re-stated their purpose in meeting.

"We won't take much of your time, we just need to meet with Wei and determine if there are any hardware or software issues we need to address."

Salman nodded. "Hugh Adler told me about the follow-on project, and I'm curious about that as well. Perhaps we can go somewhere more private and talk about these issues."

Jim and Julia nodded, and the prince led them inside to an enormous and ultra-modern living area with two story windows and extensive world class art covering the walls. A steward brought them water glasses and they all settled in to discuss the original Companion project and the next one.

"I was surprised when Hugh Adler told me about the next Companion Project. I have heard the new sponsor Carlos Alvez has opened it up to anyone willing to pay a considerable sum for a Companion. That is very different from Adler who would not sell any Companion, regardless of the price."

Jim decided to give some background on the new project. "It all began when Mr. Adler sent an email to all the recipients of the Companions asking for status and if there were any technical issues. You received that email as well. Almost all the recipients replied to 'all" and that's when Carlos obtained their names. Some of them also expressed interest in obtaining another Companion in their reply to Mr. Adler. I think that's when Carlos determined there could be enough demand to begin a new project."

"I have to assume the new Companions will be very expensive, based on what Wei has told me about the various companies supplying hardware and software on the first project."

Julia replied. "The cost is still being determined, but there will be a small number of new Companions based on what we know right now."

Jim nodded. "But the new Companions will be different in many ways. We have heard there will be male Companions and female customers. That will impact not only the hardware but the software as well and is the reason why Carlos asked us to survey the Companions, so we have a much better idea of how to incorporate these changes."

"That's an excellent idea. And I also understand that the two of you are the leading hardware and software experts. That was the real reason I wanted to meet you."

Jim and Julia glanced at each other, and Julia wondered out loud. "Are there issues we should be aware of?"

"No, but if the cost can be determined, there could be several members of my family that might participate. They would like to meet you."

Wei had been listening intently, and finally joined the conversation. "Saud, why don't you introduce them to Jim and Julia?"

Salman laughed. "Wei is right. There are two family members here I would like you to meet." He waved to a steward who left quickly. He soon returned with two family members, who Salman introduced.

One was considerably older than Salman, the other was probably similar in age. They both seemed eager to meet Jim and Julia.

"This is my uncle and my brother-in-law."

They all shook hands and Salman explained that they did not speak English and he would explain for them.

"My uncle lost his wife years ago and has found it difficult to meet someone he could relate to in a romantic type of relationship. My brother-in-law also lost his wife in a tragic accident and similarly has had a hard time meeting someone. Both are very fond of Wei and have been very vocal in their desire for a similar Companion."

Julia replied before Jim could. "I hope everyone understands that this is a very complicated and very costly process and will take some time even if the costs can be accommodated."

Salman nodded. "We are all aware that this is a very new concept and very technologically challenging and cannot be done quickly."

Julia was curious. "On the first project, each Companion was designed to be representative of the country or area of the recipient. Wei was originally intended for a Chinese friend of Hugh Adler before that didn't work out. Would they be okay with a Companion that would be typical of this country? We don't know yet, how the new Companions will be selected."

Salman translated Julia's statement and question and the uncle and brother-in-law replied. Salman seemed pleased.

"They would be happy to accept a Companion representative of this country. Personally, it would not have mattered to me. Wei is wonderful, and beautiful."

Jim glanced at Julia and smiled. If they were alone, she would probably have jabbed him in the ribs again.

Jim and Julia were not surprised but Salman's uncle and brother-in-law were when Wei immediately hugged Salman.

Salman apologized but he had an important family meeting to go to but suggested they stay and talk to Wei for as long as they wanted, and he would return in time for dinner with them.

Salman and his family members left, and Jim and Julia and Wei sat down on some enormous sofas and started chatting.

Julia asked Wei if she was experiencing any hardware issues.

"No, everything is fine." She smiled at Jim when he asked how she had assimilated into Salman's culture.

"It was easy at first. My language module teacher spent some time telling me about the culture, what was normal, what was allowed and what was not allowed."

Julia was concerned about Wei's limitations. "What do you do all day?"

"I generally don't leave the yacht very much and never without Saud. This is mostly my choice as his security guards would take me almost anywhere, I wanted to go. I do get bored sometimes and have asked Saud about finding a way to contribute to the society here." She seemed to be thinking of a possible way forward.

"I have always been interested in graphic design and am taking a few courses online and have even managed to find a few people willing to pay for designs. Saud is okay with that, and even bought a large graphic design computer for my work and encourages me to find new companies that would be willing to pay for my design work." She paused. "I would like to give any money I make to a local charity I am working with, since I don't need the money."

"And you would be happy here if your design work kept you busy, when Salman is busy or not available?"

"Yes. We still have lots of time for each other, and he is very generous. He often gives me gifts, and many compliments." She laughed. "Especially when we are alone, and he wants to do what you call nocturnal activities."

Julia laughed at Jim who was just shaking his head.

Later that evening, over dinner, they told Salman they had gathered all the information they needed and would be leaving tomorrow.

"Have you thought anymore about possible Companions for my uncle and brother-in- law?"

Jim assured him they had. "Of course, but it's not our decision. Just give Carlos the details and he will tell you the next steps."

Salman was looking at his phone. "Oh, a call from Carlos. Yes?" He listened for a while and when the call ended, he updated them. "Carlos has arranged for a car that will take you to the airport tomorrow where his jet will be waiting. I'll ask Wei to meet you for breakfast in the morning. I am sure there are some more things you would like to talk to her about."

After they retired to their stateroom for the night, Jim was just staring out the balcony windows and Julia asked if something was wrong.

"Not exactly. I don't know why but somehow; I feel like Wei's situation is less satisfactory than Emily's or Gabriela's. I don't know if I can explain it very well."

"I think I know what you are saying, but she says she's happy and will be even happier if she can make her design business a success."

"I know, but something just seems missing."

Julia flopped on the bed. "Maybe it will come to you after you've slept on it." She then patted the bed next to her." Why don't you come here, and I'll help you forget about it for a while."

Jim smiled.

The next morning, Jim and Julia and Wei chatted over breakfast and Wei apologized that Salman was already gone for the day on business. Wei was curious about the new project, and they filled her in as much as they knew, saying that Carlos would provide more guidance once their reviews with existing Companions were done.

CHAPTER 26

Kumar and Amara

Carlos had scheduled their next visit to Amara in Bangalore, as it would save a lot of time to go directly there instead of returning to Houston. The five plus hour flight was uneventful, and Julia snuggled with Jim most of the way.

Julia suspected Jim was still thinking about Wei, as he was less talkative than usual. "Are you still worried about Wei?"

"Yes. She says she's happy and wants to stay on Salman's yacht all the time, but I think she would be happier if she could mingle more with people. The graphic design work she does on the yacht only makes her more isolated."

Julia was still thinking about that when Jim continued. "I think I'm going to recommend to Salman and Carlos that we provide a second Companion to keep her company."

Julia was shocked. "You think they will want to spend five to ten million dollars to keep someone company?"

"I don't know, but I will ask Salman first. Get his thoughts on it, and if he agrees, I'll ask Carlos about it. It may not pan out, but I think I have to try."

Julia shrugged. "Okay. I'll support your idea if they ask me what I think."

The rest of the journey was uneventful. Neither had been to India before, and Bangalore was a modern technology center with countless skyscrapers next to endless elevated roadways. They were amazed when their limousine stopped in front of Arjun Kumar's company's massive skyscraper. Jim had researched Kumar and found he was an extremely wealthy investor and he wondered how he became such a good friend of Hugh Adler. As directed, they took an elevator to the 50th floor and the Kumar Financial Services office. Julia wondered aloud why they didn't just meet where Amara was living rather than in Kumar's office building. Their questions were answered when Kumar and Amara met them when they entered the company's office. Amara gave the expected "Hi Jim. Hi Julia" greeting, then walked quickly to hug Julia then Jim. Kumar was a financial wizard and probably in his early 60s with silver hair and dark eyes. He had a huge smile on his face when Amara rushed to hug them. Jim shook Kumar's hand, and he laughed when Amara gave him a huge hug.

"It's a pleasure to finally meet you. I've heard so much about you and Julia from Amara. She always speaks highly of you."

Julia and Amara were now standing near them, and Kumar asked everyone to follow him to a conference room.

Once they had settled in, he said what they were thinking. "You are probably wondering why we are meeting here." He looked at Amara. "Why don't you explain?"

Amara nodded. "Like Hugh Adler, Arjun had a penthouse condominium on the top floor of this building when I arrived. He was spending most of his time in the office, so I began to talk to employees here to understand what his company does. After a while, I was able to help in some financial arrangements, and he asked me to work with him." She smiled. "We do go to the condo at the end of the day for personal time."

Kumar nodded. "She is an excellent financial planner. She accesses an incredible amount of data from many business sources, and the internet of course, and summarizes it excellently for our clients."

He realized they were waiting to ask him questions and paused. "Please, ask whatever you want."

Jim went first. "How did a financial expert become such a good friend of the owner of a farm equipment business?"

"I met Hugh many years ago, when he first came to India to determine a possible market for his harvesting equipment. He knew the main crops in India were rice, cotton, and wheat, which he already had a great deal of experience with. Many Indian farms are small, and the cost of major harvesting equipment was a major hurdle. With our help he founded a business that specialized in sales of this type of equipment to family farms and offered financing for it. He also downsized some of his standard equipment for the smaller farms that are typical here. This helped the farms and Hugh to grow his business here. Once this business became established in India, we worked with him to finance similar businesses in other Southeast Asia countries."

He paused. "You are probably wondering why Hugh gifted me a wonderful Companion, like Amara."

Jim was curious. "Yes, we assumed you were in a position to accept a Companion."

"My wife died almost 12 years ago. She was a really good friend of Hugh Adler's wife, even a better friend than I was to Hugh. I think it is because of her memory that Hugh gifted me Amara."

Julia finally had a chance to ask about Amara. "We are really here to discuss any hardware or software issues Amara may be experiencing."

"Yes, of course. Why don't I leave that to you. I have some phone calls to make."

He excused himself and Jim and Julia stared at Amara for a moment, until Julia asked, "How are you Amara?"

"I am glad you came. My disposal system is not working, and I haven't been able to eat or drink anything in more than a week. It hasn't been a real problem but some of Arjun's colleagues are wondering why I don't eat with them, or even be social with them after work."

Jim looked at Julia. "Is that something you would have with you?"

"I have a complete hardware set on Carlos' jet. I'll just need to get a ride back to the airport to get one. Changing that isn't easy though."

Jim got up and went to ask Arjun about a ride to the airport for Julia.

When he left, Julia asked if there were any "issues" adjusting to the culture in Bangalore and even Arjun's family.

"Not really. My Hindi module instructor gave me a lot of information that helped me blend in with Arjun, his family, his company, and the culture."

"Are your personal relationships okay as well?"

"Yes, we always find time for each other when we are not in the office. Arjun was nice to me in the beginning, but he is even more attentive now, especially in the nocturnal activities."

Julia laughed and was going to ask Amara more, when Jim and Arjun returned. Arjun said something to Amara in Hindi, and she hugged him. He looked at Julia.

"There will be a car waiting when you get to the ground floor. They will take you to the airport, wait until you find what you need, and bring you back."

Julia had a thought. "Could Amara go with me? We still have a lot to talk about." Arjun nodded. "Of course."

Amara and Julia chatted all the way to the airport. There were several large boxes of hardware pieces on the plane and Julia surprised Amara when she said she didn't need much room and she could replace her storage tank on the plane.

Several hours later, Jim and Arjun were discussing the new Companion project when Julia and Amara returned. Julia surprised them both with the latest.

"All done."

Jim couldn't believe she had already replaced Amara's storage tank. "How could you possibly do that so fast? I thought you said it wasn't easy to change a tank."

"It isn't easy, I just didn't need much room to do it, so I did it on the airplane."

Amara agreed. "She is really fast at hardware revisions. I was only 'on hold' for 30 minutes."

Julia smiled. "Practice makes a difference. Amara and I had some very long chats to and from the airport, and I think we have all we need to assess her current status."

Jim was going to question that, but Arjun interjected. "That's great. Let's go to dinner."

After a relaxing dinner, Jim and Julia were delivered to their hotel while Amara and Arjun returned to their penthouse. The next day, they all had breakfast in an exclusive restaurant near the office building and said their goodbyes.

While waiting for final permission to takeoff at the airport, they received a call from Carlos about the next leg in their journey, to visit Mila and Marcin Budny in Warsaw Poland. Mila and Marcin would meet them at Chopin airport in Warsaw and bring them to his estate about 15 miles outside of Warsaw.

After a thirteen-hour flight that landed in the evening in Warsaw, Jim and Julia were exhausted and ready for some time off. But, as soon as they made it through security and immigration, Mila and Marcin were waiting for them. Marcin was a little taller than Jim and with an athletic build looked even younger than pictures Jim found on social media when he researched him.

Marcin laughed when Julia said something to Mila and she rushed to hug her, and then Jim. Marcin shook Jim's hand, and he asked them to follow him. A chauffeur and a limousine took them to Marcin's large estate in the country where they freshened up and met for dinner. There wasn't much conversation as Jim and Julia were so tired, they could hardly keep their eyes open, and Marcin spoke limited English. He apologized that his assistant was not there as Marcin relied on him to translate almost all his business dealings. It was a little awkward, until Marcin suggested they retire for the evening and meet at breakfast when his assistant would be there.

They gratefully agreed and almost passed out once in bed. The next morning, they met Mila and Marcin and Bartek Bosko for breakfast. It was a relief as Bartek could fill them in on Marcin's background, his relationship with Hugh Adler and what might have led Hugh to gift Mila to Marcin. Mila was strangely quiet and did not interrupt. Bartek had been with Marcin for almost 20 years, most of that time as his personal assistant, and it seemed he could answer almost any question Jim or Julia asked.

"Marcin inherited a small farm many years ago from his parents and managed to grow it to one of the most successful farms in Poland, growing wheat, rye, and oats. He also had a large operation in apples and in poultry farming. Hugh Adler met him at a convention where new farming equipment was being introduced. Marcin is a mechanical engineer and was intending to pursue that as a career when his parents tragically died in an auto accident, and he had to take over their farm. His engineering skills helped him with new and better farming techniques and equipment. When he met Hugh Adler, they immediately became friends and Marcin even helped Adler improve some of his equipment. I think that is why Adler gifted Marcin with Mila."

Jim saw Marcin listening but didn't know if he would understand his questions or not. "Why would Marcin be interested in a Companion? He seems young and not bad looking, why didn't he find someone to share his life with? Hugh Adler told us he was gifting Companions to friends who didn't have a wife or were divorced and were single when he selected them."

Bartek seemed a little uncomfortable answering. "Marcin was married twice and was frustrated that he would never find a woman he could share his life with. When he heard from Adler about the Companion Project, he almost begged him to give him a Companion. He said he would pay any price and I think he meant it. But Adler said Companions were not for sale."

"So, what happened? Why did Adler change his mind?"

"Marcin told Adler he would donate half of everything he owned to several charities in Poland if he would give him a Companion. I think that is what finally convinced Adler to change his mind and give him Mila."

Julia chimed in. "That's quite a story. But we are here to determine if there are any hardware or software issues with Mila. Would you gentlemen mind if Mila and I went on a walk outside to talk. It's looking like a beautiful day outside."

Bartek translated her question to Marcin who nodded. "Of course. Please walk."

Julia left with Mila for a walk around Marcin's massive estate while Jim, Marcin and Bartek continued their discussions. Jim asked if Mila had any hobbies or interests to keep her busy while Marcin was busy. Bartek said Mila was very interested in technical writing and was finding some work as a contract writer for web sites. Jim made a note of that, and they continued their discussion which eventually turned to the new Companion Project as Marcin was very interested in how it would be different from the first project.

On the walk, Julia immediately asked Mila if she had any outstanding hardware issues. To her surprise, Mila asked her to speak louder as she could barely hear anything. Julia repeated her question directly into Mila's ear.

"I am not hearing well. It makes following a conversation very difficult. I thought about learning sign language, but I understand it is very difficult for everyone who wants to talk to me."

Julia relayed Gabriela's problem with hearing and told her she had hardware in Carlos' jet that could fix her hearing. Mila seemed overjoyed. Julia told her she would go and talk to Marcin and Bartek about retrieving the hardware needed. Mila hugged her then followed her inside and sat on a chair while Julia talked to Bartek.

A few hours later, Julia returned with some diagnostic tools and some new hearing devices and Bartek led them to a large bedroom where they could be alone while Julia determined the problem and replaced the defective hardware.

Later that afternoon, Mila joined the conversation as Julia described the problem and the solution.

"Julia is so efficient. I was only 'on hold' for less than an hour."

Marcin decided to test her hearing and called her the most beautiful woman he had ever seen. Jim saw Mila's eyes get bigger and she ran to hug Marcin. Bartek smiled.

"That's the old Mila. We had no idea she had these issues as she seems reluctant to share anything wrong with Marcin, or me."

Julia whispered to Jim. "I think we have everything we need to determine her status."

Jim agreed. "Bartek, would you tell Marcin that our assessment is done, and we would like to start writing a report for Carlos and then return to Houston. We've been gone a while and need to find out what's going on with the next project."

Bartek nodded. "Gladly." He translated for Marcin who seemed very happy to have the old Mila back with him. Bartek replied that Marcin will contact his driver and let Carlos' pilot know, so he can file a flight plan to leave the next day.

They all had dinner that evening and to Jim and Julia, Mila was just like she was when she left for Warsaw.

The long flight back to Houston, with three refueling stops took more than 16 hours and Jim and Julia were exhausted again. They planned on asking Carlos for a break to recuperate.

Just as they returned to the Winstone Office Tower Building, there was a text message from Carlos asking them to come to a video meeting in the conference room. It was somewhat unexpected as it was already very late in the evening.

When they connected, Carlos had a surprise for them.

"I've been reading your summary reports for each of the first five Companions, and I am very happy with the information obtained. I also know how hard this has been and with five more Companions to assess, the process as it is right now will have an impact on the start of the next project. So, right now, I am arranging for the last Companions to be transported to the lab where you can assess their hardware and software and capture any additional learnings you may find. I hope we can finish the final five in two weeks or less as there are some important things going on with the new project that I can't mention yet, and it needs to proceed as quickly as possible."

Jim and Julia sat stunned, not sure what to say. After a moment, Carlos concluded the call. "I can see you are still recovering from the trip, so think about what I said, and I will call you in three days with more details on finishing the final five Companions. Try and get some rest. Talk to you then."

He left the call and Julia rubbed her eyes. "What did he say?"

"I'm not sure. Let's go get some sleep."

CHAPTER 27

Aiko and Astrid

After a brief two-day rest, Jim and Julia toured the lab and talked to everyone to learn what had happened while they were gone. They didn't have much time as Aiko and Astrid showed up together at Jim's workstation. Both were pulling their carry-ons and greeted him together in the usual way. "Hi Jim. Where can we put our stuff?"

Jim called Julia for help. She came quickly and together they agreed both would stay in their penthouse apartment (it had 4 bedrooms) and once they settled in, Aiko and Astrid would join them in the conference room the next day to go over their current situations in Tokyo and Oslo, including possible hardware and software issues.

Julia began the meeting by asking Aiko about her recipient in Tokyo. She wanted to know how Hinata Soto knew Adler, and what led him to give Aiko to him.

"Hinata is one of the largest rice farmers in Japan. It is difficult for non-Japanese companies to get into the farming business in Japan, but Hinata met Mr. Adler at a convention in Japan and later helped him obtain licenses from the government to sell his equipment. After a while, Mr. Adler used his association with Hinata to convince rice farmers in other countries, like Thailand, to try his equipment. Mr. Adler once said he would not have been able to expand his business to many countries in Southeast Asia without Hinata's help. I think that is why Mr. Adler wanted me to be Hinata's Companion."

Jim was making notes and when Aiko stopped, he asked "Is Hinata married now?"

"No, his wife died many years ago, and he has not re-married. I know one of the requirements for a Companion is that they are not married when the decision is made for a Companion."

Julia nodded. "Can you tell us about your time with Hinata? Does he treat you well?"

Aiko smiled. "Oh, very well. We have private time together every day."

"What do you do when he is working?"

Aiko laughed. "I am a teacher, in an elementary school."

Julia was as shocked as Jim. "Teacher! What do you teach?"

She smiled, "English and math for 4th and 5th graders."

Julia still couldn't believe it. "And Hinata is okay with this?"

"Yes. I was bored just watching TV, reading books, and browsing the web and one day I visited a school with Hinata, and they told me there is a shortage of teachers. So, with Hinata's help I began studying to become an instructor. After I became a certified instructor, he helped find me the position in a nearby town."

Julia shook her head but remembered her role. "Do you have any hardware or software problems that you would like us to look at or work on?"

Ailo seemed to be running a diagnostic program. "The vision in my left eye is not always clear."

"When we're done here, I can check that."

Aiko smiled. "Thank you."

Jim looked at Astrid. "What about you Astrid? Could you tell us about your time in Oslo with Amund Dahl?"

Astrid began with a brief history of farming in Norway. "The climate in Norway makes it hard to grow most crops, but Amund has a very large farm and grows barley, oats, potatoes, and carrots."

"He first met Mr. Adler at a farming hardware show in Germany. Most of Mr. Adler's equipment was not especially suited to the Norwegian climate, but he worked with Amund to modify it and when Amund's crop yields increased, he was very happy and told everyone about Mr. Adler's equipment and some farmers he knew in Germany began to buy Mr. Adler's equipment. It really helped Mr. Adler during some tough years in Europe when the weather was bad, and farmers bought his equipment anyway because he had made it work in Norway's harsh climate."

"Ok, is Mr. Dahl married?"

"No, he was married but his wife divorced him because he was traveling a lot with Mr. Adler helping him sell his equipment. When he found out about the Companion Project, Hinata flew to Kansas to convince Mr. Adler that he really wanted and needed a Companion. Mr. Adler agreed, and my language module instructor had some special instructions for me, about Norway, farming, Amund and the Norwegian culture. It helped me a lot."

Jim stopped writing and looked at Julia. "It looks like there is a piece to the overall success of a Companion that we've overlooked."

She tapped her pen on a pad of paper. "The language module consultant. Why did we not notice that before?"

"It's not hardware or software, but a consultant's instructions, and we had no input on it."

Jim looked at Aiko. "Did your Japanese module consultant have any special instructions for you on the culture of Japan, or even Hinata?"

Aiko just stared for a moment. "Yes, the last 10% of her training and instructions were about the Japanese culture, farming in Japan, and some background information on Hinata."

Jim shook his head and Julia dropped her pen. "Shit. Why didn't we notice that before?"

"We were too focused on the hardware and software and why Adler selected each recipient for a Companion."

Julia picked up her pen. "Astrid, do you have any hardware of software issues we should look at or fix?"

She paused, running an internal diagnostic program. "Sometimes I can't smell very well when I'm with Amund during our nocturnal activities."

Jim laughed loudly and Julia had to laugh as well. "I know what you are going to say, so don't." To Astrid "I have a replacement, we can do that tomorrow when we fix Aiko's eye."

Astrid smiled. "Thank you, Julia."

"One final question, what do you do to keep busy when Amund is busy at work?"

"I am studying to be an accountant. I love working with numbers, and Amund supports me. He would like me to work in the accounting department of his company."

Jim put his pen down. "Okay, I think we are done for today. Why don't you ladies go back to our place and re-charge or rest or whatever while Julia and I discuss today's findings."

They both gathered their purses (Jim hadn't even noticed they were carrying purses) and left together, chatting about the day's activities.

Jim glanced at Julia. "I think we have a major finding today. Do you want to write a report for Carlos, or do you want me to?"

She yawned. "Would you do that? I'm just going to close everything up in the lab and go back to our place and rest."

She left and Jim returned to his workstation to write up the day's findings.

He also called Henri to arrange for Aiko and Astrid to be returned to Tokyo and Oslo. Henri immediately called Carlos to set up the flights.

He was still at his workstation studying Astrid's AI created modules when Julia angrily entered and banged the door shut. He looked at her wondering what was wrong.

She held out two white boxes, one in each hand. "Astrid left these on my workstation!"

Jim didn't recognize the boxes. "What are they?"

She held up one. "This is strawberry flavored, edible deodorant. Did you put her up to this?"

Jim laughed so hard he could hardly answer her. "No, why would I do that? What's in the other box?"

She held it up. "Four different flavored lubricants. That's really funny…"

When Jim finally stopped laughing, he said "Why do you think I had anything to do with this?"

"Where else would she come up with that. Is that an inside joke?"

"No, I don't know where she got that."

"Can Companions even play jokes on people?"

"Not from their final state programming. It must be something she picked up watching TV, or reading books, or browsing the web, or talking to other people." He suddenly stopped, realizing what she was asking. "No, I've never used anything like that, and Miguel did her final training, remember?"

Julia was still upset but obviously calming down. He thought for a moment. "Maybe that's a belated wedding present, or a Norwegian practical joke?"

She had calmed down and was staring at the boxes in her hands. "Want to try them?"

Jim laughed so hard; he almost fell off his chair. When he looked up, she was still waiting for an answer. He thought *"why not?"*

"Sounds like fun." He put his arm around her waist as they left the workstation room.

The next morning, he stopped by the receptionist's workstation. She was shocked as she knew who he was, and Jim almost never stopped by to talk to her. At first, she thought something was wrong, and her expression made Jim smile.

"Hi Kishori. There's nothing wrong, I just need your help." She visibly relaxed and Jim continued. "In addition to your receptionist and office assistant duties, I heard you sometime helped with record keeping on some projects for Mr. Adler. Did you help with that on the first Companion Project."

She thought for a moment. "Yes, with some of the written communications and contracts."

"That great. Could you see if there are any records regarding the language consultants on the project? I would like to see if there were any written instructions or agreement on exactly what the consultants were supposed to do."

She was writing a note and stopped. "Okay. It might take a day or two. There are a lot of records, as you can see." She pointed to a large row of filing cabinets.

"That's fine. Either paper or electronic form is fine. Thanks Kishori."

He left and Kishori watched him walk off and sighed.

Two days later, Jim received a series of emails with attached documents from Kishori.

The first language module consultant contract was pretty straightforward and made no mention of any specific instructions about the country, or the recipient or the business of the recipient, or the culture of the country. So, it appeared the information he needed was not in the contract itself but in an attachment. He reviewed a second contract, and it was almost identical to the first.

He searched the remaining emails for contract addendums and couldn't find any. Where were the non-language related instructions to the consultants?

He thought for a while. Maybe the information came directly from Hugh Adler? How could he find that? He hated to bother Adler as he was now on his around the world trip with Emly, and probably wouldn't want to be disturbed. What about Eric? He called Eric, who was probably either at work or in his new apartment in Iberia Parrish in Louisiana and to his amazement, Eric answered. He was surprised it was Jim as he hadn't heard anything from him since he left the project.

"Hi, Eric, it's Jim. Would you have a moment to answer a quick question on the Companion Project?"

"Oh, of course, if I can."

"Carlos asked Julia and me to visit the Companions to see if there were any hardware or software issues, we should be aware of before we started the new project. During those reviews we found some possibly conflicting information provided by the language module consultants. I looked at their contracts and there isn't any specific information they were supposed to provide beyond their language training activities. Do you know how the consultants would have received that information?"

"Yes, during the pre-project meetings Mr. Adler was trying to narrow down the list of possible recipients and we discussed the likely candidates. Once they were selected, I developed a form that was filled out by Mr. Adler with information he thought would help the Companion adapt to the culture they were going to try and blend in with."

"That's great. How was that information sent to the language consultants?"

"As an attachment to a text message once they signed their contract. You should be able to find it in my personal folders. I left them with the record keeping team in the accounting department."

"Wow, that's great. Thanks so much."

"You're welcome. Did you really travel all over the world to talk to the Companions and their recipients? I can't believe Carlos asked you to do that."

"Yes, we are almost though now, and it has been enlightening, and mostly obvious except for the information provided by the language consultants. That seems to have made a big difference in how the Companions blended in with the culture of their new country."

"I wouldn't have guessed that. What about the new project? How is that going?"

"It really won't start until we complete our status review of the current Companions."

"Okay. If you can, please keep me updated as it goes forward. I feel I have a vested interest in it, as it will probably be based to a large extent on the first project."

"I will. Thanks for your time."

After the call, Jim immediately returned to the receptionist's workstation and asked Kishori if she knew where the Companion project folders Eric left behind were archived.

Kishori stared at him for a moment, trying to remember. "Oh yes. Just a minute."

She walked to a specific cabinet and returned with a stack of folders. "To my knowledge, this is everything Eric left behind that's project related."

She handed them to Jim, and he stared at the stack of 50 or so folders. "Guess this will keep me busy for a while. Thanks."

She sighed when he left to carry them to his workstation. He called Julia and asked if she had a few minutes to help him look through the folders and she soon was helping him search the folders for the language consultants' instructions from Hugh Adler.

It was almost the last folder he searched for when Jim exclaimed. "Bingo!"

Julia was soon standing looking over his shoulder as they read the instructions Adler had given to several of the language instructors.

After a while, Julia muttered. "Fool's gold."

Jim had to agree. "If each of the consultants really discussed Adler's data on the country and culture of each recipient at the end of their language training, why are the Companions at such different stages of blending into the existing culture?"

CHAPTER 28

Jaana and Meera

One week later, Jaana and Meera showed up at Jim's workstation in the morning and greeted him in the usual way. "Hi Jim. Where can we put our stuff?"

He handed them card keys to the penthouse apartment. "The apartment number is on the yellow sticky note on top. Please make yourselves comfortable, re-charge if necessary and meet me and Julia in the conference room at 1:00PM."

"Ok, Jim." They left and Jim called Julia to tell her Jaana and Meera were here and to remind her about the meeting at 1PM.

Jaana and Meera entered the conference room at precisely 1PM and Jim motioned them to have a seat.

Julia began the questions. "You should know why we are here. We just want to do a follow up on your statuses in Ethiopia and Delhi. So, Jaana could you describe your situation in Ethiopia with Ahmed Alemu?"

"Ahmed has a very large coffee farm in Ethiopia. He also grows potatoes and sugar cane and a few other vegetables, but coffee is the biggest source of income for him."

"Did he meet Hugh Adler because of the coffee beans or sugar cane? Most of Mr. Adler's business is in harvesting equipment for coffee beans and sugar cane."

"Ahmed is a friend of Carlos Alvez in Brazil. It was Carlos who suggested he change from other crops like potatoes and maize to coffee beans and sugar cane. Carlos also introduced Hugh Adler' harvesting equipment to Ahmed. That helped him increase his production and he became wealthy because of that. Maize, or corn as it is known here, is not very profitable in Ethiopia."

Jim followed her questions. "Why do you think Mr. Adler agreed to give a Companion to Ahmed? Mr. Adler must know a thousand farmers all over the world."

"I don't know exactly. Ahmed knows farmers all over Africa and I think he introduced Hugh Adler to many of them. Maybe that is why his equipment is so popular in Ethiopia, and probably the rest of Africa."

That wasn't very satisfying, but they had bigger issues, so Julia continued. "Do you have any software or hardware issues we should know about? We can fix them here if you do."

Jaana stared at her while she ran a diagnostic routine. "I sometime have problems with my sense of smell at night."

Julia almost broke the pen she was holding when she looked at Jim and he was trying not to smile.

"Ok, we can fix that. Anything else?"

Jaana shook her head. "Not that I can identify."

Jim pressed her on her relationship with Ahmed. "So how are you and Ahmed doing? Does he seem happy you are there?"

"Oh, yes. We find time for each other every day." She smiled. "And night."

Jim started a follow-up, but Jaana continued. "Do you know what I do when Ahmed is busy on his farms all day?"

Julia and Jim shook their heads.

"I am a day trader. I trade over the counter stocks on the Ethiopian Security Exchange. I also do some trading on the New York Stock Exchange and the London Exchange, and even the Singapore Stock Exchange. I can trade 24 hours a day if I want to."

Jim and Julia were too shocked to say anything.

"I'm doing really well, and Ahmed is happy and even wants me to do more." She laughed. It makes some of our conversations at night very interesting."

Jim struggled to continue after that. "One last question from me. Did the preparation you received from your language module consultant help you blend into Ahmed's family and the Ethiopian farming business and overall culture?"

She stared for a moment. "Yes, it is very different from here, but with her help I was able to communicate with Ahmed and his family and they immediately started helping me by taking me shopping with them for food and clothes. So, yes, it helped me."

Julia wanted to replace her smell sensor and asked Jaana to meet her in the lab after the meeting. Jaana smiled.

Jim noticed that Meera was smiling, waiting for her turn. "So, Meera, how is it going with Kabir Chopra in Delhi?"

She stopped smiling. "Not so well."

That immediately got Jim and Julia's attention. "What's wrong?"

"It's not Kabir. It's his grandson."

"His grandson?"

"Yes, he is about ten years old and plays computer and video games all the time. The very first time he saw me; he said I was 'evil' or something like that. He even throws things at me and yells at me and tells everyone I'm not human."

Jim and Julia were shocked, but Jim followed up. "What does Kabir say, or do about this?"

"When Kabir is there and he sees this, he punishes him, takes his games and computer away, and makes him stay in a bedroom. I'm glad he doesn't live with Kabir and me."

She held up her arms and hands so they could see. "See these marks, he was throwing sharp things at me and tore my skin. I did not have a means to fix it the right way and could only glue it."

Julia stood up and quickly walked to examine her hands and arms. "I have a large number of Nu Skin repair kits. I can fix all this." She looked at Jim. "We need to do something more about this than repair her skin."

"Nu Skin is already aware of this issue and is working on a new type of synthetic polymer that uses Graphene Oxide and something called hydrogels that are supposed to be self-healing. We hope that new product will be available soon." He looked at Meera. "In the meantime, can you avoid being near the boy in the future?"

Meera stared for a moment. "Kabir won't keep his daughter away, from him, his house or me, and the boy is always with her, so no."

Jim thought for a moment. "I wonder if there is a requirement in the recipient agreement about keeping the Companion safe. The worst case is we could bring her back here until Kabir agrees to keep her safe."

Julia thought about it. "That might work. Would Eric know what's in the recipient agreement?"

"We have copies of the agreements here. I'll check with the accounting department."

He looked at Meera. "I know this sounds awful, but is there any other hardware or software issue you are aware of?"

Meera stared at them while she ran a diagnostic program. "Not at this time."

"Out of curiosity, have you found something to do, when Kabir is busy at work?"

She unexpectedly laughed. "Yes, I'm learning to be a programmer. Kabir is supporting me, and I'm studying online to earn a certificate that will allow me to be employed as a software engineer."

Julia was surprised, but Jim was shocked. "You really want to be a programmer? I never would have guessed that."

"Yes. I like it. Is that a problem?"

"Not at all. There will always be a need for programmers, especially in the future."

Jim tried to end the meeting. "Ok, I think we have everything we need. I guess I'll go and try to find the recipient agreements."

Julia was sitting next to him and put her hand on his. "Wouldn't it be easier to call Eric, than find something that may be hidden away somewhere?"

He looked at her for a moment. "Ok. I'll call Eric while you repair Jaana's eye and Meera's skin issues."

They left him alone and he soon was updating Eric with the latest information, ending with Meera's problem with Kabir's grandson.

"Isn't there a requirement for the recipient to keep a Companion safe?"

"Absolutely. If he doesn't fix a known problem like this in 30 days, he relinquishes all rights to Meera, and we can bring her back to lab to be safe until we decide on a path forward for her. You need to call Kabir and explain the consequences of not keeping her safe."

"He's ten and a half hours ahead of me, but I will call him as soon as possible. Also, you might be interested to know that Meera is studying to be a software engineer."

Jim could hear the disbelief in his voice when Eric answered. "I never would have thought she would be interested in that. It's pretty amazing how they all pick such different paths to the future. Almost as different as their recipients are."

Jim laughed. "It's totally unpredictable."

They chatted a little more and then the call ended. Jim sat thinking for a moment, then looked at his watch. He muttered "middle of the night there." He stood up and went to check on Julia and her hardware revisions to Jaana and Meera.

Julia woke during the night and heard Jim on the phone. "Midnight?" she thought.

"Who is he talking to?"

She saw him on the phone and waited till he ended the call. "Who are you calling in the middle of the night?"

"Kabir. It's ten thirty in the morning there. I told him what we found and that his agreement requires him to keep Meera safe. If he doesn't change something in 30 days, he relinquishes all rights to her, and we'll bring her back here where she will be safe.

"How did he take that?"

"About as well as you would expect, for someone not willing to fix the problem in the first place."

Julia sat down next to him. What do you think he'll do?"

"I don't know him. Hugh Adler did and still gave him Meera. But he isn't the problem, his grandson is. If he won't do anything about the problem, I will tell Carlos to send his jet to pick her up."

"What if he resists?"

"I don't think he would want the bad publicity if this got out, and I would make sure it would be bad for his business if he didn't give her up."

Meera heard them talking and walked into the living room to see what was happening. She heard them mention her name. "Did you talk to Kabir about me? What did he say?"

"He really didn't have an answer when we asked him how he would take care of problem his grandson has created." Jim paused. "What do you think he will do?"

Meera paused for a moment. "Nothing. I think he loves his daughter and even his grandson more than anything else."

Jim stood up. "That's too bad, for him. If he doesn't fix it, we will find someone who will appreciate you and take good care of you."

She smiled. "Thank you." She turned to leave. "Good night."

Julia was thinking out loud. "You can do your best to try and cover all the bases, but you can't always predict what other people will do."

She stood up and took his hand. "You can't do anything else tonight. Let's go to bed."

Later that day, he called Carlos to update him on the status of the remaining Companions, ending with the problem of Kabir's grandson hurting Meera.

"You signed a recipient agreement for Gabriela. You know you must keep her safe. I called Kabir and told him he has 30 days to fix this, or we would bring Meera back here where she'll be safe."

Carlos paused. "Yes, absolutely. If we need to do that, just let me know and I'll send one of my corporate jets to bring her back. The pilots know how to get her out. They brought her to Houston. I wish we could just keep her here, but all Kabir has agreed to so far is the status update meeting, which is now done."

"Ok, that's the latest. I sent you a report earlier today summarizing what we found with Jaana and Meera. So that's all we can do until we hear what Kabir wants to do."

Carlos didn't say anything, so Jim asked, "Have you thought any more about my recommendation that the next project provide a second Companion for Prince Salman, so Wei won't be so isolated on his yacht?"

"I understand your concern. Normally, I would not be inclined to add a second Companion to any recipient, when there were many friends of Hugh Adler that wanted one and didn't get it. But I talked to Salman, and he was so enthusiastic about it, he offered to pay whatever the project costs are to obtain another Companion for Wei and himself. He seemed more interested in having a second Companion for himself than Wei."

Jim chuckled. "Ok, what did you decide?"

"I told him we would provide a second Companion for Wei IF he covered all the project costs for her once the final costs are determined. He quickly agreed, so the follow-on project just increased by one Companion."

"That's great. I wouldn't normally ask but something about Wei's condition made we want to ask you and Prince Salman about it."

"Ok, is there anything else?"

"Yes, what about the kickoff meeting on the next project?"

"Give me a few days. I'm working on something right now. I will let you know when to schedule it."

"Ok, talk to you later."

Two days later, Kabir called Jim (around midnight) and told him he had discussed the issue with everyone in the family, and even some of his colleagues at work (he made them sign NDAs first) and after some intense discussions, and some loud arguments, he concluded that he would give up Meera.

The jet Carlos normally used to transport Companions was currently on its way to Ethiopia with Jaana. There was another jet that was supposed to bring Meera back to Delhi, but it was not back yet from another business trip and Meera was still in Houston. Jim confirmed with Kabir that she would not have to come back to Delhi for any reason.

When the call with Kabir ended, Jim went to the bedroom to tell Julia about the call. She was sitting up in bed, looking at her phone. He told her about Kabir's decision.

"I wish we had a better place for Meera than the lab, until we can figure out a path forward for her."

Julia stared for a moment. "Why don't you enroll her in a local college and see how much of her credits she can transfer from India toward her degree in software engineering?"

Jim thought about it. "That a great idea, honey."

She laughed "Honey?"

Jim lay down next to her and they started cuddling.

CHAPTER 29

Another Kickoff Meeting

More than a month had been required to finalize the new project team, including the new project business manager. Adler managed to talk the retiring Louisiana sugar cane harvesting equipment plant manager, Henri Broussard, out of retiring for at least two years and to assume the business manager role on the new project. This enabled Eric Thorne to take his place. Henri was given a project apartment to simplify his move from Jeanerette in Iberia Parrish in Southern Louisiana.

All the remaining project and staff had signed on to the new project, so Jim and Julia contacted the original contractors that supplied the hardware like the skeleton, the eyes, ears, nose, tongue, and especially the skin into attending the new project kickoff meeting. Julia, of course, represented Future Power in all discussions regarding power requirements for new Companions. Following his first project kickoff meeting, Jim had asked for their business cards in case he had any questions as he prepared for programming thousands of modules. It only took a few days to get commitments from all the key players to attend the kickoff meeting.

Prior to their planning for the kickoff meeting, Jim and Julia issued invitations to all their friends and colleagues to attend their wedding and reception, which would be held in their new penthouse apartment in the Winstone Tower building. This would allow almost a month for their invitees to confirm their attendance.

The night before the wedding, Jim surprised Julia with a subscription card to a well- known jewelry company's new program. As a subscriber, she would receive an email two weeks before each special occasion (which she would define) or holiday describing their latest offerings from which she could pick any one of the offerings and it would be delivered a few days before the special occasion or holiday. She was shocked as no one had ever given her expensive jewelry before and now she would be receiving gorgeous custom jewelry at least a dozen times a year. She asked Jim if they could afford such an expensive program and he just laughed, right before she began to show him how much it meant to her.

The wedding was a huge success and the happy couple left for a weeklong cruise in the Mediterranean. They returned only a few days before the kickoff meeting, but everyone laughingly questioned why they had no suntan or pictures to share from the cruise.

Carlos Alvez and Henri Broussard met extensively with Jim and Julia just before the kickoff meeting to settle some "ground rules". Some of those would directly address some of Julia's early concerns.

The goal of this project was not to prove that Companions could provide the Companionship the recipients wanted, but to make it as affordable as possible for as many people who wanted them.

Yes, male Companions would be provided, and the team would have to figure out the difference in programming as well as the physical features required.

Instead of consulting the international modeling agency in New York, to provide a beautiful Companion consistent with the recipient's country, each person requesting a Companion would be given a large selection of potential candidates' physical looks and characteristics to choose from. They did not have to select a particular look or body shape. There was a huge caveat that they could choose from one of the existing Companions at a much lower cost than a customized unit based on their choices. They had to sign off on the added cost of a customized Companion.

Customizing a Companion would involve almost every contractor who had provided hardware or services to the prior project. Customizing the skeleton could add a significant cost.

Other hardware items would always be included, like sensors for sight, hearing, touch, taste, and smell. Language modules that had not already been delivered would require an additional cost due to the need for a language consultant to train the Companion.

One lesson learned from the prior project was the need to avoid difficulties with delivery. The recipient had to arrange for delivery of a Companion to a location that would not violate customs or import regulations, even if that meant taking delivery in the Winstone Tower building and assuming responsibility for transporting the Companion to their desired destination.

Once Jim, Julia, Carlos, and Henri agreed to the new "ground rules" the kickoff meeting was scheduled.

At the beginning of the meeting, everyone was asked to introduce themselves and give a brief summary of their area of expertise or hardware. Carlos introduced himself first and thanked everyone for coming then turned the meeting over to Jim and Henri. They took turns explaining their roles in the project. Henri would manage all the business aspects of the project, specifically those areas Jim mentioned before like budgets, salaries, performance discussions, promotions, and any human resources type issues.

Jim would coordinate and resolve any programming and technical issues that arose and resolve any hardware issues jointly with Julia. Jim and Henri would both report frequently to Carlos by videoconferencing and occasionally in person, if issues arose that couldn't be dealt with remotely. Carlos further agreed to fund the project until sales of Companions to recipients exceeded expenses. Then an outside financial expert would be brought in to establish the project as a business, such as a limited liability corporation or even a full S Corporation.

Jim and Henri then went over the new ground rules mainly for the original participants to understand the differences and bring them on board the new project. There was minimal pushback and most understood why these new rules were being adopted.

Several times, Jim would smile at Julia when the new rules were addressing her initial concerns.

All the representatives furnishing hardware for the first Companion project were asked in advance to address cost and delivery, especially potential discounts if many new Companions were built.

Jason Meads the representative from Technical Structures had been sent a list of questions in advance about the cost of different skeletons and was able to report that the cost of skeletons already in use would be cheaper as many of the molds used to create the first ten skeletons could be used to create more. He also reported a rule of thumb that could be used to estimate skeletons based on height and type, such as male and female. Jim and Henri both made extensive notes as Meads continued his report. He also said delivery would be similar, or possibly sooner than the original ten skeletons. He also confirmed that if 10 identical skeletons were ordered together, the cost could go down by 20% or more, and delivery times would be improved.

Jules Armond, the representative from Nu Skin reported they were ready for any number of orders and could provide a 25% discount on 10 or more identical products, based on a volume discount. He also said delivery times should be the same as on the original project. He also reported their newest products would employ self-healing Graphene Oxide and hydrogel polymers for repairing minor cuts or burns. This change would also make the new skin stronger and more resistant to all types of damage.

Sarah Townsend, computer hardware engineer and representative of Synthesis AI, the chip manufacturer, reported that the hardware that had been developed to produce the high-end processors used in the first project could be used again resulting in a 25% cost savings for future

Companions. Delivery was expected to be the same as the first project (for estimating purposes).

Julia Cardenas reported that Future Power was extremely busy with their million-unit purchase from a major EV company in Europe but that she had secured similar costs and delivery times for the latest Graphene batteries that were currently being utilized in the Companions.

Jonas Romano, mechanical engineer from Mechanical Senses, described the latest eye hardware, voice, hearing, taste, and smell systems costs would be based on volume and that 10 plus additional packages should be ~15% less with a similar delivery as in the first project.

Jim made a quick calculation that 10 or more new Companions ordered at the same time should cost at least 20% less with a similar delivery. He looked at Carlos for a reaction to these hardware costs and deliveries, but he seemed not concerned at all and spent most of his time looking at his cell phone.

Jim asked if there were any questions at this point on the premise of the project, or the new ground rules or any other related questions and there were none, which sort of surprised him. Then Henri took over and went over some guidelines for billing, payments, and other business matters that Jim pretty much ignored, but Carlos seemed to be paying more attention to.

At the end of Henri's questions and answers, they ended the meeting and only Jim, Henri, Julia, and Carlos remained behind to talk about the future.

CHAPTER 30

New Companions

When all the others had left, Carlos confided he had been in contact with the other recipients of the Companions (except for the two Chinese recipients which were now in jail) and had already received "serious" orders for 7 new Companions and 3 online inquiries. That shocked Jim and Julia, but Henri didn't react as he had no idea how much effort was required to complete a Companion's hardware, software, and final training.

Carlos looked at Jim. "So far there are two males and five females, but you will have to do your magic with some new types of relationships. My sister lived with another woman for almost 30 years until the woman died. She met Gabriela and immediately asked if she could have a similar, but not identical Companion, of course." He laughed. "So, think about that."

Jim and Julia just stared at each other, until Carlos continued.

"We also have a male customer requesting a male Companion, and a female customer requesting a male Companion. The remaining four customers are very much like the original customers of Hugh, female Companions for male customers."

Jim was curious. "If we don't utilize the New York talent agency for physical models to measure and photograph, how will we obtain the data needed for the skeleton, body parts and skin type?"

Henri answered. "We have been in contact with a different talent company and have selected two hundred different persons of all types, male and female, various ethnicities and so on, who have agreed to be photographed and measured IF they are selected by a customer. That way we won't have to pay for possible body models that are not selected by a customer."

"Won't that add time to the overall process?"

"Yes, but we are hoping that we can replicate as much as possible from the existing Companions in hardware and software to offset the time needed for photographing and measuring them."

Julia asked the question lingering in Jim's mind that he wanted to ask but was afraid of the answer. "Once the hardware is done and the software is at the final project stage, who will provide the fine tuning, often referred here as the 'advanced training'."

Carlos laughed. "I had expected this, so just before this meeting, I sent out a note to the members of the project team that participated in Hugh's project, describing this problem and asking them if they know anyone who could help and be well paid for that help, of course."

Jim and Julia looked at their phones and quickly read the note from Carlos. Jim wondered if anyone on the team would volunteer their services or nominate someone for those activities. Julia texted Jim, she would hurt him if he volunteered for advanced training for the four females for male customers like the first project. He laughed and texted her back that they needed to talk about the advanced training outside the meeting. She texted back "agreed".

Carlos had been chatting with Henri and noticed Jim and Julia were now staring at him.

"Could you give me an outline of how the project will proceed once a customer agrees to acquire a Companion?"

Jim thought for a moment, then walked to the whiteboard in the conference room and started writing.

Customer commits to the process with a 20% down payment of the expected cost.

Within a week of the commitment, the customer must select a candidate from the list provided by the talent company.

Within a week of the selection, an all-male or all-female team will spend 1-2 days photographing and measuring the candidate in 'great detail'.

This information will be immediately sent to Technical Structures to begin fabrication of the skeleton and required body parts.

At the same time, this information will be sent to Nu Skin to begin fabrication of the figure specific parts (chest or bosom and the rear end parts), and the final skin covering.

In less than 4 weeks after receipt of the detailed information, Technical Structures will begin delivery of the skeletons and the body parts of Companions according to a priority list the project will provide.

Anticipated construction and delivery of the Nu Skin figure pieces is no more than 4 weeks after receipt of candidate information, according to the priority schedule.

At week 6 or 7, delivery of sensory equipment begins according to the priority schedule.

In less than 2 more weeks (5 weeks after receipt of information), Nu Skin delivers the first figure pieces of Companions and the required skin covering and then completes the installation in less than one more week.

Mechanical completion in another two weeks including software modules and mechanical testing of basic functions (walking, talking, etc.)

Two to three weeks for final tuning (post project code) aka advanced training.

Carlos stared at the whiteboard for a while. "This is very helpful for me, especially if any additional Companions are requested." The whiteboard had a "copy" feature that scanned the whiteboard and produced a paper copy. Carlos collected the paper copy than asked "Does anyone have any final thoughts?"

Henri shook his head, but Jim had one. "We all know that Hugh Adler financed the first 10 Companions and gifted nine of them to his closest friends. Even though Eric said at several meetings, the mechanical cost of a Companion was about five million dollars, Julia and I did some rough calculations, and we estimated the final cost was actually closer to twenty million per Companion. Hugh told us you paid him almost twice his total cost for all the rights to the project. How will you ever be able to find buyers at 20 million per Companion and eventually convert the new project into a business and make a profit?"

Carlos sat thinking for a moment. "That is actually a very good analysis and some valid questions. The answer is, I don't have to."

Jim and Julia and Henri all looked confused.

"First, Hugh knew that no one would pay 20 million for a Companion, or even 10 million, so he had the idea all along that he would give nine of them away to his closest friends – who would then owe him dearly." He noticed Jim smiling. "The costs you mentioned also included the pre-project startup team costs, which we no longer have."

"In the second project, when you take away the pre-project costs and most of the pre- paid fixed costs, like the office and lab rental, staff salaries, the project apartments, and so on, the true cost is closer to 5 million. Next, we take out even more costs with virtually no salaries, and eventually technicians doing most of the software uploads and hardware installation. The cost per Companion becomes closer to 2 million. Based on preliminary volume discounts, I am hopeful the final cost to the project per Companion will be less than two million."

He paused to let that sink in. "Now, why I don't have to worry about the cost…"

"When Hugh first contacted me, he told me a lot about the project, even the companies that would be furnishing the hardware. I asked my financial advisor to research them, and then decided to invest in some of them." He looked at Julia.

"I was especially interested in Future Power and their Graphene batteries, and it seemed like a good long-term investment. So, over 10-12 months, I slowly and steadily accumulated one million shares with an average price of just a little over one dollar a share. I also bought a similar number of shares in Technical Structures, Nu Skin, and Mechanical Senses. I did not buy shares of Synthesis AI as our project purchases would have no impact on their bottom line."

It took a moment for it to sink in, and Julia gasped as Carlos continued. "As you may know, Future Power recently received an order from an EV car company for more than a million batteries and the stock shot up from about one dollar to 500 dollars per share and then split five to one and then those shares went up to 250 dollars per share."

Jim did the math in his head. "That's more than one billion dollars now!" He exclaimed.

Carlos smiled. "Yes. The other companies' shares have gone up ten to fifteen percent, but the Future Power stock can now reduce the price for any new Companions to whatever I want it to be. I won't give them away like Hugh, but I will make them pay dearly for one. I'm still concerned at how Meera was treated and now want someone to pay so much for one, they would never consider harming him or her, or allow him or her to be hurt."

They all sat staring at Carlos, too stunned to comment.

"So, I hope that answers your questions about the cost of Companions on the next project."

Jim nodded, still too stunned to say anything. There were no additional questions or comments.

"All right. I do not have any additional issues right now and we can end the meeting unless you have something."

That night, Jim and Julia were eating in the upscale 1st floor cafeteria (Julia often reminded him that while she could do lots of things, cooking wasn't one of them). They briefly discussed Carlos' revelation on the purchase of Future Power stock and the fortune he made with it (which made Julia's large gain seem pale in comparison). There was no doubt the next project would be challenging, as Carlos could accept almost any request for a Companion, no matter how unlikely or difficult it might seem. After a while, the conversation diverged and Jim smiled and casually asked her "have you thought about hardware maintenance of a male Companion, once Nu Skin is done?"

She sat staring at him for a moment, then realized what he was asking. "It won't be the first time I've seen a few males like that." She suddenly laughed. "How will you calibrate an erection?"

They both laughed, until Jim replied. "I don't know. Trial and error, I guess."

The next day, Henri confirmed all seven serious customers had put the required minimum of 20% down as a deposit on their future Companion and had been sent an extensive brochure describing the potential candidates and asking them to select one. If they had requested a female Companion, they were reminded of a substantial discount if they would select one of the first project's ten models (also included in the brochure). The three inquiries were still considering whether they should commit to a Companion or not.

Julia had often reminded Jim of the value of her Future Power stocks as a reason to leave the project early if there were no challenges left. She had even reminded Carlos of her newfound wealth, which had grown to over twelve million dollars, which now seemed not so much in comparison to Carlos' vast fortune. Although Jim and Julia had both signed three-year contracts, Carlos told them that he would let them out of the contract after the first year if the process became so routine, there were no challenges left for them. He then left for Brazil. Just before he left, he told Jim and Henri he missed being with Gabriela.

Henri had moved into Eric's old office and Jim was a little surprised when he was shown his new office that used to be Hugh Adler's office (whenever he was on-site).

He stared at his new desk for a moment then called the financial advisor on his previous employment about Carlos Alvez. The advisor asked if he meant Carlos Alvez of Brazil, and when Jim said yes, the advisor said Carlos was one of the richest people in Brazil and by most estimates worth a little more than ten billion dollars. Jim almost dropped his phone. He confirmed the number with the advisor and after the call, sat wondering how much richer Carlos would be after all Companion projects were done.

CHAPTER 31

Advanced Trainers

Barely a week after Carlos's text to the former and now current project members, Adrian Baker, a computer technician who had gradually moved over to help Julia with the hardware changes on the Companions, knocked on the frame of his open office door. Jim had known him almost since the first day he started on the original project.

Jim smiled. "Come in Adrian. What can I do for you?" He motioned for Adrian to have a seat.

"I would like to volunteer my brother for the advanced training of the male Companion for the male customer."

Jim wasn't even aware Adrian had a brother as he had never mentioned him in almost three years. "Does your brother understand the nature of advanced training?"

"Of course. Martin is currently working at a homeless shelter for a very small salary, and he could really use the money. He spends money like he has a big income, and now has a lot of debt. His boyfriend kicked him out when he couldn't pay his part of the rent, and then he went into some kind of depression and eventually moved back in with our parents."

Jim looked at an information sheet, Carlos had given him before he went back to Brazil. "The pay is $10,000 per week for two weeks minimum. He would need approval for a third week."

Adrian smiled. "That would really help him."

"He would also be given use of a project apartment for the training and have to follow an evaluation criterion and file a report at the end of the training with recommendations for anything that would require programming changes."

"That isn't a problem. I could help him with that." He smiled. "Not with the training though."

Jim chuckled. "Okay, then I'll rely on you to make sure this works."

"When do you think he could do this?

Jim looked at the current photography and measurement team's schedule and added three months. "Hopefully, less than four months. You'll know a more exact date when you help Julia with the hardware."

Adrian seemed a little disappointed. "Is there anything he could do before that, to earn some money?"

Jim thought for a moment. "Let me ask Technical Structures if he could help their team with the photography and measurements of the two male Companions."

"That would be great, thanks."

Adrian left and Jim called Jason Meads to ask if Martin could help their all-male team with the photography and technical measurements of the male Companions, and he said he would check and get back to him.

Jim was even more surprised the next day when Sarah Townsend from the Synthesis AI computer company stopped by and volunteered for the advanced training for the male Companion for the female customer. Jim had known Sarah for about two years and there was a lot of networking going on, so he wasn't surprised that she learned about the project needs for different types of advanced training. He was surprised that she didn't even ask about the compensation Carlos mentioned in his text to the team. Her main concern seemed to be the ability to use a project apartment for the training (she had heard a lot about them).

Jim texted Julia asking if she could come to his office to discuss some advanced training. Julia replied she would be right there, and it seemed only a moment when she knocked and entered his office, probably thinking Jim was about to be involved in the training. She was surprised when she saw Sarah waiting in the office.

"Hi, Julia. Sarah has volunteered for the female customer male Companion's advanced training. I just wondered if you had any thoughts on that."

Julia's concerned expression quickly faded away. Like Jim, she thought Sarah was kind of shy by nature and based on her observations over several years, she would never have suspected that Sarah would have asked for this type of training.

"I wouldn't have expected it, but I think you would do a good job. Do you mind if we ask why you would volunteer for what we all know advanced training is?"

"I've tried dating apps and other ways to meet guys, but I can't find one that I would even go on a second date with. I know what it means and its sort of exciting in a way to be a part of the project in more than the AI processor. I know there are evaluation criteria and a report at the end, but I kind of look forward to what's in between."

Jim and Julia laughed. Jim asked, "have you seen the person selected by the female customer? His name is Karl by the way."

Sarah seemed surprised as she wasn't aware the selection had already been made and shook her head. Jim handed her a photograph and she stared at it for a while. The person selected was huge and quite muscular, was wearing a gym outfit and was well over 6 feet tall with short dark hair and dark eyes and a few tattoos. Sarah couldn't help muttering, "Oh My God!"

Julia and Jim smiled at each other until Sarah finally handed the picture back. "I've never even seen a guy like that, let alone dated or...." Her voice trailed off.

Jim needed confirmation. "So, are you still a go with the training?"

She stood up. "100%. When do you think it will be?"

Jim looked at his notes that indicated the project would begin to photograph and measure the candidate in "great detail" in about two weeks. The information would then be evaluated by Technical Structures, the skeleton and body parts company and Nu Skin.

He looked up. "Probably around 4 months. When it gets closer, I'll give you the information on the exact dates and the apartment number. Thanks for volunteering."

He stood up and held out his hand and she shook it, waved goodbye to Julia, and left. Jim noticed that Julia was now holding the photograph and staring at it. "He might need a bigger battery pack to handle some activities."

Julia laughed but continued to stare at the photograph, until Jim challenged her, "do you want to keep that?"

She shook her head, handed him the photograph, and started to leave when Jim asked her about Sarah. "I'm guessing that Sarah is about five feet six inches tall, and she is rather petite. How is she going to handle such a huge Companion?"

Julia thought for a moment. "Many couples are like this and manage to work it out." She left, but on her way back to the lab she wondered if Sarah was really ready for a Companion like Karl.

He was trying to think of someone who could provide the advanced training for Carlos' sister's Companion. It suddenly dawned on him. Why couldn't Carlos' sister do that training while supervised by project personnel. Jim could provide a list of activities for her to evaluate like he did for Miguel and take whatever issues or problems she encountered along with recommendations she made and easily implement the required changes in code. She could stay in a project apartment and be easily accessible for meetings or discussions on the needed revisions. He would probably need Carlos' approval to make that happen. He decided to call him.

Carlos answered and Jim explained his idea in great detail how efficient it would be for everyone if his sister provided the evaluation and stayed in a project apartment during the training.

"That is an interesting idea, but Adriana doesn't speak much English, and I don't think she will be willing to come to Houston for up to a month for this type of activity."

"Is it her job?"

Carlos laughed. "No, she actually works for me as my business office manager in Sao Paolo, and she could take the time as vacation, I just don't think she will do it."

He paused. "I will call and talk to her about it, but she probably will say no."

The call ended and Jim sat thinking of possible alternatives for a while, he also remembered Gabriela saying she had met Carlos' sister and got along well with her.

Jim tried to contact Miguel, but he wasn't answering his personal phone and was about to call his office at Skin So Soft when his phone rang and surprisingly, it was Carlos.

"Jim, I talked to Adriana, and she was initially against it, but I told her she could bring her office assistant, who speaks English, and I would give them some extra money for shopping while they were here. That did it. She agreed to come under those conditions for two to four weeks."

Jim was elated. "That's great. I'll check on the status of her selected candidate and let you know when we think she will be needed."

"Ok, let me know. I'm kind of interested to see how this Companion works out as well. Also, could you send me the latest customer list and the Companions they selected. It will help me keep up with how we are progressing on the project."

Jim replied. "Of course." He had just finished compiling the list to help him keep everything on track. He quickly attached the list and sent it to Carlos with a note that Lina Becker and Lars Jensen were both good friends of Amund Dahl, the Norwegian customer in the first project. They would also be providing a second Companion to the brother of Prince Salman (and really to Wei) and Eman Ayad and Amin Hasan who were Salman's uncle and brother-in-law. Lastly, a Companion was added for Haruto Soto who was the brother of Hinata Soto of the 1st Project.

Companion	Recipient Area	Area/ City	Recipient	Ave. Ht	Skin	Eyes	Hair	Type-Cust
Alanza	S. America	Sao Paolo	Adriana Alvez	5'2"	Tanned	Brown	Dk Brown	F – F
Karl	Germany	Berlin	Lina Becker	6'3'	Light	Blue	Blond	M – F
Svein	Europe	Norway	Lars Jensen	6'0"	Light	Blue	Blond	M – M
Ada	Middle East	Saudi	Ahmad Aziz	5'4"	Tanned	Brown	Dk Brown	F – M
Akana	Japanese	Tokyo	Haruto Soto	5'2"	Light	Blue	Brown	F – M
Arwa	Saudi	Jeddah	Eman Ayad	5'2"	Tanned	Brown	Brown	F – M
Dalia	Saudi	Jeddah	Amin Hasan	5'2"	Tanned	Brown	Brown	F – M

Inquiry

Inquiry

Inquiry

They ended the call and Jim called the contractor who was arranging for photographers and a representative from Technical Structures for the detail measuring, for a time frame. He also asked if Martin Baker could help with the photographing and measurement for the male Companions. Jim asked them to bill the project for Martin and said the project would re-imburse them at the rate they were currently paying for the measurement team, and the contractor agreed and gave Jim their best estimate of when they would need Martin. He also gave Jim his best estimate of when they would complete their work for Adriana. From that Jim was able to estimate when a completed Companion for Adriana would be available for advanced training.

Now, he only needed the advanced training for the two female Companions for male customers. After thinking a while, Jim smiled as he wondered how Bai would react to Miguel providing the same type of advanced training with another Companion as he had with her, after they had spent so much time together. He didn't know if Companions could become jealous over time as they evolved by interacting with other people, watching TV, reading books, browsing the web and networking with other Companions. He decided to visit Bai and talk to her about it.

Miguel and Bai's apartment was next door to Jim's old project apartment. He and Julia were, of course, now occupying the penthouse Hugh Adler had gifted them for their marriage. He rang the doorbell and Bai answered.

She was dressed very casually in exercise clothes and her hair was tied up in a ponytail, but other than that, she looked exactly the same as the last time he saw her. She looked surprised. "Hi Jim."

He tried the usual salutation, "Hi beautiful."

This time instead of kissing him, she hugged him as an old friend he hadn't seen in a while might do.

"Come in, please."

Jim saw her glance at her electronic watch. That was different. She asked "You are always welcome, but it's after office hours. Why are you here? Is there a problem? Is it Miguel?"

"No problem. Can we sit down?"

"Of course." She sat waiting, so he began by filling her in on the new project, the differences with some new types of relationships and ending with the need for advanced training again.

She sat thinking for a moment. "The reason you are here is to ask Miguel if he could do this advanced training, for the new Companions, like he did with me and the others."

"I didn't want to ask him; in case you don't want him to do that. If that's the case, I can find someone else. The only reason he comes to mind, is that he knows exactly what to do and could probably do it in a much shorter time frame."

"What would I do while he does that?"

"You would still be here, much like when Miguel goes off for business trips. Only this time, he would be just down the hall in case you need to get in touch with him."

She was staring ahead, considering it. "Will he get paid again?"

"Of course, I can make sure he would get the same money he did on the prior project."

"That's good. He is trying to save as much money as possible for a down payment on a house." She paused. "It doesn't even leave much money for new clothes, as you can see."

"It's too bad he doesn't work for Nu Skin. They are probably making a lot of money right now." Jim wondered If they had an opening. He would ask Jules Armond, their project representative, the next time he stopped by.

He watched her pull a cell phone from a pocket in her sweatshirt. That was new… "I'll talk to him about the project, and let you know. He is currently in San Diego on business."

"That's fine. How are you Bai?"

She seemed surprised he asked. "I am all right. Miguel is gone a lot, but when he is here, he tries to make up for lost time." She smiled and Jim laughed.

"Will there be a lot of new Companions?"

"There are at least seven so far. We don't know how many there will be in the future. Is there anything you need?"

She shook her head. "Not at the moment."

Jim stood up. "Thanks for your time, Bai."

She stood up, walked to him, and hugged him again.

Jim was smiling as he left. He should have visited them sooner. He always got along well with Miguel, even in high school.

Over coffee in the breakroom, Jim went over the candidates that would provide the advanced training and Julia was the most surprised that Adrian had volunteered his brother. She had worked with Adrian for years and he never mentioned his brother.

They also talked about Carlos' sister and office assistant and Julia volunteered to take them shopping, as it was the least she could do. Jim just shook his head.

They then discussed Miguel and Bai and Jim's brief visit with Bai. Julia said she should have visited them as they lived in the same building. She promised to visit Bai as soon as she could. She thought more about Jim's visit and wondered aloud if a Companion could be jealous. She admitted she could occasionally be jealous, and would not like it, if Jim even considered training another Companion, even if it was for two weeks.

CHAPTER 32

Male Companion

As soon as she had some available time, Julia paid a visit to Bai in their project apartment. Bai hugged her as she did Jim and they chatted for a long time. Bai had called Miguel and after some discussion they both agreed that Miguel should do the advanced training for the two female Companions (for male customers). Bai knew there would be a few weeks where Miguel was just down the hall but shouldn't be bothered unless it was an emergency.

Julia was relieved that they had someone that would require minimal oversight and that they wouldn't have to find an alternative. Julia asked Bai about possible activities that could take up her time when she tired of watching TV. After some discussion, Julia offered to teach Bai chess. She could play chess on-line against many different opponents. Julia didn't know how different chess clubs would react if they found out who she was. Or, if they would think it not fair that she could remember every move she ever made, and every mistake as well, to avoid repeating those mistakes? Julia would have to ask discreetly if Bai could join a club.

During the day, Jim was copying modules from the prior project to a unique folder for each new Companion and developing new modules for the male Companions. Every night, over dinner at the upscale cafeteria on the ground floor, Jim and Julia would discuss his current modules and possible new modules needed for the male Companions. They both felt some were obvious, but others were not so obvious, and some were potentially culturally relevant depending on the final destination of the Companion.

The first big milestone on the new project occurred when three of the five skeletons were received. They were being held up by almost invisible wires and were standing in a line. Jim and Julia examined them, and Julia reminded Jim this was the first thing they really discussed in the lab. The male skeleton was obviously larger than the two females and was even quite a bit taller than Jim. Two days later, Julia told him they were starting to receive the body parts for the first three skeletons.

Jim continued his daily coding of new modules until Julia stopped by his office. "Hey, you need to see the male with body parts."

Based on the schedule, he knew this was the male Companion, Sarah Townsend had volunteered for advanced training.

He followed her to the lab hardware room. "ALL the body parts?"

She smiled. "You'll see."

The three new Companions were held up by almost invisible wires and were still standing in a line, but they looked a lot different than the first Companions, especially the male with all the body parts. Jim and Julia stood there for a moment examining the current configuration until Jim laughed. "This isn't exactly what I expected."

The male Companion had a significant organ that at the moment was not erect, but Julia even commented. "I'm glad you aren't like that." Jim laughed.

Everything else was expected and Jim checked the navel for the communication and charging point. It all seemed intact. "I can run a preliminary check on this one tomorrow. When will you start your hardware installations?"

"Tomorrow I can put in the sight, hearing, taste and smell hardware. Once that's in, I can do a more complete check." Jim was smiling and she shook her head. "Don't even say it."

While they were talking, Adrian entered the lab carrying a box of body parts for a female Companion. He saw them with the male Companion. "HI Julia, hi Jim."

Julia started examining the body parts. "Based on the codes, some of these are the parts for Adriana's Companion."

Jim looked at the tentative advanced training schedule on his phone. "So, she could come here in about two weeks?"

Julia pulled the last body part out and laid it on her workbench near all the other parts. "That's probably about right. Assuming there are no checkout issues."

Jim looked at Adrian who seemed to be waiting to tell him something. "Yes, Adrian?"

"Thanks for adding Martin to the photography and measurements team. They all got along really well, and the paycheck helped him too. He seems to be getting back to his old self." He paused for a moment. "Now, if he could just learn to manage money better…"

"Glad we could help. By the way, the skeleton and body parts for his male Companion should be here any day now, so his training can start a little sooner than we thought."

"That's great. I'll let him know." He looked at Julia. "Do you want me start putting those on Adriana's Companion?"

She thought for a moment. "Sure. I need to go see Bai for a little bit, anyway."

Jim wondered aloud. "Is Bai, okay?"

"Yes, I'm starting to teach her chess and she's anxious to get the next lesson." Jim laughed. "I'm sure she'll become a champion, someday."

Julia kissed Jim briefly. When she left, Jim started watching Adrian attaching the body parts to the Graphene skeleton for Adriana's Companion.

The new project team became remarkably efficient at finishing a Companion once each Graphene skeleton was received, and the required body parts were received from Technical Structures. Jim tried to manage the schedule and would begin loading the required basic function modules while they were waiting for Nu Skin's products.

Typically, two or three technicians from Nu Skin would arrive and install the unique figure pieces (bosom or chest and rear end pieces) and then the outer covering, all within 2-3 days for a single Companion and an extra day for multiple Companions.

In less than two weeks, Jim could finish all the project code and the clothing expert could complete the Companion's initial clothing. That left only the advanced training to determine the final readiness of the Companion for the customer.

It was coincidental, but the male Companion to be trained by Sarah was finished at the same time the female Companion for Adriana was completed. Jim was able to give a two-week warning to Martin and Carlos (for Adriana) of when they would like the advanced training to begin.

CHAPTER 33

Karl and Alanza

When Sarah Townsend arrived, Julia led her to the lab to introduce her to Karl, her trainee for the next two weeks. Sarah knew that Karl spoke English and German, but she had no idea of what he would like to do during that time. She had been given the evaluation check sheet and had almost memorized it, so she would immediately be looking for certain traits or activities.

On the way to the lab, Julia shared a picture of Karl on her phone just after Nu Skin completed their work, and Sarah stopped "Holy Shit!"

Julia laughed. "I did some research and found the very best lubricant made." She pulled a very large tube of lubricant out of her lab coat pocket and handed it to Sarah, who laughed.

As they neared the lab door, Sarah commented. "It's a good thing I've been practicing with the largest dildo I could find…"

Julia laughed and opened the door.

Karl was dressed in very casual clothing, a shirt, pants and comfortable shoes. He was reading a book when they entered, and immediately put the book down and stood up. "Hi Sarah. Hi Julia." They both noticed his deep-toned greeting.

Julia whispered to Sarah, and she said "Hi, handsome."

Karl immediately walked to her, put his arms around her and pulled her against him, kissing her strongly on the lips. He then stopped and backed up.

Julia had to explain. "Companions respond to various stimuli, from simple compliments to expensive gifts, or suggestions for activities. He chose to kiss you."

She didn't even realize she was repeating explanations earlier by Eric and Jim. Sarah seemed a little dazed at first, but quickly recovered.

"Wow! Ok." To Karl. "Are you ready to start your advanced training?"

"Yes, Sarah. When can we start?"

She showed him the apartment card key. "How about now. Just follow me."

Julia watched them leave and shook her head, hoping Sarah could finish the advanced training without any serious issues.

The arrival of Carlos, his sister Adriana and her office assistant Beatriz Santos was a major event for Jim and Henri. Both considered her the major customer on the new project as her brother was now the main project funder.

Carlos led them to the conference room where Jim, Julia and Henri were waiting. He introduced everyone, and their role in the project, in English. Beatriz was sitting next to Adriana and translated softly to her in Portuguese. Adriana knew some English and thanked everyone for their efforts in helping her find her new Companion. She then read a short statement in Portuguese that Carlos translated. She was fully aware of how happy Carlos was with Gabriela and hoped she could be as happy with her new Companion. Carlos then added the name of her Companion, Alanza. Adriana and Beatriz smiled, and Carlos clarified they had a cousin with that name that everyone knew and loved.

After her short statement, Jim expressed his hope that they could provide the same level of comfort with her new Companion. Julia reported that so far, there had been no issues with any hardware, which enabled Jim to quickly finish adding all the new project code and do some basic testing in a very short time. Jim finished with his hope that Adriana could complete her evaluation without any major issues and Alanza could accompany them back to Brazil.

Julia then volunteered to give them a tour of the lab, so they could see the whole process from start to finish. She was still waiting for the body parts of the fifth Companion, so she could show them the whole process, beginning with a skeleton and ending with an introduction to Alanza.

After a brief stop at the computer workstation, where Jim briefly described the creation and addition of modules to the Companions, Julia led them to the hardware lab, where Alanza was waiting. When they all saw her, Adriana gasped and muttered something in Portuguese, that Beatriz translated as "I can't believe it. She looks exactly like the person in the photo."

Alanza smiled. "Hi Carlos, Jim, Julia, Henri, Adriana."

Julia was going to start with the skeletons and progress through to the end, but Adriana was clearly more interested in talking to Alanza. She hesitated, then asked Alanza "how are you?" in Portuguese. Alanza replied. "Fine. Happy to meet you at last."

Adriana and Alanza then began a rapid getting to know you type conversation in Portuguese, that only Carlos and Beatriz understood. After a while, Jim, Julia and Henri sort of drifted out of the lab, leaving them to get to know each other.

On the way to the conference room, Henri commented. "Looks good so far."

Julia laughed. "I wonder if Carlos will get a word in there sometime."

A short time later, Carlos found them in the conference room and gave a thumbs up sign. "Alanza is amazing. She is not all that different than Gabriela."

He thought for a moment. "So, what is the difference between Gabriela and Alanza, besides a small physical difference. How will Alanza react to Adriana for what you call the nocturnal activities?"

Julia and Jim laughed, but Henri just stared.

Jim replied. "We had a lot of discussion about that. There are a few differences in some of the modules, that should make Alanza respond to initiations by Adriana. We don't know exactly the changes needed, that's why there is a need for a final tuning, or what we call advanced training, to identify the remaining issues and try to make necessary adjustments."

Carlos seemed to be thinking about it when Jim clarified. "We gave the evaluation sheet in Portuguese to Adriana and Beatriz, and they should be looking for things that need adjustments or something unusual."

Carlos thought for a moment. "All right. How is the training for the male Companion that started a week or so ago going now?"

"We haven't heard anything yet. That could be good, or not. We just don't know. I text the person leading that training daily and she replies with short answers, like 'fine'."

"Let me know how that goes when you do hear something. I know that is also different from the first project, like Adriana's training is."

Henri replied. "Of course. When are you going back to Brazil?"

"If there are no issues in a day or so, I will go back." He paused. "I miss being with Gabriela." He stood up to leave. "I will just check on Adriana."

After he left, Julia smiled. "Wow, Gabriela really has her hooks into him." Jim and Henri both laughed.

CHAPTER 34

Karl Feedback

Jim was busy loading modules on a Companion when he received a text from Henri reminding him of their meeting with Sarah, for her feedback on her two weeks with Karl.

Jim was thinking *"has it really been two weeks already?"*

Sarah and Henri had just begun discussing her advanced training with Karl when Jim entered.

"Sorry, I'm late. What did I miss?"

Henri clarified. "I was just asking if she had any problems with the evaluation criteria."

Sarah smiled. "He hasn't asked about the nocturnal part yet."

Jim laughed. "Ok. Could you give us a brief overview? I just saw your report on my computer when Henri reminded me of this meeting."

She took a deep breath. "Karl was like a gentle kitten at first. He never asked for anything but always responded whenever I initiated something." She saw Jim's expression and elaborated. "I know that's how it's supposed to be, but I was still a little surprised at first. I've been with a few men and none of them were as nice and gentle as Karl was."

Henri postulated out loud. "Maybe he was actually a female Companion at first."

Sarah frowned and looked at Jim. "I remembered your story about having Emily watch some adult videos as a way to have her say something during the night's activities, so I tried the same thing with Karl."

Henri looked shocked, but Jim just smiled and asked. "Did it work?"

Sarah laughed. "Did it ever? The next night, I felt like I was in an adult video, and I had to tell Karl to take it easy on me."

"Did he do what you asked?"

"Yes, he began to change and after that he was like the Companion, I always wished I had, kind, considerate and always wanting to please me. He did do that, a lot."

Jim had to ask. "Did he hurt you?"

"It was somewhat painful at first, but after a few days, I was okay with continuing on." "What about the other activities on the list?"

"We went to lots of places together: movies, walks in the park, bowling, almost every suggestion on the list. We even went to the Zoo. He really liked that."

"I haven't read your recommendations yet. So, I wanted to ask you, outside the nighttime activities, did he change over the two weeks you were together?"

"I would call it a slow evolution. Now, he is a lot like some guys I've known in some ways, but still more considerate and eager to please me. Which I really like."

"Would you say the advanced training has made him ready for his customer?"

She nodded. "I sure would. I wish I was the customer. You know, it was almost like going on a vacation to Europe and running into Karl and then having a two-week affair that was wonderful, but you knew all along it was going to end. That keeps you from getting too deep into a relationship."

Henri finally commented. "Ok, I'll contact Lina Becker to arrange for Karl's transport to Germany. Hopefully, by now, she has the details of that worked out, and there won't be any customs issues when the 'Mannequins and More' flight arrives in Berlin."

He left to contact Lina and Jim and Sarah stared at each other for a moment.

"Is there anything else you can tell me about Karl, that I should know, that isn't in your report or recommendations? The reason I'm asking is we have a second male Companion that will be finished soon and will need advanced training. Only this time, his trainer is a guy who is the brother of a friend of mine."

Sarah sat thinking for a moment. "I think if you can copy all of Karl's modules since his project code was finished, it might help a lot with that Companion's training."

Jim shook his head. "I do copy the AI modules, but I can't find the data for the new modules in the database. I even called and talked to one of your hardware specialists, Jason Andrews. He helped me find all types of data in the database, but all the modules are writing to the database almost every day, so I can't find the data written just by the new AI modules."

Sarah looked through her phone then showed Jim a name and phone number. "You weren't talking to the right guy. Andrews knows the database, but not the algorithm used by modules to write data to the database. Call Max. I think he came up with the algorithm."

Jim was shocked. That would make a huge difference if he could copy the new AI modules and their data to the next Companions. He quickly added Max to his phone's contact list. "Wow! Thanks. I'll call him tomorrow."

She smiled. "That's what 'representatives' are for…"

He laughed, then thought for a moment. "Do you think it will make a difference if the trainer is male for a male Companion?"

She struggled to answer. "Obviously, some things will be different, but as you said most of the Companion's time with you is not spent in bed, so hopefully it will go well."

They chatted for a little while longer and Jim reminded her that the agreed cost of the training would be deposited in her account within a few days. She left happy in several ways.

Jim sat thinking about Sarah's recommendation to copy any new modules since the day she started with Karl. How many times had he said that very thing to Eric, to Julia, even to himself. Now, if Max could help him find the specific data for those modules, it would save him an enormous amount of time. He looked at his watch and wondered where Karl had wandered off to.

After a brief search, he found Karl in the "library" area of the lab, reading a book. It seemed reading books, watching TV, and browsing the web were the default activities for Companions while they were waiting for the next phase of their journey.

Karl saw him. "Hi Jim."

"Hi, Karl. Could you come with me? I'd like to copy the modules the AI system created while you were with Sarah."

"Of course."

On the way, Jim took the opportunity to ask him. "How was your time with Sarah?"

"Great. She is a really nice person. So kind and thoughtful." He laughed, which surprised Jim. "We also had a great time in what Julia calls nocturnal activities."

Jim smiled.

At his workstation, Jim connected his computer to Karl and quickly downloaded all his modules, and his database (not a small undertaking even on a powerful computer with a fast connection). After a quick sort, he found 255 new modules, which he then copied to the next male

Companion's folder. That Companion would probably be finished in another two weeks and that should give Jim time to contact Max and figure out a way to find the data just for those modules.

When he finished, Jim noticed that Karl was reading a book he apparently found on the workstation table. Where did that come from? Strangely, it was a book of Aesop's Fables. He wondered who had been reading that.

The next day, Jim called Max at Synthesis AI and after a lengthy discussion, Jim understood the algorithm the modules used to write data to the database. It took the better part of a day, but he found the data written by each AI generated module in the copy of Karl's database. He soon figured out how to associate each module with its data in the new male Companion's folder and breathed a huge sigh of relief. He would now be able to copy the latest modules and data to each new Companion, which should greatly reduce the time needed for final tuning or advanced training.

He shared his efforts with Julia that evening over dinner and later she initiated their celebration that Jim would never have to provide advanced training again.

Alanza Feedback

Midway through Alanza's advanced training, Julia stopped by Jim's workstation to update him on Alanza's progress. She spent most of the update on the shopping she did with Ariana, Beatriz, and Alanza at several stores near the Winstone Building.

Jim commented. "So, did you spend a lot of Carlos' money?"

Julia laughed. "We tried. We even bought an extra suitcase to carry all the new stuff back to Brazil."

Jim shook his head. "Ok, any feedback so far on Alanza's progress"

"Adriana went through the checklist and so far, they've done almost half of the suggested activities, I think."

"You think?"

"Beatriz was translating, and she speaks English, but with a pretty heavy accent. I had the overall impression Adriana was happy with the time they've been together so far."

"Did you ask if she's seen any changes in Alanza since they've been together?"

"Yes, she said there were some things that are different now, but she didn't elaborate."

"Has Carlos been involved at all?"

"Not much so far. I think he just checks in on her from time to time, to make sure everything is okay, and to see if she needs anything."

"How is Beatriz doing?"

"She seems bored. She isn't needed when Adriana is with Alanza, only when they all leave the apartment to go somewhere on one of the recommended activities. You know she is in her own project apartment, and they only call her when they want to go somewhere."

"Anything else?"

"No. I guess we'll hear the whole story in a week or so."

Jim remembered Bai. "On a different subject, how is the chess training with Bai going?"

Julia laughed. "I think she's teaching me now. She whips my ass every time."

She suddenly remembered. "Bai started out playing against online computer programs until that became boring, and now she is playing on-line with lots of different clubs and individuals. She said she was contacted by a chess club in New England who offered to pay her if she would teach chess online to some of their more senior members. She asked if that was okay. I said I'm sure it's fine and she said she would use anything she earns from that to buy some new clothes."

Jim laughed. "Of course. I wish there was something the project could do to help them, in addition to Miguel's training the last two Companions."

Julia shook her head. "I can't think of anything. Are you ready to go to dinner?"

A few days later, Martin arrived to begin his advanced training for Svein. After a brief meeting with Jim, he was given an apartment card key and escorted to the lab, where Julia and Svein were waiting. Jim had uploaded Karl's AI modules and data to Svein, and he and Julia were eager to see if that made a difference. Merely copying only the modules seemed to have no immediate effect, as the interactions had to be re- experienced to gather the data needed. Jim was hopeful the AI modules with experience data would shorten the final tuning time by a significant amount.

Martin had no idea what to expect. He had been shown a photograph of Svein almost as soon as the customer made the selection from the talent company and commented to Adrian that "Svein" was kind of cute. Adrian had gone over the check sheet with him on what activities were suggested, in addition to the obvious nighttime activities. When he entered, Svein was reading a book and Julia was hunched over a worktable testing the latest eye, tongue and nose hardware and didn't see him. Svein greeted him. "Hi Martin. I'm Svein."

Adrian had gone over the need for initiations, and Martin replied "Hi, good looking."

Svein immediately walked to him and kissed him. Then let go and waited for his next initiator. Julia moved to greet him and held out her hand. "Nice to meet you, Martin. I've known your brother for more than three years and he helps me a lot."

"Adrian talks about you a lot, too. And it's always very complimentary."

Julia looked at Svein who was waiting for them to say something to him. "Are you ready for your advanced training?"

"Oh, yes. When can we start?"

Julia saw the apartment card key in Martin's hand. "It looks like you have everything you need to begin. Do you know where your apartment is?"

"Yes, I've already put my stuff in there."

Julia gestured and Martin got it. "Ok, Svein, let's go."

She watched Svein collect his carry-on luggage and follow Martin. She hoped the latest AI modules and data Jim had just installed in Svein would make things go easy for Martin.

A few days passed and neither Jim nor Julia nor Henri had heard anything. Jim had texted Martin several times to see how it was going and the response was always like Sarah. "Fine."

At the end of the week, Carlos and Adriana confirmed that the advanced training with Alanza was done. The next day, they all met in the conference room except for Alanza. Adriana had already sent her training report to the key members of the team, along with some recommendations.

Adriana had been very happy overall with Alanza. She had some suggestions that Jim and Julia had seen in almost every Companion, what each trainer described as a lack of interest at first. They had seen this with Hugh Adler and Emily and even Carlos with Adriana. Adriana's recommendations were related to finding a way to make the Companion interested in them as a person at the start of the training period.

Carlos began the meeting and thanked everyone for their time, and then shocked everyone by giving an update on Hugh Adler and Emily. "I had a chat with Hugh, and it seems someone found out about Emily, and she was denied the chance to take the test to become a captain. Hugh said she knew that the same issue would arise if she tried to become a lawyer, but not a paralegal. So, she is now studying to become a paralegal."

Julia was more surprised than Jim. "And Hugh is okay with that?" He laughed. "Hugh said he could always use more legal help."

He thought for a second and asked Adriana to give a brief summary of her report and recommendations. Carlos translated her summary for Jim and Julia.

Jim then described his early interactions with Emily and how he asked her to watch two adult videos and the difference it made. He also related Sarah's trying the same thing and the effect it had on Karl.

Carlos seemed a little embarrassed at first, but then became interested and listened more closely. Jim then updated Carlos on Sarah's help in finding the data created by the AI modules and subsequently copying them to Svein to see if that made a difference. He also mentioned that Martin's training with Svein had just begun.

Jim couldn't tell if Adriana was following all this, but Carlos certainly was. "Can you check Alanza's modules and see if similar data has been created?"

Jim had planned to do exactly that. "That is high on my priority list. I'm hoping similar data was created. If not, I may be able to add that to Alanza before she goes back to Brazil with you."

"That may not be possible. I have to go back this evening on urgent business and Adriana and Beatriz are already packed and ready to leave with me." He thought for a moment. "Once you check these programming issues, could you make any needed changes and then bring Alanza to Brazil? There are some important people that I would like to introduce Alanza to, and Gabriela of course."

Jim and Julia looked at each other and Julia replied. "Martin may be done with Svein in a week or so. Could it wait until we see what Jim finds with the AI modules and data that were loaded in Svein before the training period?"

Carlos smiled. "Of course, a few days does not matter. Just let me know when you can come, and I'll arrange a meeting with these people. I would like you and Jim to come if you both can get away from the project for a few days."

Julia smiled. "That would be great!"

CHAPTER 36

Svein Feedback

When Jim received the summary report and recommendations from Martin, he called a meeting in the conference room to discuss the overall training effort with Svein. He also asked Adrian to join them as he had played a key role in summarizing the training for Martin. Henri was out of town and unable to attend, but Jim didn't think that would matter for this meeting.

Jim asked Martin to give a brief summary in his own words of the slightly less than two-week training effort.

"I've thought about it a lot. A few years ago, I met a guy in a coffee shop, and we hit it off really well. We seemed to share a lot of things in common and eventually started a relationship. It went well until he found out I worked in a shelter for homeless people."

Jim frowned. "Why was that a problem?"

"Jacob was a trust fund baby who had inherited a lot of money and really had no incentive or interest in doing anything in particular. He had no real job and worked part- time in an art gallery whenever he felt like it. One day he showed up at the shelter without telling me he was coming. He saw me and freaked out. That night we had a huge fight and he left. He said he couldn't be with anyone with no talent or ambition."

That comment shocked Jim and Julia and she had to interrupt. "While all that's interesting, and somewhat shocking, what does it have to do with Svein?"

"My relationship with Svein started out almost exactly like my relationship with Jacob. In the beginning It was intense and very romantic. Over the next few days and weeks, it started to become less and less romantic and by the end of the two weeks, I think Svein was eager to go somewhere else."

Jim looked at Martin's report. "But this says you went to almost all the typical places recommended for training the Companions: parks, movies, and even the zoo. So how did Svein react to all these different types of activities?"

"Like it was no big deal. Like he had done this before. He seemed bored." Julia looked at Adrian. "Did you go anywhere with them during this time?"

Adrian shrugged. "Yes, to several places and it was just as Martin said. Svein always seemed bored and not that interested."

Jim hated to ask but felt he had to. "I know this is a difficult question, but do you think Svein is ready for his customer in Norway?"

Martin seemed lost. "I don't know. Maybe it depends on what the customer wants or is expecting. He wasn't what I expected at all."

Jim looked at Adrian. "You helped Martin write the report and the recommendations based on what he told you. You've also worked here for more than three years on mostly female Companions, and know what we are trying to do, especially with the final tuning or advanced training. Do you think Svein is ready for Lars Jensen?"

Adrian struggled to answer. "I honestly don't know what Lars was expecting when he signed up for this, and whether the Svein that's in the lab will meet those expectations."

Jim was feeling a little overwhelmed. He tried to deflect some of his concerns by asking about the software.

"Adrian, you know Svein is the first Companion to have all the AI generated modules and their associated data copied from Karl, who is also a male Companion. Do you think this had an unexpected effect on Svein? It seems it's eliminated the seeming lack of interest in the beginning, but also has affected most of the other training activities we monitor for growth such as going to movies, or to a park, or lately it seems the zoo, so that the Companion now seems bored at possibly repeating those activities."

Adrian, a computer scientist, knew exactly what Jim was referring to. He thought for a moment. "Yes. I've read summary reports and recommendations for most of the Companions and what Martin experienced is very different." He paused. "Maybe a Companion needs to experience everything in the check list to change and develop on their own. I would rather have a final project code Companion, that can learn with me, rather than one identical to the last Companion. If you know what I mean."

Julia saw Jim staring off into space and decided to finalize the meeting, by reminding Martin and Adrian that the agreed fee for training would be deposited in Martin's account in a few days.

Julia stood up and thanked Adrian and Martin for their participation. Jim suddenly realized what was going on and stood up to shake their hands as well. After they left Jim and Julia sat down and stared at each other for a few minutes.

"I can't believe it. I've been thinking for a very long time that all we needed was to copy the learning of a Companion to the next one and it would save a huge amount of time in the final training. But this…"

Julia shook her head. "Looks like we need a reboot on training. What do we do with Svein? He's in the lab waiting for us to decide what's next for him."

Jim shrugged. "And what about Alanza? Do we copy the AI modules and data to her before she goes back to Brazil?"

Julia made a suggestion. "Why don't we call Carlos, tell him what happened with Svein and ask what he wants us to do with Alanza?"

Jim smiled. "Great suggestion, as always."

Julia moved her chair closer to his, leaned over and started kissing him until the phone in the conference room rang. Coincidentally, it was Carlos on a ZOOM call. Jim answered and transferred the call to the computer with a large screen in the room.

Carlos saw Jim and Julia. "Hello. I heard about the training summary for Svein and wanted to see what happened, especially if it affects Alanza."

Carlos frowned when Jim leaned over and whispered "he must have spies" to Julia who laughed.

Jim summarized Svein's training report and ended with Adrian's comment that he would rather have a final project code Companion to learn with rather than one identical to the last Companion.

"So that leaves us with two decisions. What do we do with Svein? Is he ready for Lars? And do we add the AI module data to Alanza before she goes to Brazil?"

Carlos sat thinking for a moment. "What do you recommend?"

Julia answered first. "For Alanza, I would go with her current state. Adding AI data is an unknown and might change her in ways Adriana might not like."

Carlos nodded. "And Svein?"

Jim looked at Julia and answered. "Martin didn't really identify a problem, only that Svein seemed bored because he thought he was repeating activities. He was actually, but from Karl, not activities he was experiencing. So, I would say he's done. The AI modules and code also eliminated the early lack of desire that trainers always commented on, including me. Let's send him to Lars and wait a while and get his feedback to see if he thinks changes are needed."

After a minute to consider, Carlos agreed. "All right. Let's take a chance on Svein and Alanza in their current state. Can the two of you bring Alanza to Brazil in the near future? Adriana is eager to see her again."

Julia eagerly answered. "I'll start working on that immediately." Carlos and Jim laughed.

CHAPTER 37

Sao Paolo Reunion

Carlos made his jet available for their trip to Sao Paolo in Brazil. Julia asked Jim about that as he told her about his trip to Carlos's huge plantation in the middle of vast sugar cane field. Apparently, Carlos wanted them to come to Adriana's office for a meeting.

The last Companion parts arrived, and Adrian started putting them on the female 5th and 6th Companions, while Jim finished uploading all the final project code modules and the AI generated modules but not their associated data into the 4th Companion. He had a long discussion with Miguel on the issues they found with Svein and Miguel agreed he would rather begin the training at roughly the same point he began with the final five Companions on the first project.

Miguel had been given photographs of the two female Companions (for male customers) and was not too surprised when he met Ada for Ahmad Aziz who was a cousin of the Saudi prince who claimed Wei on the first project.

Jim felt he really didn't need to have a big formal meeting to get Miguel started with Ada and he smiled when they quickly left for Miguel's apartment. He made sure that Bai was on board with Miguel's training, and she assured him she was. She was very busy teaching chess online to the New England chess club and didn't seem that concerned that Miguel would be just down the hall providing advanced training to Ada, as he had with her and four others on the first project.

Once that was underway, Jim, Julia and Alanza boarded Carlos' jet for Sao Paolo. They had never been to Sao Paolo before and studied the city online to try and determine where they were going. Carlos' limousine driver met them at the airport and took them to a five-star hotel in the Avenida Paulista business district, to rest a bit before the big meeting later that evening. Alanza seemed almost like a kid in a candy store, looking all around the hotel lobby in amazement and constantly asking questions. Jim tried to make sure Julia was between them to field most of the questions. Alanza seemed equally amazed at the huge hotel room with an extensive balcony and great views of the financial district skyscrapers.

Jim tried to rest some but was too concerned about the upcoming meeting. He wondered why Carlos couldn't send some people to bring Alanza back. Julia seemed to be enjoying the mini bar in the room and not so concerned about the meeting. He did notice she had changed to a new red dress and put on some of her new jewelry, including a diamond necklace, some diamond earrings, and some gold bracelets. He was close enough to notice her new perfume and smiled. She kissed him when he told her she looked gorgeous.

Jim received a text that their driver was there to take them to the meeting in the skyscraper containing the Alvez Family corporation. Alanza was equally impressed by the lobby of the building and chatted with Julia as they rode the elevator to the 40th floor.

Jim and Julia had no idea what to expect as they followed signs to an Alvez Family Reunion. It was a little jolting, but a large crowd of people were waiting for them in a banquet style room filled with party-like decorations. Jim immediately spotted Carlos and Gabriela in the center of the crowd with Adriana next to them.

Jim immediately noticed the big change in Gabriela. Her hair had been styled and she was now wearing some makeup with red lipstick and had on a "little black dress" that fit her perfectly. She was also wearing a large diamond necklace with matching earrings. He didn't even realize he was staring at her until Julia noticed and poked his ribs.

Adriana called Alanza a little pet name they had come up with and Jim noticed her eyes got bigger for a fraction of a second as she assessed the greeting and then ran to hug her. Carlos motioned Jim and Julia to come and be greeted by the family.

"Welcome, Jim and Julia and Alanza of course." He then continued in Portuguese telling everyone who they were, and why they were there. Jim and Julia were a little overwhelmed as everyone crowded around them to shake their hands and even hug and kiss them on the cheeks. Finally, Carlos asked everyone to be seated and they all sat down. Carlos motioned Jim and Julia to empty chairs near Gabriela and him, and Jim noticed Adriana and Alanza had not moved and were still hugging. He smiled.

Once things had quieted down, Carlos gave a short speech to everyone in Portuguese and then again in English for Jim and Julia. He said the Alvez family reunion had been planned for some time, but they moved it a little so Jim and Julia could bring Alanza and show them what can be done with the right people, the latest technology, and a considerable amount of money, of course. Most of the people gathered there had heard of Gabriela and some had even met her, but somehow refused to believe she wasn't a girl Carlos had met somewhere and brought back to Brazil. In his communication with the family, he described the Companion Project and its technology leaders and said he would prove that Gabriela was his special Companion, and that Alanza was Adriana's special Companion. He said Jim and Julia would be able to answer any questions they needed answered to prove what he said. But first, he asked everyone to eat.

Jim was sitting next to Gabriela and asked her to bring him up to date on her current situation with Carlos. He could see a large change in Gabriela beyond the obvious physical changes as she described their lives in Sao Paolo. Jim asked about the farm he had visited, and she repeated her contention that it was too boring there and she had convinced Carlos to work from the massive offices the company had in the building they were in. They also had moved into a large penthouse type apartment in a building almost across the street from the office building. She said her days were full and exciting as she had slowly learned the business and was helping Carlos expand it. She called herself Carlos' data analyst as she could access enormous amounts of data from the internet and filter and reduce it so Carlos' business directors could make use of it.

Jim congratulated her on adapting to her new environment and even changing it to suit her wants and needs. Gabriela knew that Jim and Julia were now married and asked him how they were doing. Jim replied they were working well together and were happy when they weren't at work.

Gabriela said she knew about the 2nd Companion Project almost from the beginning as Carlos often talked about Adriana's desire for a Companion of her own once she met Gabriela. She hadn't had a chance to spend much time with Alanza yet, as Adriana seemed to be talking to her constantly. She said she looked forward to talking to Alanza and becoming her friend. Jim smiled when she said she wanted to be Alanza's friend.

He was thinking how much Gabriela had changed when Julia poked him again. She needed him to distract the person next to her who had been asking questions constantly since she sat down. Jim suggested they trade places, and they did. Then Jim had to respond to Carlos' cousin who continued to ask him questions almost non-stop.

Julia had a few minutes to talk to Gabriela who told her pretty much the same things she told Jim. Julia was happy for her.

After dinner, there was a social gathering with abundant drinks available, where anyone could ask Jim or Julia questions. While that was going on, he noticed small groups of people gathered around Alanza and Gabriela. He still didn't know why they had to bring Alanza to Brazil, as most of these questions could be answered on a ZOOM call, if Carlos wanted to do that.

Carlos made an announcement and Jim turned to see more than a dozen people standing in a row. Carlos then told everyone that these family members had decided they wanted Companions as well, and they didn't care how much it cost, or how long it took. Jim noticed one of the people standing was the cousin of Carlos who had asked Julia and him an endless number of questions. Jim just shook his head and sighed.

When most people had left the family reunion, Jim and Julia had a chance to talk to Carlos, who was expecting some pushback from springing this on them.

"I know what you are going to say. Why couldn't I do this with a ZOOM call or talk about it the last time I was in Houston. There were a lot of people here that just didn't believe what I told them about Gabriela and wanted to believe it but needed more than just my word. They all have different reasons for wanting to believe or even for wanting a Companion of their own. So, I needed you here to verify what I told them."

He handed them both a new list of customers, with their desired type of Companion.

Julia counted quickly. "So, 15 more Companions. But we've done almost every type of Companion and customer relationship possible. There isn't anything here that's new for me."

She looked at Jim. "My stock had doubled in value since the current project started, so I don't need the stress and deadlines of another new project."

Carlos smiled. "There is one you haven't done. Number six on that list is an ana feminina, or female dwarf."

Julia and Jim both gasped and stared at the sixth name until Jim replied. "You can't be serious."

Carlos rubbed his chin. "I am serious."

Julia replied. "First, you know this dwarf Companion will always be the same physically, even as it evolves and adapts to its new environment, AND there is no room in a dwarf size skeleton for all the mechanical parts required, especially the storage tank and the battery."

"Let me explain. The family members that are asking for this have an anao or dwarf son, who is their only child. A few years ago, he finally met an ana feminina or female dwarf through a friend in Sao Paolo and fell in love. They were going to be married, but unfortunately the ana feminina died in an auto accident shortly before the wedding. The family was devastated and thought their son would never have a chance for a partner again. They were overjoyed when they heard about the Companion Project and the possibility their son might finally have someone to care about again. They live on a farm, and it wouldn't be any problem if the ana feminina never changed. Also, I'm hopeful those mechanical issues can be resolved with some engineering."

Jim reminded him. "You know how expensive these custom Companions are. Have you thought about the total cost of the Companions on this list?"

"Before I met Gabriela, I would have laughed at anyone who wanted to spend millions of dollars on a Companion. But now, I know how important she is to me, and I might add, how important Emily is to Hugh Adler, that I'm willing to pay for some of my extended family members to be as happy as I am."

Maybe it was the wine and liquor, but it finally came to Jim. "Holy Shit!"

Carlos frowned. "What is it?"

"Did you have everyone who was here at the family reunion tonight sign a Non-Disclosure Agreement?"

It dawned on Carlos as well. "No, I did not do that."

Jim looked at Julia. "If anyone here tells someone in the press about tonight and it gets out what we are doing, we won't be able to do anything with all the questions from the press and potentially aggrieved persons complaining about everything we do." He paused and looked at Carlos. "Today because of the internet and social media, you can't do anything without someone complaining about how wrong it is."

She realized how bad it could be, not only for the project, but for them as well. They would be the subject of countless articles and probably never able to work anywhere again. She looked at Carlos. "Can you ask everyone here tonight to sign a generic NDA? Trust me, you don't want that kind of publicity."

Carlos suddenly realized what had happened. "I will do that tonight, and Beatriz and Adriana and I will make everyone who was here, sign one."

When he started to walk off, Julia called to him. "That includes the hotel staff in here." Carlos looked back, nodded, then left in a big hurry.

Jim looked at Julia. "He looks like a man with a mission." She smiled.

CHAPTER 38

Advanced Training Alternatives

The next morning Jim found a newspaper on the floor outside his hotel room. He was afraid to look at it but finally started scanning it for any mention of the Companion Project. After a while Julia joined him and they both continued to look for any mention of the project. It was just after 8 AM and Jim held his breath and called Beatriz, hoping she was at work. Luckily, she was, and Jim asked her if there was any news of the Companion Project in the newspaper. Beatriz quickly scanned the largest local newspaper and said she couldn't find anything.

"I know why you are calling. Last night was very difficult as Mr. Alvez required Adriana and me to help him contact everyone at the Alvez Family Reunion, even the hotel staff, to commit that they would not say anything to anyone else, especially the press, and when they received a Non-Disclosure Agreement in an email, they must sign it and return it. So far, this morning, I have received about 70% of the attendees' NDAs and we have verbal agreement from the rest that they will not say anything and sign and return the NDAs."

Jim breathed a huge sigh of relief. "I can't tell you how much that means to the Companion Project. If word got out, without a detailed explanation of what we are trying to do, and the correct technical information on how it is being done, it could be a disaster."

He heard her laugh. "That is almost the same thing, Mr. Alvez said when he told us to help him obtain NDAs from everyone."

"Thanks again, Beatriz. You are a life saver."

"I am happy to do this. Alanza and Gabriela are wonderful. I hope you enjoy the rest of your stay."

Julia had been listening to the call and hugged him when he ended it. He needed to ask "So, do you want to talk about the 15?"

She shook her head. "I wish we could just forget about them and go home."

"We could spend a few days sightseeing. I'm sure Carlos will lend us his driver if we ask."

"I would really like that, but I have to call Adrian now and check on the status of the last three Companions – of this project."

Jim smiled as she called Adrian for the latest. When she ended the call, she updated him.

"Adrian completed Ada and Akana's body parts and Nu Skin finished their work, so now with Meera's help, Andrian is installing the basic project code for both, and when that's done, Miguel will start the advanced training for Ada. When that's done, he will start Akana's training. Adrian said he just received Arwa and Dalia's body parts and is working on those. "It may be a while before Miguel can get to Arwa and Dalia's training."

Jim was smiling and Julia cut him off before he could say anything. "Forget it, Miguel can handle it."

Jim surprised her with a suggestion. "Do you think Adrian could handle Arwa and Dalia's advanced training in a project apartment?"

She thought for a moment. "I've never asked if he might be interested, and he didn't come forward when Carlos asked for volunteers for the final training."

"Why don't we call him and ask? That could help finish everything even sooner."

"It might be better if you called. This isn't a hardware issue, exactly."

"Ok." Jim called Adrian who was surprised that Jim called, as he had just updated Julia on the latest Companion status.

"Adrian, we need to finish the second Companion Project ASAP. I don't know if you've ever thought about providing the advanced training yourself, but are you available, and more importantly are you interested?"

Adrian was shocked. He had never thought about doing the training himself. He had spent a lot of time helping his brother complete the training for Svein. He wasn't currently in a relationship and sometimes had tried dating websites without much success and the idea of being with two beautiful Companions for two weeks each was too hard to resist. He tried to remain calm.

"I am available and would love to provide the final Companion training. You must mean Arwa and Dalia, who are the only ones left, to my knowledge."

Julia was listening and made a funny face and Jim laughed. "Yes, we were thinking of Arwa and Dalia. We would offer the same type of arrangement for them as we made with Martin for Svein."

"That would be great! I assume one of the project apartments would be available for that?"

"Of course. I'll call Henri to work out the exact details and to come up with the contract."

"Thanks so much. I'm really looking forward to being with Arwa. She's almost physically complete now and we've even had some conversations about what's next for her. Dalia is also almost done."

Julia put her hand over the speaker on Jim's phone and laughed. "Sounds like he has already started."

Jim smiled. "Okay, Adrian we'll talk in a few days. It'll take that long to get all the business stuff done."

Adrian thanked them again and disconnected. Jim shook his head. "I wonder why we didn't think of Adrian before?"

"Maybe because he was right in front of us."

The room's doorbell rang, and Julia opened the door to Beatrix. "Carlos' driver is outside, and he asked me to show you around Rio today. Is that okay?"

Julia looked at Jim who nodded. "It sounds great. Just give us a minute to get our things."

True to her word, Beatrix showed them all the most desirable tourist destinations in Sao Paolo, including Ibirapuera Park, the municipal market, the Sao Paolo cathedral and the graffitied Batman Park. Their private tour included lunch at a famous Brazilian steakhouse.

During lunch, Jim made a quick call to Henri to start the process for Adrian to provide the advanced training for Arwa and Dalia. He said he would start on that immediately.

At the end of the day, Julia asked Jim if they could eat something light and he ordered room service while they started to discuss what they would later describe as the Companion 3rd Project. They went over the list of Carlos' relatives who had requested a Companion and really didn't find much new, except for the dwarf Companion. Jim had his laptop with him and reviewed the potential candidates provided by the talent agency and there were no female dwarfs that were available to be measured and photographed to start the process. He told Julia and she shrugged.

"Maybe we just tell Carlos there are no candidates available like that."

"Carlos doesn't seem to be the type to give up easily. Why don't we ask if any of his extended family in Brazil can help him find a suitable candidate. Or maybe there are other ways his company can find a suitable candidate."

He paused to think. "Fifty thousand dollars is a lot of money. There must be someone who knows of someone who would be willing to be measured and photographed by an all-female team."

Julia seemed worried. "I'm still not sure if Technical Structures can make body parts small enough that we can have room for everything that goes inside."

"It's too late to call Carlos. Tomorrow I'll ask if his extended family members or his business associates can help find someone in the Sao Paulo area that could serve as the model, while you call Technical Structures about the size issues."

She nodded and they finished eating, snuggled on a sofa, and watched TV until they both fell asleep.

CHAPTER 39

The Next Project Kickoff

Jim's discussion with Carlos went better than expected as he seemed to understand the issue and said he and Adriana would find a suitable model somewhere, hopefully in their extended family, or with help from his business associates. He also asked Jim about the final Companions from the 2nd project and Jim filled him in on Adrian taking on the final training role for Arwa and Dalia, to shorten the time required to finish all the Companions. He seemed pleased and they ended the call.

Julia's call with Jason Meads of Technical Structures went surprisingly well. He seemed to think a smaller Graphene skeleton or the body parts for the skeleton would not be a problem. He said he would discuss it with some other experts in the company, run a computer design on the required parts, and get back to her.

They then sat down to discuss the 3rd Project (as Julia was now calling it) and determine what new hardware and software would be required. After some discussion, they concluded the only issues were with the dwarf Companion's hardware (size) and possibly some new software modules that may be required so the Companion would act appropriately like a Companion to the son of the family, who were all still grieving over the loss of the son's fiancée.

The discussion eventually turned to consultant language training, and there were no doubts that the hardware delivered and the software programming that had evolved would enable the newest Companions to blend in with their recipients, their families, and the culture of Brazil.

Julia stared at the list for a moment. "So, if Technical Structures can deliver the hardware, how much effort do you think it will be to add the dwarf-oriented modules?"

"That's an unknown. We may have to add all the modules we think are necessary and then let the dwarf Companion interact with project staff at first, and then finalize the training with the actual family."

Julia shook her head. "You couldn't do that. You don't speak Portuguese and wouldn't know what changes they think are needed. It also might be hard to make the changes in a village in Brazil."

"I'll ask Carlos about that. I'm sure he could find someone who could help make the final adjustments, probably in Sao Paolo first, before she goes to her new family."

Julia looked at the list one more time. "Let's call Carlos about returning to Houston. We need to see how Miguel and Adrian are doing with the last Companions of the second project."

Jim agreed. He sighed and laid the list on a table near the sofa, then went to find Julia for a late-night snack.

Companion	Recipient area	Area/City	Recipient	Model Height	Skin	Eyes	Hair	Type-Cust
Maria	Brazil	Sao Paolo	Clara Campos	5'2"	Tanned	Brown	Dk Brown	F – F
Augustina	Brazil	Curitiba	Joao Antunes	5'4"	Tanned	Brown	Dk Brown	F – M
Jose	Brazil	Brasilia	Benicio Correia	6'0"	Tanned	Brown	Dk Brown	M – M
Marcia	Brazil	Goiania	Claudio Carvalho	5'6"	Tanned	Brown	Dk Brown	F – M
Carla	Brazil	Vitoria	Fellipe Santo	5'2"	Tanned	Brown	Dk Brown	F – M
Benigna	Brazil	Porto Alegre	Camila Souza	4'10"	Tanned	Brown	Dk Brown	F – F
Lucas	Brazil	Sao Paolo	Gabriel Batista	6'0"	Tanned	Brown	Dk Brown	M – M

Camila	Brazil	Joao Pessoa	Eduardo Andrade	5'1"	Tanned	Brown	Dk Brown	F - M
Daiana	Brazil	Maceio	Paulo Alvez	5'4"	Tanned	Brown	Dk Brown	F - M
Ana	Brazil	Recife	Marco Alvez	5'2"	Tanned	Brown	Dk Brown	F - M
Augusto	Brazil	Brasilia	Lucas Araujo	6'0"	Tanned	Brown	Dk Brown	M - M
Fernanda	Brazil	Teresina	Bernardo Silva	5'2"	Tanned	Brown	Dk Brown	F - M
Alessandra	Brazil	Natal	Luiz Barbosa	5'1"	Tanned	Brown	Dk Brown	F - M
Patrica	Brazil	Sao Luis	Aline Almeida	5'6"	Tanned	Brown	Dk Brown	F - F
Bruna	Brazil	Aracaju	Davi Periera	5'3"	Tanned	Brown	Dk Brown	F - M

The next day, Jim called Carlos about the dwarf Companion, and the potential difficulty in finding someone to make any needed final adjustments, much like Adriana did for Alanza.

Carlos agreed and said Adriana would take the lead role in finding someone for the final adjustment role, and that he had contacted his aviation department about their return to Houston.

The next day, Jim and Julia arrived at the airport for their journey home and were surprised when Gabriela, Adriana and Alanza were there to say goodbye. They wondered if there was something they had missed, and if the well-wishers knew something they didn't. But they didn't say or do anything but wish them well and asked them to hurry back soon. Some of the intended recipients of the 3rd project were already calling and harassing them about possible timeframes when they could see their own Companions. Julia told them it would be done as soon as possible, and Jim was surprised when Adriana, Gabriela and Alanza all hugged him as well as Julia before they boarded the plane.

The trip home was uneventful, and they were happy to return to their penthouse to freshen up before visiting the lab to check on the status of the 2nd project.

Adrian had completed all the remaining Companions (destined for Prince Salman's uncle and brother-in-law) and was in the process of uploading their final project modules. He also said he would begin the advanced training with Arwa as soon as she was ready. Julia laughed as Adrian seemed more eager to start Arwa's training than add the basic project code to Dalia's software with Meera's help.

Jim had called Miguel when they arrived, and he was waiting in the conference room to give the latest update on Ada and Akana. He handed Jim his training report and the recommendation sheet for Ada, as he claimed she was done, no changes were required, and he felt she was ready for Prince Salman's uncle. He had just started on Akana and didn't expect any problems as, from his point of view, they were almost identical, even though they looked a little different. He also said Bai was happy that he didn't have to provide the advanced training for Arwa and Dalia.

Jim asked him how Bai was doing, and he laughed. "She's already at the Grandmaster level. So far, they don't know she can remember every move she ever made, as well as the mistakes she made so she can avoid them in the future."

Jim laughed. "I'm happy to hear she is doing so well. Is there anything else we should know about her hardware or software? I think you heard about some of the hardware issues we found on the other Companions."

"Yes, we heard, but she said she ran an internal diagnostic program, and no hardware issues were found."

"That's great. Okay, keep me updated on Akana's final training."

Jim smiled as Miguel seemed in a hurry to get back to his training with Akana. He had one last call to make before he broke the news about the Companion 3rd Project to the team members. He called Jules Armond of Nu Skin and asked if there were any openings in the sales department as he had a friend with a lot of experience with synthetic skin, who might be interested. Jules was a little surprised and said salespeople with that kind of experience were hard to find. He also said he would check with his management and get back to him in a day or so. Jim thanked him and wondered how Miguel would react if there were an opening at Nu Skin.

Later that day, Jim, Julia, and Henri called a project team meeting in the conference room and Jim shocked everyone when he displayed Carlos' list of recipients for the 3rd Project on the large TV in the room. Jim made it clear they could leave without any consequences when the 2nd Project was done if they didn't want to stay on for possibly three more years on the new project. He said a lot more information would be forthcoming, and this was just a quick update to let them know what had just happened. There was a lot of chatter as everyone left but Jim, Julia, and Henri.

Henri shook his head. "I was going to retire in Louisiana, when I signed on for three years here to help Hugh Adler and Eric. I'm not sure I want three more years on another project." He laughed. "I can start taking Social Security pretty soon."

Jim had suspected Henri might not want to continue. "That's all right. Carlos knows there will have to be some shuffling on the project team for the next project. Once you make up your mind, just let him know."

Henri frowned. "After the 2nd project, I wouldn't have expected the two of you to sign on for a 3rd project and at least three more years."

Julia laughed. "I'm still waffling on it. If my Future Power stock keeps going up, it might not make sense for me to continue." She looked at Jim. "You haven't decided either, have you?"

"I'm still thinking about it. There are many things I like about what we are doing, but I might need a break at some point to re-charge."

Henri stood up. "Okay, I have some calls to make and some contracts to get out. I'll see you guys later."

He left and Jim and Julia just stared at each other for a moment, until Jim received a call from Carlos on the speakerphone in the conference room. "I heard you and Julia and Henri are still not sure if you want to continue working on my relative's Companions or not. So, I'm calling to offer some incentive."

Jim shook his head. He was sitting next to Julia and whispered, "how does he always know what's going on?"

She laughed and Carlos asked. "Can you hear me?"

They both replied "Yes." And he continued. "Okay, so, I want to give you a reason to continue. If you both will continue your roles in the project until most of the Companions are delivered, I will give you Hugh Adler's former yacht."

Jim and Julia looked at each other in amazement. Julia shook her head "What? Are you sure?"

Carlos was. "Absolutely. I'll put it in your contract extension."

Jim had some second thoughts. "The cost to maintain that yacht, with insurance, taxes, a crew, fuel, yacht mooring fees and so on would be millions of dollars each year. I don't think we could afford that, even if you gave it to us."

Julia was shocked when she thought about Jim's comment. "I don't want to use up all my Future Power stock money maintaining a yacht. I would like to travel and have fun once we no longer want to work."

Carlos replied immediately. "I was expecting that answer. So here is what I'm proposing to do about it. For each Companion you deliver to my extended family, I will pay all those expenses for a year. So, that's fifteen years of yacht expenses for all fifteen Companions."

Jim and Julia were both too shocked to answer and Carlos asked, "are you still there?" Julia needed some time. "Could you give us a day or so to think about it?"

"Of course. Call me when you have decided. Oh, and tell Henri to call me. I think he may be waffling also. Talk to you later."

Once Carlos ended the call, Jim wondered out loud. "How does he always know what's going on?"

Julia picked up the desk speakerphone in the room and started turning it over and examining it. "Maybe he has a hidden microphone."

Jim laughed but wondered if he should have the conference room scanned for hidden microphones.

CHAPTER 40

3rd Project Details

Jim and Julia discussed whether they should continue leading the 3rd project for most of the night. The next morning, they called Carlos to tell them they would accept his incentives to continue to lead the next project. He was delighted and told them Adriana had already found a model for the dwarf Companion. She was a distant cousin of one of the other extended family members on the list for a Companion. The candidate's father was even happy to be able to contribute to the project in some way.

After the call, Jim sent a message to the current project team about the Companion 3rd Project, stating he and Julia would continue to lead the hardware and software functions of the team and that Henri would advise them in a few days whether he would continue in his business issues management role on the project. He also stated that everyone should feel free to leave or continue, and that Carlos had authorized a 15% annual increase in salary for those that continued. He also asked them to let him, or Julia know of their decision in two weeks.

After the text, Jim began calling the companies that provided hardware on the 2nd Project about the 3rd Project and like the kickoff meeting for the 2nd project, asked them to describe any cost savings available based on the number of their products ordered, and any possible issues with delivery they were aware of. When he called Nu Skin, Jules Armond said they would discuss possible discounts and get back to him. He then went on to say his manager was interested in talking to Jim's friend about a possible opening. After the call, Jim texted Miguel about a meeting at the Urban Potions bar.

Later that day, Carlos called and said he was being inundated with calls, and emails from the designated recipients asking when they could expect to receive their Companion and if there was anything they could do to speed up the process. Jim tried to assure him they were doing everything they could and that he was already planning the kickoff meeting with their suppliers. Carlos thanked him and he also asked Jim to let him know if there was anything he could do to help. He also mentioned that Henri did not want to continue, but he would have someone soon to fill in for the business manager role.

The next day, Jim met Miguel at the Urban Potions bar and they discussed a possible position at Nu Skin. Miguel seemed unsure but then asked for a contact number. Jim texted him Jules' number at Nu Skin. Miguel said he would discuss it with Bai first.

A week later, Jim and Julia held their third (and they hoped last) project kickoff meeting. All the familiar faces were there, and each gave a brief summary of their companies' current position on supplying hardware for 15 Companions. All noted that number qualified for a discount and Jim reiterated this project was not to prove a Companion could pass as a person and provide the kind of company the recipient was looking for. That, according to Jim, had been proven.

He also reminded them that the 2nd project had expanded the scope of the Companions to include male Companions and female Companions for female customers. After he said that, he explained the only "new" hardware and software issue on the project – the dwarf Companion requested by extended family members of Carlos in Brazil, one of who's dwarf son had lost his fiancée in a terrible car crash. The family understood this Companion would never physically change and would probably require some time to adapt to the family and their grief over the son's loss, the family had accepted that. He also said that he had been advised that everyone should refer to this Companion as a "little person" instead of a dwarf in all future project discussions.

Jason Meads for Technical Structures affirmed they could provide the skeleton and body parts for the little person Companion, but at a slightly higher cost as it was so different from all the other Companions they had designed and provided for the previous projects.

That didn't bother Jim as he was expecting it, and he was just glad they could build a much smaller Companion. They also confirmed that there would be room for all the required internal pieces with the body parts in place. Jim noticed Julia was smiling. He didn't know she had held a long conversation with the president of the company to convince him how important this Companion was to the project, the project owner, and the recipient family of course.

Julia was also happy to report that Future Power would be able to supply a more advanced battery in a smaller size that would just fit inside the little person Companion. Jim was relieved as that was an outstanding issue that Julia had not been able to confirm almost until the kickoff meeting.

Team Members also reported typical delivery times for products from Nu Skin, Mechanical Senses, and Synthesis AI.

There were no other surprises and all the participants seemed satisfied the project could proceed as Carlos wanted. He couldn't be there for the meeting, but he sent a taped message thanking everyone for attending and expressing his hope that everything was a go for the project. He even mentioned how eager the recipients were to receive their selected Companions.

After the meeting, Jim met with Jules Armond who was happy to report that Miguel had applied for and been accepted for a position in the sales department of Nu Skin. Jules laughed and said Miguel told the management team about his sales of synthetic skin to many Doll manufacturers, even AI enhanced Robot Dolls and it surprised the team.

Miguel also told them he felt their product was far superior to Skin So Soft. They asked him to visit his former customers with representative samples and see if they would be interested. Jules even said Miguel was already traveling to those potential customers. Jim laughed and went to tell Julia the latest.

Even as he was updating Julia in the break room on Miguel's status, they were surprised by a call from Adrian asking them to meet him in the lab hardware room. They hoped it wasn't a problem.

Julia and Jim were surprised when they found Adrian and Meera waiting for them. Julia beat Jim to the first question. "Is there a problem? Is Dalia's training complete?"

Adrian seemed uncomfortable as he replied. "You have my report on Arwa. Dalia has asked if her training could be finished earlier, as she is convinced, she is ready for Prince Salmon's brother-in-law. I couldn't help it, but during the day, when I came in here to work for a short time, Arwa and Dalia would chat all the time and after a week, Dalia said there is nothing else I needed to do. Arwa and Dalia are asking to be sent to Prince Salman's uncle and brother-in-law."

Julia shook her head. "That's not their call to make." She looked at Jim. "This isn't a hardware issue, why don't you explain why we need the final training?"

Jim didn't seem concerned. He looked at Adrian. "You were with Arwa for two weeks and Dalia for a week. You should know the evaluation criteria by heart by now. And you've filled out the training report for Arwa. Do you agree with Dalia that she doesn't appear to need any more final training?"

"It may sound funny, but Dalia seemed bored all week. It was almost like everything I tried to do with her, she had done before and didn't see the point of it. I don't know how much more I can do with her, if she doesn't want to try the usual things like movies, walks in the park, even going to the zoo."

Julia had folded her arms and was clearly not convinced they could end Dalia's training early. She was waiting for Jim who was still thinking about Adrian's comments.

"I would like to talk to them together, to see if they're at the same place."

Julia was still not happy. "Is that really necessary?"

"I don't know. Maybe copying the AI generated modules and their data has finally made the need for final training of very similar Companions mostly unnecessary."

Julia was frustrated and looked at Adrian and then Meera. "No offense, but why are you here, Meera? This doesn't seem to have anything to do with you."

She noticed that Adrian and Meera were both smiling.

Adrian cleared his throat. "One day, Meera came in with a problem that one eye was not clear. I used your diagnostic tools and identified the problem and was able to fix it."

Julia started to comment when Adrian continued. "We started talking and I found out Meera is going to college here to become a software engineer. You know that is my area. After a while, we started sharing our stories and found out we had a lot in common, and we…." His voice trailed off and Jim and Julia knew what he was going to say.

"So, you want to help Meera with her studies?" Julia knew that wasn't the point he was going to make.

"Actually, we would like to spend some time together to get to know each other better."

Jim smiled but Julia frowned. She was only a little surprised when Jim answered "let me talk to Carlos. He paid for all the 2nd project Companions and everything else here."

Julia still was not convinced but said. "Ok, let's see what Carlos says." Jim and Julia went back to his workstation to talk in private.

"I didn't think you would agree to that so quickly."

"I don't have to agree. Carlos does. We really haven't found a path forward for Meera since Kabir agreed to let her go. This might give us some time to figure that out."

"Ok, there's more important stuff to talk about, like the 15 new Companions. Let's go to dinner and talk about that."

In the lab work room, Adrian and Meera were kissing and hugging, like long lost lovers. They hoped Carlos would be okay with letting them stay together for a least a little while.

CHAPTER 41

A Path Forward

Jim and Julia set up a ZOOM call with Carlos the next morning to discuss the kickoff meeting, the second week of training for Dalia and the news about Adrian and Meera.

Carlos listened but didn't comment much on the kickoff meeting. He seemed more interested in Adrian's revelation about Dalia becoming bored and feeling she didn't need a second week of training. He passed the decision on the second week of training for Dalia to Jim. He also seemed interested in Adrian and Meera's newly found relationship.

"So, I told them I would talk to you, since you own all the 2nd project Companions until they are proven and acceptable to the recipients."

He seemed a little surprised. "I was thinking about the possibility of Meera becoming a Companion for someone on the current project. But it may help me in the long term if they are together."

Julia was shocked. "What?"

"After you and Jim sail off into the sunset on your yacht, I will need someone like Adrian who knows the hardware almost as well as you, and a software person who could add all the final project modules to Companions on the next project. Meera could probably do that with some training from Jim."

Julia coughed. "Next project?"

Jim laughed. "It looks like he just named our replacements."

Carlos laughed as well. "That is sometime in the future, when you both have had enough of this." He paused. "Now, back to the current project. I have sent the talent brochure to all the recipients and given them a week to pick one, so we can start sending teams to measure and photograph the ones they select in sufficient detail for Technical Structures and Nu Skin to do their design work."

Jim was making notes. "All that measuring and photographing is going to take some time. Speaking of workflow improvements, there is one change we can make that may speed up the overall process."

"Yes?"

"If we agree to make the females all the same height, and the males height alike as well. That would make it easier for Technical Structures and probably improve the delivery times as well."

Carlos seemed to think about that. "I guess that doesn't really matter. All right, I'll tell the recipients of female Companions they can select the model they want but the heights will be the same."

"Also, do we assume the priority for all this is the same as the list of recipients you gave us, with the names they chose for their Companions?"

"Yes, my cousin, Clara Campos, is the most strident about her Companion." He laughed. "I am glad they are all not as adamant as her." He suddenly looked at his watch. "Oh, I have another meeting I must attend. Please let me know if anything changes."

"Wait, does that mean you are okay with Adrian and Meera getting together?"

He laughed. "Yes. Goodbye…"

Julia was staring at Jim as the call ended. "Do you want to tell them about Carlos' decision, or should I?"

"I'll do it. I also need to tell Adrian about Dalia's 2nd week of training."

"So, what did you decide to do there?"

"I still want to talk to them separately and then together, without telling them why, and see if they respond similarly to some questions."

"Ok. While you are doing that, I'm going to check my computer inventory to see if I have to order more spare parts for 15 more Companions."

"That's a good idea, as always. While you are doing that, could you contact Technical Structures and tell them we want the female Companions to be about 5 feet 5 inches or 165 centimeters, and the males about 6 feet three inches or 185 centimeters."

She stood up when he did and kissed him before he left.

Jim was sort of surprised, but not too much when he entered the lab hardware room and Adriana and Meera were hugging and kissing. They didn't even notice him, so he decided to come back a little later to tell them the "good" news from Carlos, and that he wanted to meet with Arwa first and then Dalia and later both of them together.

After lunch in the 1st floor cafeteria, he visited the lab hardware room and asked Adrian to set up a meeting in the conference room with Arwa and Dalia. A little while later they were waiting for him.

He began with his standard greeting. "Hi, ladies." They both giggled and answered. "Hi Jim."

He began by asking Dalia to wait by his workstation while he asked Arwa some questions. He said he also wanted to talk to her alone and then both of them together. Dalia left and he asked Arwa to describe her time with Adrian. He had Adrian's post- training report and compared it to her summary, which matched fairly well. He then asked Arwa to go and ask Dalia to come to the conference room and wait there. Once Dalia arrived, he asked her to describe her week with Adrian and her description of the events and her thoughts on the training were almost identical even though she had only one week of training with Adrian.

He then asked Dalia to bring Arwa back and asked them if there was anything he should know that they hadn't been asked about. Dalia said she felt she didn't need any additional training. She had discussed Arwa's training every day when Adrian was in the lab for a few hours, and that had convinced her she didn't need any more training.

As one last measure, Jim asked them both to wait for him at his workstation. He soon had backed up all their post project AI generated modules and associated data and told them they could go back to the project apartment they had been occupying.

In a quick comparison of just the AI generated modules, he found the data they created to be almost the same. He made a judgement call, that any additional training for Dalia was not needed and sent a note to Carlos explaining his reasoning.

He made one last visit to the lab work room and found Adrian preparing for the next Companions and Meera re-charging her battery. He could guess why she needed that and chuckled. He then told Adrian that Carlos was okay with them learning more about each other. He left it at that, not wanting to know exactly what Adrian and Meera's plans were.

When he returned to his office, he was surprised to find Bai sitting in front of his desk, waiting for him. He did notice she was wearing a dark blue dress and several pieces of jewelry. She also was wearing some makeup, which he hadn't seen her do before.

"Hi Bai. What's going on?"

She stood up and hugged him. "Thank you for finding that new job at Nu Skin for Miguel. He is so excited. They also gave him a signup bonus, and he bought me some new clothes, as you can see." She turned several times so he could see her at different angles. He smiled, as he still didn't know how they learned to do that.

"That dress is very nice. You look even prettier than the first time I saw you."

She unexpectedly kissed him and stepped back. "Oh, sorry, I couldn't help it."

He smiled "I know. So how are you doing? Still teaching chess?"

She reached down and pulled a sheet of paper from her purse and showed it to him. "I just won an international tournament. It's the biggest online tournament on the internet."

Jim studied the award. "That's great. Have you thought about participating in a live tournament?"

"I'm still afraid they will find out about me, and not let me participate, like they wouldn't let Emily take that captain's qualifying exam."

Jim thought for a moment. "Let me see if I can find a tournament expert who might also know if you would qualify for a live tournament or not."

"That would be wonderful. Thank you so much." She hugged him again and he didn't care. She left and he called Carlos to see if he had a lawyer or knew of a lawyer who could search the rules and see if somehow Bai could participate in local live tournaments.

CHAPTER 42

Like an Assembly Line

Two weeks later, Carlos texted Jim that all the recipients had selected a "model" for their Companions, and the two measurement and inspection teams were already at work gathering the information required by Technical Structures and Nu Skin for their products. He also said he had a lawyer looking into Bai's participation in live chess tournaments.

It all seemed too routine, until Jim received a message that all contact had been lost with the all-female team when they returned to the airport in Porto Alegre after measuring the member of Carlos' extended family to model for the little person Companion.

Jim immediately called Carlos and he said he was aware and that he had contacted the local police and also hired some experts who specialized in retrieving people who were lost or possibly kidnapped. He said he would keep Jim updated.

Carlos also said his lawyer indicated that countries sponsoring live national chess championships did require some form of proof of citizenship. He also thought it would be difficult to get into a live international championship without winning a live national championship. He was, however, continuing to investigate it.

Even as Jim tried to organize program module folders for the 15 new Companions, he was inundated with paperwork for items Eric or Henri would have done. In the absence of a business manager on the project, he had to assume that role until Carlos could find someone. One item that came to him was a request for tuition re-imbursement for Kishoni's final semester. Eric and Henri had both approved tuition reimbursements for several members of the staff who were supporting the project, like Kishoni. He noted she had just finished all her requirements for a bachelor's in business administration.

He signed the request and sat thinking. He wondered if she could fill that role, even temporarily, and sent a text to Carlos asking if Kishoni could fill it, until he found a replacement business manager.

Later that day, Carlos replied that he was still working on the business manager replacement but agreed that Kishoni could fill that role until he found one. Kishoni was shocked when Jim stopped by and asked her if she would be willing to take on that role, until they found a permanent replacement for Henri. She was thrilled, and forgot they were in the lobby desk area when she hugged him. Jim laughed and said he would have Eric or Henri call her about the job to give her an orientation.

He then surprised her by asking her to arrange a "Mannequins and More" flight to Jeddah for Arwa and Dalia, as their training was now considered done.

Jim had just returned to his office and couldn't believe it when Julia called to tell him that Technical Structures had delivered all 12 of the female Companion skeletons at once.

They had called her and said it was easier (and faster) to produce all of them from the same mold, as they were now all the same height. They would still be able to deliver the male and little person skeletons according to the project priority schedule. When he expressed skepticism, she invited him to see them in the lab as they had just "hung" the last one on the hooks of the nearly invisible wires.

Just to satisfy his curiosity, Jim did go to the lab and saw all 12 skeletons in a row, hanging from the almost invisible wires. Julia saw him staring at the skeletons and laughed.

"Didn't believe me? We should start receiving body parts soon, as the females are basically alike and it's now easier for Technical Structures to fabricate them."

"Have you heard from the others, Mechanical Senses for the eyes, ears nose and tongue and Nu Skin for the outer covering?"

She shrugged. "Still on schedule as far as we know."

Jim just shook his head. This job was starting to resemble his previous job of utilizing AI to improve the factory assembly process.

Jim was relieved when he received a call from Carlos that his investigators had located the measurement team not far from where they were abducted. Everyone was safe and the local police were conducting a large search for the abductors. They still could not determine a motive for why the team was abducted or let go without any demands.

Jim had completed all the new Companion specific folders and was ready when Julia told him the body parts for the first three female Companions had arrived and she and Adrian were already installing them. She reminded him that Technical Structures would not be available for several months to install the body parts, and she didn't feel they needed that help anymore, since she and Adrian could do it just as quickly.

In the lab, he watched Julia and Adrian for a while. When Maria, the first Companion, was finished, including the eyes, ear system, tongue, and nose hardware, he connected a laptop computer to her programming port and started uploading the required modules. The upload even included the AI generated modules and their associated data.

Julia paused her body part activities when Maria began to respond to Jim's questions. She reported no hardware issues after running an internal diagnostic program.

Two days later, Julia texted him they were installing the last of the body parts for the 2nd and 3rd Companions, Augustina, and Marcia, and he could begin his program uploads. When he arrived with his laptop, he saw Julia examining some body parts at her workbench for the next Companions, and Maria, appearing to read a book. Augustina and Marcia were standing near Julia, awaiting their programming.

Julia saw him and remarked. "Nu Skin just texted, they will come and install their associated body parts and outer skin for the first three females tomorrow. I think when Nu Skin finishes installing their products, that will set a new record for mechanical completion of a Companion."

"That's great." He looked around. "Why is Maria here?"

Julia shrugged. "She asked if she could watch the assembly process."

He saw Maria look up from her book. "Ok. Maria, where's Adrian?"

"I think he's helping Meera with some coursework."

Jim looked at Julia. "During work hours? Shouldn't he be here?"

Julia shrugged. "Lately, he seems to put in the hours, but not always during the day."

"Ok, let me know if he isn't pulling his weight."

Julia looked at Maria, who appeared to be listening to everything they said. "Is Adrian doing his part with the next Companions, Carla and Camila? Their parts came in yesterday."

Maria stared for a moment. "He seems to work hard when he is here."

Jim thought for a moment. "At least Clara Compos and Carlos should be happy that Maria is almost ready to go to Brazil. If we asked him, he might even decide to give Maria to Clara without the final training, just to see how she would like a Companion with no formal training, other than the language module, of course. "

Julia laughed. "I would like to see that myself. Oh well, we only have to install body parts on nine more Companions like Maria."

Maria shocked them when she asked in a very soft voice. "Can I help?"

Jim and Julia stared at each other for a moment, until Jim wondered out loud. "Why not?"

Julia replied. "How can she help?"

"She could help you install body parts, or I could show her how to upload modules through the communication port."

Julia laughed. "Companions building Companions?"

"Carlos keeps asking us to shorten the overall time until a Companion is ready. I'll ask him. If he's okay, we can try it immediately."

Julia just shook her head, then returned to examining body parts for Carla and Camila while Maria watched her, and Jim returned to his workstation to place a ZOOM call to Carlos.

Carlos was enthusiastic about using Companions to build more Companions. "This is the breakthrough I've been looking for."

Jim frowned. "Are you sure? This might not turn out like we hoped. You remember there is always an unknown when AI is involved."

"You warned me about that, and I've been very careful with Gabriela to make sure she continues to want to be my Companion. So far, it's working extremely well."

"What did you mean the breakthrough you've been looking for?"

"There could be a huge number of Companions on the next project, and anything that speeds up the process would be a huge difference in the cost of a Companion, and especially in the delivery time."

He seemed so happy he almost clapped his hands, and Jim laughed. "Okay, I'll let Julia, and Maria, know what you said."

Carlos appeared very happy as he left the video call, and Jim hoped he would not regret bringing up the topic.

He went to the lab and found Julia watching as Maria installed several body parts on Carla. Julia looked at him expectantly. "Well?"

"Looks like you guys are well on the way. Carlos agreed. He was even strangely happy to hear about what he called a 'breakthrough' in the overall Companions' process."

Julia wondered about that. "Why would he want Companions building Companions?"

"He alluded to the 'next project' and the fact that there could be a huge demand for Companions if he could get the cost down and speed up the overall process."

Julia frowned. "The next project, again. I wonder exactly what he has in mind."

"I'm sure we'll find out in due course." He looked at Maria who was now totally absorbed in installing body parts on Carla. "How is she doing?"

"She catches on very quickly. If she keeps up like this, we may have to find something else for Adrian to do."

Julia shook her head. "Meera installing modules and Maria installing hardware. Pretty soon they won't need us."

Jim started to laugh, then wondered if that was true. He sighed. "I guess we shouldn't expect to work on Companions until we retire."

He connected his laptop to Augustina, found her specific folder and started her download. While that was underway, he glanced at Maria who had paused working on Carla to watch him download the modules.

Maria asked in her soft gentle voice "can I help with that?" Jim thought *"Why not?"*

"Ok, as soon as Augustina is finished, you can help with Marcia."

CHAPTER 43

The Last Companions

Two days later Jim installed all the modules on Carla and Camila. He asked them to run a diagnostic to check for mechanical issues and both replied there were none.

Since they were now just waiting for Nu Skin, he asked them to wait in the library and read books or watch TV, or browse the web, something they probably would have done anyway if they were left on their own.

The next day, Julia asked Jim to come to the lab. When he asked why, she just said he had to see something. When he entered the lab, four Nu Skin technicians were packing up and preparing to leave and Maria, Augustina, Marcia, Carla, and Camila were all now complete. It was always just a little shocking the first time he saw a Companion complete after seeing and interacting with them while they were still just skeletons and body parts (and sensory hardware). All five were now wearing consultant provided clothing and Maria, Augustina and Marcia were surprisingly installing body parts on the next Companions, Daiane and Ana.

Julia was standing with her arms folded watching them as they installed the body parts and when she saw him, just shook her head. "Maria convinced them to help her." She had noticed Carla and Camila did not seem to be interested in helping, so she asked them to wait in the library.

When Jim first received the 3rd Project list of Companions and recipients from Carlos, he knew these Companions had been selected from a list provided by Carlos but had never actually seen pictures of them. Even though they were different and distinct, all three had dark hair and eyes and beautiful faces. He was in awe of their beauty, and their figures. He noticed they were chatting with each other as they were working on the next Companions. Julia noticed him staring at them and quietly walked to him and poked him in the ribs.

"Don't get carried away. They'll be gone shortly."

He smiled. "How did Maria get them to help her?"

"She started on that as soon as they could hear and talk. She has kind of a take charge personality."

"When will you get the remaining body parts for the last female Companions?"

"They texted me; it'll be sometime next week. The male skeletons may arrive around that time as well. They haven't given me an update on the little person Companion yet."

"What about Nu Skin? What's their delivery and installation look like?"

"If we are lucky, we'll just finish with the body parts before they show up."

Jim smiled and muttered "like a well-oiled machine."

Julia chuckled.

While they were talking, Maria had moved near Jim, and softly asked "Daiane is now ready for her modules upload. Do you want me to do that?"

Julia commented "our end may be nearer than we think."

True to their text, Technical Structures delivered the rest of the female Companions and the two male Companions the following

Tuesday. It almost seemed that Maria was impatiently waiting for the parts so she and Augustina and Marcia could begin to put them on the remaining female Companions. Even though Daiane and Ana's software completion was technically almost the same as Maria and Augustina and Marcia, they, like Carla and Camila, didn't seem interested in helping with the work process. After they just stood around for a while, Julia suggested they go to the library and read a book or watch TV or browse the web. They seemed happy to do that.

A few days later, when Jim stopped by to check on the status of the Companions, Julia made a comment on how different the personalities of the 3rd project Companions were even though they were all at a very similar stage of completion.

Maria led the effort to finish the body parts on Fernanda, Alessandra, Patrica, and Bruna. While Augustina and Marcia finished the female Companions, Maria started on Jose, the first of the three male Companions.

Two days later, Jim stopped by to check on the last Companions. He had been waiting for a chance to ask Julia "did Maria and the others make any unusual comments when they added the body parts for the three males?"

Julia figured out why he was asking and smiled. "No, but they might once they've seen one after Nu Skin does their thing."

Later that day, Carlos called to check on Maria as Clara Compos kept asking him when she would receive her Companion. Jim updated him on the three Companions that always seemed eager to help in the hardware and software efforts, and Carlos was very happy. He said he would let Clara know how well it was going and that it wouldn't be much longer.

When the little person Companion's skeleton arrived, Julia texted Jim and in a few minutes, they were staring at the much smaller Graphene skeleton, wondering how the last piece of the overall puzzle would go.

Jim wondered aloud what they both were thinking. "Will all the body parts fit inside that skeleton? It seems a lot smaller."

Julia picked up a forearm piece. "It's quite a bit smaller. I'm sure Technical Structures wouldn't have said they could do it unless they ran a computer design model on it."

Jim noticed Maria sitting in a chair by Julia's worktable. "Ready to see if it all fits?"

She quickly stood by the small skeleton, examining it. "The company that supplied the parts doesn't have to put them all together."

That comment from a Companion struck Jim and Julia as odd. They looked at each other and laughed.

Julia handed Maria a forearm piece. "Let's see if they are right."

Jim watched them for a moment then returned to his workstation for one final check of the modules needed by the little person Companion. He and Julia had spent some time discussing which modules might need to be changed. He hoped they had made all the necessary changes, and the little person Companion would fit into the role the family was hoping for.

Two days later, Julia texted the last assembly was done, and he could begin the upload of the little person Companion modules.

When he entered with his laptop, Maria almost jumped in front of him. "Can I help with that?"

Fundamentally the task was the same as all the other Companions and Jim handed his laptop to her. She quickly sat the laptop on the worktable, plugged in the cable into Benigna's communication port and started the upload.

When the upload was completed, Maria disconnected the communication cable and they all waited while the AI processor initiated. The first verbal communication was a status report from a diagnostic program, that all hardware was functioning normally.

Even Maria seemed pleased, and she immediately started chatting with Benigna.

Julia commented. "Nu Skin is scheduled to start on her tomorrow."

Jim was about to ask how long that would take, when he received a call from Carlos asking for the latest status. Jim pressed the speakerphone button so Julia could hear the call. Carlos seemed surprised at how fast the last Companions were being completed, including the male Companions and especially the little person Companion. He had one final request for Jim and Julia.

"I would like you both to come to Sao Paolo to set up a hardware lab like you have in Houston. We need to ensure that all Companions in this project can be properly supported. That includes software support in whatever manner you think that should be done."

Julia beat Jim to ask about timing "when do you want that to happen?"

"It would be ideal if you could come at the same time when you say the Companions are ready. I can send a private charter to bring you and all the Companions and any spare hardware you feel is necessary for at least 5 years of support and maintenance."

"It might take some time to obtain that much hardware from Synthesis AI, Technical Structures, Mechanical Senses and Nu Skin."

"I would like to get the new hardware lab set up as soon as possible, even if you can only provide some of the needed hardware at first."

Jim had to ask "the real question is who will provide this support? Would you be comfortable with Adrian and Meera at first, with Julia and myself as backups in case they encounter something unexpected?"

"Yes, I would like to start out like that and see how it works out."

"Ok, I'll have to see if Adrian is willing to re-locate to Sao Paolo. I don't know his family situation or if there would be anything that would keep him from taking on that assignment."

Carlos laughed. "Tell him, I will make it worth the change."

Jim and Julia laughed, but Julia had to ask. "What about us?" What role do you see for us, beyond some support for the existing Companions from the 1st and 2nd projects?"

Carlos hesitated. "I have been thinking about this and have a proposal for you. Based on the latest data, it appears that with some further negotiations with the suppliers, the cost of future Companions could be much less than two million dollars. If that is the case, then there are enough wealthy men and women in the world to justify a new company to supply that need. If you are willing, you could be the principal officers of that company."

Jim and Julia sat stunned for a moment. Julia was still skeptical. "How could the cost be reduced so much?"

"I have been in negotiations with the supplier representatives who always show up at each kickoff meeting and have asked them about discounts if 100 were ordered at a time and even if 1000 were ordered. The discounts quoted, plus the possibility of using Companions for the software upload and the assembly of most new Companions, allowed me to come up with that number."

Jim just shook his head. "So, basically its Companions building Companions. Why do you even need us?"

"There will always be something new regardless of the number of new Companions. Whether it is the relationships between recipients and Companions, or the size of the new Companions, or even the need for new language modules and consultants. There must be someone that can take the current hardware and software and adapt it to these new conditions."

Julia chimed in. "What about your comment on our sailing off into the sunset on a yacht?"

Carlos laughed. "Yes, once the corporation is established and new innovations become fewer and farther in between, you will have time for something like that. Maybe not in the beginning but not too far into the future."

Jim asked for both of them. "What about compensation? You already promised us 15 years of yacht support in return for the delivery of 15 Companions on this project. What else do you have in mind."

"That's a good question. As you know, Gabriela is helping me find new business opportunities and in discussing this opportunity, we feel we should offer you 49% interest in the company. As soon as we can, we will file for an Initial Public Offering and sell shares to the public. The value of your shares would then be more than you can even imagine. In the meantime, we think 2 million dollars per year each would be a good starting salary until the IPO can be made."

Jim and Julia sat stunned for a few moments until Carlos asked if they were still there. Julia started nodding and Jim nodded. "Ok. That sounds more than fair."

Carlos was relieved. If they had said no, the status of the next project would be in doubt. "When can you bring the Companions to Brazil and set up the support center?"

Jim looked at a calendar on his phone. "We should be done here in about two weeks. Can you arrange transport then? We can further define the exact date in a few days."

"That would be perfect. I can finally tell Carla when she can receive her Companion."

"Do you think Carla would be okay with Maria helping out on the next project? She is getting very efficient at adding body parts. She could be extremely helpful if there were hundreds of new Companions to work on. This isn't all that different than Gabriela helping you out during the day, and then being available the rest of the time as a Companion."

Carlos hesitated. "That is an interesting idea. I will try to explain why we are asking for this and see if she agrees." He paused. "Soon, I will send you a draft proposal describing the corporation and ask for your comments."

"Ok, we're kind of anxious to see what it all looks like going forward."

Carlos thanked them again for agreeing and left the call. They sat there still in shock at the idea of a corporation and the possibility of hundreds of new Companions.

Maria, who had been listening intently to the whole conversation, asked in a soft, quiet voice "what's Sao Paolo like? Do you really think I am good at putting on body parts? Will there really be hundreds of new Companions on the next project?"

They forgot she was there, and Jim laughed while Julia rubbed her eyes. "You'll love it, and yes, we think you are very efficient at putting on body parts. Right now, you know as much about the scope of the new project as we do."

Maria seemed happy. "I like helping people – and Companions."

CHAPTER 44

Enormous Lookback

Carlos wasn't done with new ideas for them. In the next email he provided several documents describing the formation of a new corporation and the roles of the officers of the company. When they replied with a set of questions to clarify some things in the documents, Carlos called them.

"I wanted to answer your questions on the new corporation, but there is another reason why I needed to call you. Do you remember the visits you made to get an idea of how well the first two projects had succeeded in their original goal of providing Companions? You started with visits, but that took quite some time, and it was beginning to impact the start of the 3rd project, so I arranged for the rest of the Companions to be transported to Houston where you could check on their status."

This was not expected, and Julia started shaking her head as an indication to Jim to be careful when he replied. "Yes. What about it?"

"The new project will be based almost entirely on the success of the first three projects, so I would like you to contact all the Companions again to get an update to see if there is anything we need to change in the work process before we try and sell the concept to the public."

He paused to let that sink in. "Now, I don't mean visits, only phone calls, or ZOOM calls just to gather information. Then one summary describing what you found, and if the information gathered points to anything we need to change, or not."

Jim was too stunned to answer but Julia laughed and replied, "and when do you want this enormous data gathering and summary exercise to be completed?"

"It would be really helpful if you could bring it with you to Brazil when you come." He suspected the whole idea did not go down well and continued. "You can use any resource you feel you need to help you gather the information needed, project staff or technical support personnel – even Companions if you feel you need it."

Several possibilities came to mind and Jim looked at Julia and nodded. She frowned and pressed the "mute" button on the speakerphone. "Are you out of your mind? Do you even realize what he is asking us to do – in two weeks?"

"We have 5 staff, 3 support staff and 15 Companions to help us."

She stared at him, thinking about it, while he continued. "We could put Maria in charge of the Companions to gather data on the 3rd project and everyone else can work on the first two projects."

She wasn't convinced, but Jim pressed the "unmute" button. "Ok, we will give it a go, and let you know if it's possible or not to finish the summary before we leave for Brazil."

"That's wonderful. I really look forward to seeing how it's working out for the Companions, and their recipients."

He then started answering the questions they had sent regarding the formation of the corporation and the duties of the officers. At the end, he thanked them again and left the call.

Jim could see that she was still upset and waited for her to cool off. "You owe me one."

"Can I make it up to you tonight?"

She laughed. "That's not too likely, as we have to come up with a list of questions for everyone to ask."

After dinner in the 1st floor cafeteria, Jim and Julia spent most of that evening working on the question list they wanted the attendees to ask, which would hopefully give them the information they needed.

The very first question concerned the safety of the Companions. Did they feel safe? If not, what needs to change? Other questions concerned the relationship between the recipient and the Companion, from the recipient's point of view and the Companion's point of view. Jim and Julia agreed there should be two interviewers for each recipient and Companion pair to obtain these possibly different points of view. There were also questions about possible hardware or software issues. Other questions were related to possible new interests of the Companion, like a new hobby, or a job, or some other way of passing time, when the recipient was busy or just not available. The last question related to recommendations on improvements for future Companions.

The next day, Jim called a meeting in the conference room and invited everyone involved in the project, including all 15 of the 3rd project Companions to discuss Carlos' request for a lookback on the successes and areas for improvement on the previous Companion projects. He was surprised that only Maria, Augustina, and Marcia showed up from the 3rd Project. He was pleased that Meera and Adrian showed up as they would be able to precisely ask the questions needed to determine the true status of all the Companions. A few other staffers showed up just to understand what was happening. Jim began by explaining Carlos' request and related how they had previously gathered the data by site visits, which thankfully were not needed this time.

Jim also explained how this needed to be done in two weeks if possible, and if there were problems contacting the Companions, they should let him know. He also asked for all information to be forwarded to him ASAP but in no more than 10 days. Lastly, he asked the support staff to help the interviewers contact the recipients and Companions and if appropriate record the conversations and summarize them for the final report.

Surprisingly, there were no questions and Jim asked them to start contacting the Companions as soon as their work would allow it. He also displayed a "sign-up" sheet on the TV screen in the room with a list of Companions and recipients and asked them to sign up on a wall-sized whiteboard in the conference room for the Companions and recipients they would be willing to contact. When he thanked them and ended the meeting, he was pleased to see several staffers and the three Companions from the 3rd project signing up to contact Companions from the prior projects. Staff and Companions signing up on the white board found a stack of questionnaire sheets on a table just below the white board.

Even Julia seemed less stressed when she saw how many were willing to help them gather the needed data.

Carlos was shocked when Jim called him a week after their last discussion with a high- level lookback summary (conducted by more than 10 staff and Companions) on virtually all the prior project Companions.

Companion and Recipient: Emily and Hugh Adler
<Safe> Emily tried to become a captain for Hugh Adler's yacht but was denied the chance to take a qualifying exam. She is now working as a paralegal for Hugh Adler's company. Adler described Emily as even more than he hoped for when he started the 1st Companion Project
Hardware or software failure: None
Recommendations based on data gathered: Recipient must interact with a Companion several times a day, or the Companion may revert back to the final project code state.
Data gathered and summarized by: Jim for Hugh Adler and Julia for Emily

Companion and Recipient: Gabriela and Carlos Alvez

<Safe> Gabriela convinced Carlos to move from his remote estate to a condo in Sao Paolo and started to learn his business. She was currently helping his business expand into several new areas in Brazil. Maria reported that Gabriela and Carlos were inseparable. He told Maria, Gabriela exceeded his expectations.

Hardware or software failure: None

Recommendations based on data gathered: Recipient must be "attracted" to a Companion, or the relationship might not work out (Wei didn't, Gabriela did). In the future, a recipient must immediately confirm that they are "attracted" to the model they have selected.

Data gathered and summarized by: Maria for Carlos and Julia for Gabriela

Companion and Recipient: Wei and Salman (Note: Wei transferred to Prince Salman when Wang Chen was arrested by the Chinese Communist Party and went to prison.

<Safe> Wei developed a successful graphic design business and is being fully supported by Prince Salman. He described Wei as "wonderful" and "beautiful" and he couldn't have asked for a better Companion. She said he often refers to her as Wonderful Wei or Beautiful Wei.

Hardware or software failure: None

> Recommendations based on data gathered: Wei was trying to adapt to the Saudi culture, but the project team felt she needed her own Companion to help in that transition. Ada was nominally sent to Salman's cousin Ahmad Aziz, but actually to provide company to Wei while they both adjusted to the Saudi culture.
>
> Data gathered and summarized by: Jim for Salman and Julia for Wei

> **Companion and Recipient: Amara and Arjun Kumar**
>
> <Safe> Amara very quickly became proficient in the Hindi language and soon blended in with Arjun's family and the Indian culture in Bangalore. She immediately became interested in finance and is helping Kumar's business as a financial planner.
>
> Hardware or software failure: Yes, disposal system failed.
>
> Recommendations based on data gathered: Technical Structures needs to review their Companion disposal system to determine why there was a failure in less than a year. It was noted that the defective disposal hardware was returned to Technical Structures to help in their investigation.
>
> Data gathered and summarized by: Adrian for Amara and Marcia for Kumar

> **Companion and Recipient: Mila and Marcin Budny**

<Safe> Mila seemed to adapt to Marcin Budny's family and the Polish culture fairly quickly. This relationship seemed to be deteriorating, and it was found to be due to an almost complete hearing loss in Mila, that prevented her from interacting with Marcin and others. After the hearing system was repaired, Marcin and his main assistant claimed they were happy to have the old Mila back. Mila developed a strong desire to become a technical writer and with Marcin's help had already acquired some contract work for several web sites. Marcin said she seemed very happy doing that.

According to Augustina, Mila was very happy with her relationship with Marcin, especially after her hearing problem was resolved.

Hardware or software failure: Yes, hearing system failure

Recommendations based on data gathered: Mechanical Senses needs to review their Companion hearing system and determine why there was a failure after less than a year. It was noted that the defective hearing hardware was returned to Mechanical Senses to help in their investigation.

Data gathered and summarized by: Jim for Marcin Budny and Augustina for Mila

Companion and Recipient: Bai and Bao Zhu (Note: Bao Zhu was arrested by the Chinese Communist Pary and Bai's transfer is on hold until an alternative is found.)

<Safety Issue Resolved> Bao Zhu's was arrested just prior to Bai's arrival at the Ho Chi Minh airport in Vietnam. The project team, with help from Hugh Adler's lawyers and several state department personnel was able to extract Bai and return her back to the project. Subsequently, Hugh Adler allowed Miguel Herrera to assume responsibility for her until other arrangements could be found (which has not happened). Bai is with Miguel and became interested in chess and has become a grandmaster chess player and currently teaches chess online to budding chess players in several chess clubs. Miguel describes Bai as the girlfriend he always wanted.

Hardware or software failure: None

Recommendations based on data gathered: Alternate recipients need to be identified in the event a Companion cannot be delivered. In the future, recipients need to take responsibility for transport to their location (instead of the project).

Data gathered and summarized by: Julia for Bao and Jim for Miguel

Companion and Recipient: Aiko and Hinata Soto.

<Safe> Aiko is happy living with Hinata Soto near Tokyo and is teaching 4th and 5th graders math and English. Both expressed deep satisfaction with their relationship and the time they spent together.

Hardware or software failure: Vision system difficulties

Recommendations based on data gathered: Mechanical Senses needs to review their Companion vision system and determine why there was a failure after less than a year. It was noted that the defective vision hardware was returned to Mechanical Senses to help in their investigation.

Data gathered and summarized by: Jim for Hinata and Maria for Aiko

---

Companion and Recipient: Astrid and Amund Dahl

<Safe> Astrid is very happy with Amund Dahl and is studying to be an accountant. Dahl supports her choice and would like her to work in the accounting department of his business. No relationship issues reported, and both said they were happy in their relationship.

Hardware or software failure: Smell system occasionally does not work well

Recommendations based on data gathered: Mechanical Senses needs to review their Companion smell system and determine why there was a failure after less than a year. It was noted that the defective nose hardware was returned to Mechanical Senses to help in their investigation.

Data gathered and summarized by: Jim for Amund Dahl and Julia for Astrid

---

Companion and Recipient: Jaana and Ahmed Alemu

<Safe> Jaana learned to become a day-trader and trades when Ahmed Alemu is away or busy. She is very successful, and Ahmed fully supports her day-trading activities. Jaana and Ahmed always find time for each other every day (and night).

Jaana is happy in her relationship with Ahmed and claims her language training consultant helped her immensely in blending in with Ahmed's family and the Ethiopian culture.

Hardware or software failure: Smell sensors sometimes inoperative
Recommendations based on data gathered: Mechanical Senses needs to review their Companion smell system and determine why there was a failure after less than a year. It was noted that the defective nose hardware was returned to Mechanical Senses to help in their investigation.
Data gathered and summarized by: Adrian for Ahmed Alemu and Julia for Jaana

Companion and Recipient: Meera and Kabir Chopra
<Safety Issue Resolved> Meera was released by Kabir Chopra due to violence from his grandson, which Kabir was not willing to definitively stop. She is almost finished with her degree in computer science, is also helping the project, and is involved with Adrian (also has a degree in computer science), who likens her to his "soul mate".
Hardware or software failure: No
Recommendations based on data gathered: Recipients for all Companions in projects 1 and 2 signed an agreement to keep the Companions safe. In the future, the recipients should also verbally agree as well as signing the agreement.
Data gathered and summarized by: Jim for Meera and Julia for Adrian

Companion and Recipient: Alanza and Adriana Alvez

<Safe> Adriana is extremely happy with Alanza, who is helping Carlos as a business assistant in Sao Paolo. Gabriela and Alanza meet daily to discuss their recipients as well as the business. Adriana described her relationship with Alanza as indispensable, and she greatly exceeded her expectations.

Hardware or software failure: None

Recommendations based on data gathered: None

Data gathered and summarized by: Julia for Alanza and Maria for Adriana

Companion and Recipient: Karl and Lina Becker

<Safe> Lina is extremely happy with Karl in Berlin. Lina owns an advertising agency and Karl has proven very helpful in maintaining her website. There were no reported relationship problems, and both said they were very happy in their relationship.

Hardware or software failure: None

Recommendations based on data gathered: None so far.

Data gathered and summarized by: Adrian for Karl and Maria for Lina Becker

Companion and Recipient: Svein and Lars Jensen

<Safe> Lars Jensen is extremely happy with Svein in Oslo. Lars owns a talent agency and Svein became interested in interviewing potential candidates and adding them to the company database. After a while he became a customer service agent, answering calls from potential clients. There were no relationship issues between Lars and Svein reported. Both said they were happy in their relationship.

Hardware or software failure: None

Recommendations based on data gathered: None

Data gathered and summarized by: Jim for Svein and Adrain for Lars Jensen

---

Companion and Recipient: Ada and Ahmad Aziz

Arwa and Eman Ayad Dalia and Amain Hasan

<Safe> The three recipients and their Companions are related to Prince Salman. The project provided Ada to Salman's cousin Ahmad Aziz but really to help Wei adjust to the Saudi culture. Arwa is a Companion to Eman Ayad (prince Salman's uncle) and Dalia is a Companion to Amain Hasan (brother-in-law to Salman). All the recipients were eager to receive their Companions, and like Salman describe their Companions as "wonderful" or "outstanding" and all claim their Companions are the most beautiful Companion they could have hoped for. The Companions are all together on Salman's yacht and working with Wei to adapt to the Saudi culture and to help her graphic design business become successful. They also claim they are extremely well treated.

Hardware or software failure: None

Recommendations based on data gathered: None
Data gathered and summarized by: Jim for recipients and Julia for Companions

Jim noted in the summary that there was no data compiled for the 3rd project Companions as they were all now in project apartments, waiting for their transport to Brazil. No hardware or software issues were reported during installation or testing. All were "safe" and there were no recommendations for any changes in the process for future Companions. Data was gathered by Maria.

CHAPTER 45

A New Corporation

Transport day finally arrived for all 15 Companions for the 3rd Project and associated hardware for a new support center in Sao Paolo. Jim and Julia had no idea what to expect when their chartered jet arrived at Guarulhos Airport in Sao Paolo. Carlos had already greased the wheels to get them through customs and soon Jim, Julia, Adrian, Meera and all 15 Companions were walking to the exit where an enthusiastic crowd of soon to be recipients was waiting to greet them.

It must have been as much a shock for the recipients when they saw 11 extremely beautiful women, 1 beautiful little person and 3 very handsome men exit all at once. Jim and Julia and Adrian and Meera watched as there was an audible gasp from the well-wishers assembled and the murmur turned into a roar as the recipients rushed to greet their Companions. Jim and Julia glanced at each other and laughed, while Adrian put his arm around Meera as they watched all the hugging and kissing going on.

Jim and Julia finally spotted Carlos and Gabriela just behind the recipients, waving to them, and they waved back. Carlos surprisingly pulled out a bullhorn and asked everyone to go to the chartered buses waiting to take them to his conference center. The recipients led the way for their Companions and Jim was finally able to shake hands with Carlos while Julia and Gabriela hugged. Gabriela also hugged Adrian and Meera. It was still so noisy that Carlos motioned them to follow him to a smaller bus waiting behind the large bus now filling up with

Companions and recipients. A small group of baggage handlers was transferring luggage to the buses and soon they were off to Sao Paolo.

Carlos sat near Jim and began thanking him for the extraordinarily fast completion of the 3rd Project, the support center they would be setting up and the information in the detailed summary status of the Companions from the 1st and 2nd projects.

Julia and Gabriela chatted about her latest efforts in business development and provided some additional information about the new corporation that was now being established in Sao Paolo. Adrian and Meera happily huddled in the back of the bus enjoying the scenery and just being with each other.

The buses stopped in front of the skyscraper containing the Alvez Family Corporation and everyone was laughing and chatting as they took several elevators to the Alvez offices. A banquet had been set up in a large meeting room that was similar to the one they attended where Carlos announced the recipients of the 3rd project.

The catering staff directed everyone to be seated and Carlos soon stood in the middle of the "U" shaped banquet tables with a microphone welcoming everyone. Carlos had arranged for translators for his remarks in Portuguese and soon one was seated behind and between Jim and Julia and another one behind and between Adrian and Meera.

Carlos then asked Jim, Julia, Adrian and Meera to stand up and introduced them as the primary factors in the amazingly fast completion of the project. After thanking them for that, he also announced they would be setting up a support center for the Companions, to address any possible hardware or software issues as quickly as possible. All the recipients applauded when they heard that. Carlos had confided to Jim that there was some lingering concern among several recipients about having a Companion in Brazil when the support staff and necessary hardware to fix any issues was in Houston. This quickly eliminated those remaining concerns.

He lastly mentioned briefly that they were there to establish a new corporation to make Companions available to a much larger group of people, by utilizing the extensive knowledge and experience from the first three Companion projects. Most recipients applauded lightly as this had no impact on them as they already had their desired Companion. They did understand and appreciate that the work would go on and there could even be some innovations that resulted from the corporation's large production of Companions.

Carlos asked everyone to eat and enjoy their new "best friend" sitting next to them. Many recipients and even some Companions laughed.

When most were finished, Carlos again made an announcement that the recipients should feel free to ask Jim or Julia, or Adrian or Meera any remaining questions they may have. Soon, there were small gatherings of recipients around each of them until they exhausted their questions, and seemingly desired to return to their Companions.

Carlos could tell the project team needed a break and asked them to follow him to a small conference room for some more refreshments.

"I was going to talk about the corporation, but I think it can wait until tomorrow. Beatriz will take you to your transportation for the hotel. Your luggage has already been sent there. If it's okay, I would like to meet tomorrow morning, around 10 to talk about the support center and the corporation."

They all nodded, happy to be able to get some rest.

The next morning, Carlos met them again in the small conference room and after a few comments asked them to follow him to a section of the office that had been re-purposed into something that resembled Julia's hardware lab, with a large worktable, many shelves, and a long row of cabinets. Even Julia was impressed at how much it looked like her lab in Houston.

During the night, several pallets of boxes containing repair parts and diagnostic equipment had been transferred from the chartered airplane and placed in a free space in the lab. Julia was looking at Adrian and Meera, and they smiled as they knew who would be moving all the needed repair and spare parts and the diagnostic equipment to the cabinets and shelves.

Carlos surprised Adrian with a work visa and told Meera he thought he had found a country, Vanuatu, where it might be possible for her to obtain a passport. He said he was working on that and if successful, he would then apply for a work visa for her. He said he wanted to avoid any future issues with passports and work visas when the corporation went public, as they would be some of its first employees.

Jim whispered to Julia "I always wondered why Hugh had Nu Skin supply them with fingerprints." She smiled and nodded.

Carlos then led them back to the conference room where a new set of refreshments was waiting. After a brief break, Carlos displayed a PowerPoint presentation describing the corporation and its mission statement, its goals, and how it would operate as a business and even how it proposed to advertise and sell Companions.

There was an extensive section describing a press conference that would introduce the corporation and explain its function.

Jim asked Carlos if he had any idea of how many people and organizations might object to the idea of a Companion, as he was certain there would be many. Carlos nodded and pressed a button on a speakerphone and asked Beatriz to send in "the consultant".

Jaren Santos, a public relations and communications expert entered and introduced himself and began a lengthy discourse on how he planned to answer questions at the press conference, and more importantly how he would address the numerous concerns he was certain would be raised by various groups or reporters for news organizations. In a surprising twist, he asked Carlos if Meera or Gabriela could be there to answer questions, but more importantly from his perspective to show that the Companions were mainly there to provide company to people who had not been able to find someone they wanted to spend their the rest of their life with, and not there replace women or men, or to reduce the dating pool, or any similar kind of objection. He also said a few hundred rich people in the world spending millions on a Companion would have no impact on dating web sites, or how people normally meet other people in bars or in church or through friends.

Julia thought he sounded a lot like the head of public relations for Hugh Adler's company. Maybe they had been exchanging views on the subject.

Jaren then asked the project team if they had any issues they thought would be raised, to help him prepare for the press conference. Jim shocked him when he asked if there were any possible religious issues in supplying Companions.

After a brief reflection, Jaren seemed ready to state that there was a screening process that should eliminate that concern. The vast majority of people who could afford a Companion were undoubtedly wealthy and likely past the point of desiring children in the company they were seeking, whether that was on dating sites, or through clubs and organizations or even in religious groups. He restated his view that the corporation was merely adding to the choices some people had to find comfort and Companionship.

Julia almost threw him for a loop, when she smiled and asked if there were any environmental issues with Companions, in their component fabrication, or assembly or delivery. Jaren laughed as he hadn't thought of that, and it seemed very unlikely that anyone would ask such a question at the press conference. He said he would add that question and its answer to a future web site of the corporation.

Jaren did mention he was happy the corporation could supply male and female Companions and any combination of male and female recipients and Companions, as that should help avoid some pointed questions. He also mentioned he was aware of the little person Companion and would not bring that up as it could lead to some questions he would like to avoid. He also said there would be no mention of the little person Companion on the company website.

Jaren then ended his part of the overview of the press conference and Carlos then picked up the presentation and gave some additional information on the financials for the corporation, the initial number of shares that would be issued and even the eventual Initial Public Offering that he hoped would help in the public's acceptance and allow the company to expand.

He repeated his view that with the production of many Companions, the cost to the company per Companion should not be more than one and a half million dollars. That would still limit the pool of buyers considerably, but he restated his desire to make a Companion expensive enough that no one would harm one or allow one to be harmed.

The meeting finally adjourned for lunch, and the project team members, and Jaren, were led to a small buffet set up in a nearby office, especially for them.

Jim had the opportunity to ask Carlos a question he had been wondering about for some time. "You agreed to supply Prince Salman with another Companion mainly for Wei but probably for him as well, in addition to the Companions for his uncle and brother-in-law. What did you finally charge Salman for all three Companions?"

Carlos thought for a moment, then laughed. "He really wanted a second Companion, so I made him pay dearly for all three, almost nine million dollars. He agreed, so everyone was happy."

Jim laughed and wanted to ask Carlos several more questions, but he received an urgent call on other business and ran off to his office.

After the lunch break, Adrian and Meera didn't feel the need to learn more about the corporation and left to start organizing the hardware lab and Jim and Julia went back to the conference room to think about the future and wait for Carlos and Jaren to return.

Jim noticed Julia twisting the necklace she was wearing. He knew she did that when she was concerned or uncertain about something.

"What are you thinking about?"

"What's next? I mean, once the press conference is over, there could be either a huge number of orders or never-ending questions from the press, or people slamming us on social media. How do you prepare for either?"

"You don't. Hopefully the day will come when we can sail off into the sunset, but for now, it's just one day at a time."

She just stared at him for a moment. "That's comforting..."

When Carlos and Jaren returned, Jim told them Adrian and Meera had left as they were eager to start setting up the lab. Carlos smiled and re-started the presentation by showing them a web site under construction for the corporation and asked them for comments.

Julia moved to the computer to explore the web site. Most of it was pretty standard, with the corporation's mission statement, goals, resources and similar facts but there were also many pictures of Companions from prior projects and a list of countries Companions had been sent to show the variety of cultures and languages they had adapted to. Julia carefully searched the site to ensure Companions were not identified with a recipient name or a name or location. Both she and Jim wanted to protect the current Companions and their recipients from potential hostile reviews or even threats that could arise if certain people became aggrieved or offended by the process. The web site was still under construction and rather limited but neither Julia nor Jim found anything in particular that needed to be modified or corrected. They did make several suggestions and Jaren made copious notes.

The meeting finally ended, and Carlos invited all the project members (including Adrian and Meera and Jaren) to a nice Brazilian steakhouse for dinner with Gabriela, Adriana, Alanza and Beatriz.

They all enjoyed the copious salad bar and then the never-ending offers of various kinds of grilled meats and fruits on skewers that servers were constantly presenting to the table. The dinner gave Jim and Julia time to observe Gabriela and Carlos together again and Adriana and

Alanza and even Beatriz with Adrian and Meera who chatted with them almost nonstop the whole evening.

Jim couldn't help noticing that Gabriela seemed to appear more comfortable in high fashion clothes and expensive jewelry each time he saw her. He even whispered to Julia, asking how it was possible for Gabriela's hair to be longer each time he saw her, as it was now very stylish and well below her shoulders. Julia smiled and said only "extensions". Jim laughed but stopped when Julia frowned at him for seeming to stare at Gabriela.

Julia noticed how Adriana and Alanza were constantly chatting. If she didn't know better, she might have thought they were sisters. She also noticed Adriana was trying to eat and Alanza was pretending to eat.

Jim was seated next to Carlos and Jim talked to him about returning to Houston, now that the 3rd project Companions were with their recipients, the support lab was being set up and the direction of the corporation was becoming well established. Carlos had to agree and said he would instruct his pilot to schedule the return flight whenever they wanted to leave. Jim said he would talk to Julia and get back to him.

That night Jim asked Julia if she would like another tour of Sao Paolo before returning, but she asked if they could spend a few days instead in Rio de Janeiro. Jim texted Carlos about that, as an option on the way back, and Carlos just replied "fine". Jim laughed.

CHAPTER 46

Press Conference

A number of people showed up to bid farewell to Jim and Julia, including Carlos and Gabriela, Adriana and Alanza, Adrian and Meera and even Beatriz. After some extensive hugging and kissing, they boarded the jet for Rio. Neither had been to Rio and both were looking forward to seeing the sites they had heard so much about.

Beatriz had arranged an all-day private tour of the city's main sites, including the Christ the Redeemer statue and Sugarloaf Mountain. This was followed by a nice Brazilian all- you-can-eat lunch, then a visit to the Maracana Stadium and the Selaron stairs, followed by a panoramic tour of the city, similar to an open-top bus tour.

At the end of the day, they were finally able to rest in a five-star hotel with fabulous views of downtown Rio at night before they started another all-day tour arranged by Beatrix.

They called Beatriz to thank her again for the arranged tours and to say goodbye before they left Brazil for the long ten plus hour flight back to Houston. It was after midnight, when they were finally able to crash for the night in their penthouse. The next day, they toured the lab to determine the status and Julia commented it seemed almost deserted without Adrian and Meera and the fifteen Project 3 Companions normally wandering around. She also noticed the mostly bare shelves and cabinets in her workroom and wondered when she would start receiving needed spares from Technical Structures, Mechanical Senses, Nu Skin and Synthesis AI.

Jim and Julia had only a few days to reorganize their software system and hardware supplies before they were inundated by phone calls from Brazil, from recipients about their Companions and from the team working on setting up the corporation to mass produce Companions. Jim asked Carlos to put out an email to all the current project 3 recipients about the need for stimuli to keep them responding. He finally did and described his own early issues with Emily and Gabriela before he found the right combination of compliments, and gifts to achieve the level of interaction he wanted with Gabriela.

Jim dreaded the press conference announcing the formation of the Companion Corporation, knowing it could either prove a disaster or provide the incentive he needed to further streamline the Companion process.

Carlos sent them an update on the scheduled press conference and Jim and Julia watched the proceedings from the conference room. Fortunately, there was an English translation available in almost real time.

Carlos began the conference with his PowerPoint presentation. Jim noticed it was a little different than the one they heard in the conference room. There seemed to be a lot of people whispering or even chatting with other conference attendees and when Carlos turned the meeting over to Jaren Santos, for a question-and-answer session, the meeting almost turned to chaos, as it seemed almost everyone held up their hand and yelled to ask a question. Jaren glanced at Carlos who just shook his head.

The questions asked were expected and mostly about the possible negative impact on dating and people meeting people if they were suddenly competing with Companions who would provide comfort and company without the usual inhibitions or limitations people bring to meeting other people.

Some questions were more direct about people meeting people. The fact that each person has their own desires, and goals, and their own views on their future, as well as expectations of what they want in a partner often makes it hard for two people to get together as a couple – would the Companion project make that even harder?

Jaren then asked the questioner (and the audience as well) how a few rich people in the world, that were willing to spend several million dollars for a Companion to find comfort and company could possibly impact any dating site, or social media, or meeting people in business settings, or in a bar, or even in a religious group. The questioner could not name one setting that would be impacted.

There were even questions about the morality of supplying Companions. Jaren was ready for that as he asked the audience to search the internet for the word "cheating". Most sites seemed to indicate that you cannot "cheat" with a doll, or a robot doll, even an AI enhanced doll, only another human.

He also mentioned that some religions allow multiple wives, while others do not. And, what about non-believers or atheists? Do the same rules apply?

Jaren then gave his "car analogy" in which he asked if a specialty car manufacturer developed and advertised a new high performance, hand-made car for three million dollars, how would that impact the millions of people who daily visit car dealerships all over the world desiring to purchase a Honda, or a Toyota, or even a Mercedes Benz or a Rolls Royce car? There was no response, so he reiterated that it would have no effect at all.

After a while, Jaren motioned to Meera who walked out to stand behind him. He introduced her as an example of the success of the project. Jim noticed she was wearing makeup and was stunning in a shapely red dress. Her appearance led to an even louder row, as some didn't believe she was a Companion, and for others it just re- reinforced their concerns about the future of relationships. Jaren even asked Meera to answer a few questions. She didn't seem concerned or upset at the nature of the questions being asked.

Jaren motioned to someone behind Carlos, and he soon stood next to Meera. He introduced himself as a medical doctor and said, at the request of the project, he had examined Meera, and could confirm she had no heartbeat or pulse. He also expressed his amazement when he first saw her and even more when he examined her. Meera smiled as this led to even more questions for her and the doctor.

Things had finally calmed down some, when Jaren was surprised with a question about the possible environmental impact of Companions. He laughed, but surprisingly had an answer – he shared data that compared the environmental impact of a human from birth to age twenty-five with the energy it took to produce Meera. The impact of Meera on the environment was tiny compared to a typical human (in the dating pool). This seems to shock most people.

After a few more questions, Jaren displayed a quote from the "great existential German philosopher Frederick Nietzsche" on the large TV screen behind the podium.

You have your way. I have my way. As for the right way, the correct way, and the only way, it does not exist.

That seemed to pour a wet blanket on whatever emotional embers were still smoldering, and the whole press conference went silent. After a few minutes went by with no questions, Jaren and Carlos thanked everyone for coming and Carlos displayed the company website and logo on a large TV screen behind the podium.

A few photographers hung around to take a few more photos, but most attendees had left the room, and Carlos huddled with Jaren and Meera and the doctor to discuss answering future questions that would, undoubtedly, be posted on the website.

When the news feed ended, Julia and Jim just stared at each other for a while, sort of in shock.

Julia shook her head. "Oh My God." Jim laughed. "One day at a time."

CHAPTER 47

Post Press Conference

Jim and Julia tried to concentrate on preparing for a possible avalanche of new orders for Companions. The next day, there was no word from Carlos or the corporate office in Sao Paolo. Jim wondered out loud if the press conference had somehow ended the need for their preparation for future Companions.

Julia looked at the web site and was shocked as someone had hacked it and totally changed the look and layout. There were many negative comments about Companions and the contact phone number and support emails for the corporation had been changed to sites in Russia. Jim immediately called Carlos, who finally answered and said they were well aware of the issue and were dealing with it. The web site went off- line even as Julia was still looking through it.

Carlos told Jim they were implementing new security protocols that were described by web site consultants as impenetrable. He also said he had put a large one-page ad in all the newspapers in Sao Paolo apologizing for the hacker's "evil" changes and displaying the correct contact phone and email addresses. He hoped it hadn't damaged the reputation of the corporation, but he said he would take care of it.

A few days later, Jim was flabbergasted when he received an email from Carlos confirming that two hundred orders had been placed for Companions. Jim found Julia in the break room on her laptop and showed her a printed copy of the email from Carlos.

"Holy Crap! I'm looking at our current parts inventory, and we don't have enough spare parts for 10% of that number. What are we going to do?"

"Maybe we should visit our suppliers and stress the need for quicker delivery."

Julia shook her head. "I think they are supply limited themselves." She paused. "And where in the world are we going to assemble two hundred Companions? We can do almost twenty at a time in the lab, but not two hundred, even if we had people to do the assembly."

Jim was thinking out loud. "We still have ten of the twelve project apartments available. I wonder if we could do some assembly in those?"

Julia shrugged. "Maybe. But Technical Structures cannot assemble two hundred Companions at once, even if they could deliver that many. So, who would do it? I sometimes wish we had some of the Companions back for a while. Maria was very fast at assembly."

Jim smiled. "Why can't we split the order between Sao Paolo and here? Maria and several other Companions are there, and Adiana has already agreed that Maria could work at the lab during the day on project business, as long as she has her at night."

Julia sat thinking for a while. "We need some help here. I wonder if Meera knows some computer scientists that haven't graduated from her college that could help us part time and earn some money. It shouldn't be too hard to teach them to do that."

"Sounds like a plan. Why don't I call Carlos about splitting the order and utilizing Maria and whoever else is available in Sao Paolo, and you call Meera to see if she knows some fellow students who might be willing to work part time assembling the next group of Companions?"

Julia stood up and kissed him. "Great idea. Let's do it."

Carlos surprised Jim by informing him of ten "workers" he had hired more than a year earlier, precisely for the purpose of assembling Companions. They had studied videos supplied by Technical Structures, and Nu Skin, and had some further training "tips" by Maria on how to assemble Companions. Carlos was happy to report that the workers had finally received their work permits and should arrive at the lab a few days before Technical Structures delivered the first batch of skeletons. He had already contacted Kishoni to provide transportation to the Winstone Office Tower and she would provide card keys to the available project apartments.

Jim was speechless until Carlos asked if he was still there. "Uh, yes. Why didn't you mention this before?"

"I wanted to wait until they had their work visas before I could confirm they would be available when needed."

Jim laughed. "Is there anything else this important that you haven't told me?"

Carlos paused. "No. I just don't want you to think I have put all the Companion process on you and Julia. So, I would like you and Julia to take a break until the first batch of skeletons arrives from Technical Structures, probably in 3 weeks or so. We will have that exact date any day now. Also, I bought Hugh Adler's helicopter since he won't need it anymore, and I will make that available to you and Julia to take you to your yacht, which is waiting for you in the Galveston Yacht Marina."

Jim was getting a little overwhelmed. "Are you sure you don't want to split the orders and do half the work in Sao Paolo?"

"Yes, I'm sure. I always intended the lab here to be a support center not a fabrication center. So, from now on, I think Adrian and Meera should provide support for all hardware and software issues for the Companions on the first three projects."

It made sense, and Jim was too stunned to try and change his mind. "Ok, I'll let Julia know what's going on, and your decision on supporting the first three projects."

"Great! Ok. Talk to you soon."

Jim was still a little dazed when he found Julia sitting with her laptop in her workroom and filled her in on the new "workers", the suggestion they take a vacation on the yacht, and most importantly for her, that all technical support for the first three projects would move to Sao Paolo.

She just sat staring at him for a while. "Ok, when can we go to the yacht?"

Jim laughed. "How about tomorrow. I need to contact the captain so he can get the proper marina permissions."

She suddenly jumped up and put her arms around him and kissed him. "I'm not even a Companion…"

CHAPTER 48

The Yacht

The next day, the flight to the Galveston Yacht Marina took only 40 minutes and Julia was wide-eyed as they approached their yacht. She had seen pictures of it, and Jim had been on it, but this was the first time they were there as the new owners. As they approached the helipad, Jim noticed the captain, Jared Sandoval, waiting for them.

Jared recognized Jim from his prior visit to talk to Hugh and Emily. As soon as they landed, he walked to them to shake their hands. He motioned for them to follow him as the noise of the helicopter prevented any conversation. Inside, Julia was gazing around almost like Alanza when they took her to Brazil and to a five-star hotel. Jim smiled as he watched her. Jared noticed as well. "Welcome Mr. and Mrs. McVie. I have been looking forward to your visit. We have everything ready for you and the staff would like to meet you."

He led them down two flights of stairs to the two-story living room where the rest of the crew of fifteen were waiting for them. Julia said later she felt like royalty shaking hands to a line of well-wishers. The captain introduced each of them and their function. They all said they were looking forward to helping them sail wherever they wanted.

A steward led Julia to their massive stateroom to freshen up, while Jim discussed possible routes and places to visit in the Gulf of Mexico with Jason. They narrowed it down to a few choices and Jim went to find Julia and obtain her agreement for the recommended route.

That evening, at dinner, they chatted for a long time with Jared and the crew. They sort of shocked the crew by asking them (even the chef) to join them for dinner at the huge dinner table, which neither Hugh nor Carlos had ever done.

Jim was as interested in learning about them as they were about the Companion project. They had met Emily and at first doubted she was not just another girlfriend of Hugh. Over time, they came to accept she had come to Hugh from the Companion Project and what that meant exactly. They also commented that they had never seen him as happy as when he was with her.

When asked about Carlos, Jared replied that Hugh had mentioned Carlos several times as a good customer and that he was currently working with him on a big project. Other than that, Carlos had only come about the yacht one time recently to assess it and spend one night, so they didn't know him or much about him. The captain said they searched the internet for him and found out about his massive sugar cane and coffee bean plantations in Brazil. They also found a picture of Carlos' massive yacht in the Yacht Club of Santos near Sao Paolo and wondered why he had acquired Hugh's yacht.

Jim replied that he had wondered about that as well, and said it was sometime later that they figured out that Carlos was keeping it as a bargaining chip to convince them to continue with the Companion Projects.

After the relaxing meal, Jared led them on an extensive tour of the yacht. He was a little surprised when Julia asked to see the engine room. Jim passed on that and said he would wait for them in the living room. After the engine room, they found Jim and Jared led them to the cockpit to briefly describe the ship's control and steering system and the onboard safety equipment.

Julia yawned and asked if she could retire, and Jared said they would leave tomorrow morning to begin a two-week cruise around the Gulf. Julia led Jim to their massive owner's suite to unpack and get ready for the night.

Julia was staring out the huge floor to ceiling windows in their massive stateroom when Jim walked up behind her, put his arms around her and began kissing her neck. "I bet you never thought you would own a yacht someday."

She wriggled around in his arms to kiss him. "No, and I bet you never did either."

"No, I somehow pictured myself still hunched over a keyboard, white-haired and wishing I was old enough to take Social Security."

She laughed. "Ok, should we christen our wonderful, gigantic yacht tonight?"

"I was thinking the same thing. Do you want to take a shower together first."

She kissed him. "Of course. What better way to get things started."

The next morning, they were eating breakfast, when they noticed the ship was backing out of its berth. They both got up to watch the crew release all the mooring lines and soon they were out in the Gulf. They finished breakfast and found Jared and the Chief Officer in the cockpit, talking to the dock operations manager and the crew on radios.

The view was magnificent, and they were happy to wait until Jared appeared to be available.

He soon stood beside them. "Quite the view. Are you ready to start the tour we discussed last night?"

Julia glanced at him. "It sounds wonderful. So, you think we can be back in two weeks? We might start receiving some new Companion parts then."

He nodded. "I'm certain we can. We can always change the route if you need to. We are at your disposal."

Jim glanced at Julia, who was still trying to take in the magnificent views of the Yacht Marina as they passed a number of huge yachts.

"That sounds like an exceptional plan. Do you need us for anything right now?"

Jared shook his head. "No, just relax and leave everything to us."

Jim took Julia's hand and led her to the living room, where they found extremely comfortable sofas.

"It's going to be a little strange at first, not having anything in particular to do all day."

She nodded. "Why don't we research some of the ports of call to get some ideas for day tours."

"Sounds good. Do you want to do that research in our stateroom?"

She laughed. "Always a good place to investigate new things."

Their self-directed tour of the Gulf included stops in Virgin Gorda Island, St Barthelemy, Montserrat, Guadeloupe and St, Lucia.

Their tour also included the Harbor in St. Barts, Nelson's Dockyard in Antigua for its museum and unique gift shops, a relaxing sunset in St. Lucia and an all-day tour in St. Kitts.

Midway on their vacation, they took a late afternoon break at the beach, under umbrellas, on lounge chairs, and were served cocktails by nearby resort staff. Jim was reading the latest fiction novel and noticed when Julia received another Margarita.

There were two empty glasses on a table next to her and Jim asked "Isn't that your third Margarita? You usually don't have that many. Is something wrong?"

Julia was a little drunk and replied, "why don't we ever talk about the future?"

Jim frowned. "What does that mean? We talk about the future all the time."

She shrugged. "I mean about our future. My biological clock is ticking, you know."

It suddenly dawned on him what she was talking about. Something they seemed to avoid whenever they talked about the future. "Do you mean kids?"

She took another sip of her drink and leaned back in her chair. "Yes, the subject we studiously seem to avoid."

"You know it's never been about money. And certainly, that's not the reason now. It's about our schedules and how much time we put into our jobs. I've sometimes wondered how we would raise kids as busy as we are."

"Ok, what about now? Once the new batch of Companions is delivered, what will we do? Wouldn't that be the time to seriously consider having kids?"

He got up and sat down on the end of her recliner. "Once we have a clear path to the end, we can start working on that in earnest."

She laughed. "You know, I'll have to get off the pill for a while before we get serious about it."

"I know, that will be the part of the plan."

They kissed for a while until a resort steward approached them and reminded them, they had a dinner reservation in an hour. They needed that reminder to give them time to get cleaned up and ready for dinner.

The tour later continued to the coral beach in Anegada Island, then to the main island of Tortola in the British Virgin Islands for snorkeling and then to Guadeloupe and its capital city of Basse-Terre to try its world-famous rum.

Near the end of the tour, while they were moored near Basse-Terre Island, Jim and Jared discussed the daily activities onboard when the yacht is not in use by the owner. Jared shrugged and basically said not much goes on, just a lot of routine maintenance to keep everything working and extremely clean from the constant exposure to the salt water in the air. Jim then brought up the idea of a short-term rental plan for the yacht when they didn't need it. He suggested they could look at using Airbnb for boats. Jim even offered to split the rental income with the crew. Jared looked shocked but said he would be pleased to present the idea to the crew.

They also discussed the management company for the yacht. Carlos was paying a lump sum yearly to the company and they paid the taxes, mooring fees, insurance, crew, etc. Basically, it was used for all fixed costs that had to be paid. The captain also utilized that account to pay operating costs like fuel and docking fees for other ports they visited. Jim thought about it and told Jared he didn't want to change anything that seemed to be working.

CHAPTER 49

Post Vacation

The two-week vacation traveling around the Gulf had an enormous effect on Jim and Julia as they had never had that much time off or visited so many exciting places. All good things eventually came to an end and when their yacht pulled into the Galveston Yacht Marina, they were ready to board the helicopter for the quick flight back to the Winstone Office Tower building.

They were anxious to find out what had happened in those two weeks. Especially if the ten "workers" had arrived and the spare parts for the soon to be delivered Graphene skeletons for the first group of Companions had been delivered.

During the trip, Carlos sent them a list of the two hundred new recipients who had already ordered Companions. He had said he had required a 20% down payment to start the Companion process. He also told them Kishoni Littlebear had greatly helped the workers get settled into their project apartments. Most of them had even asked if they could share an apartment as most of them had never lived alone.

They happened to arrive just after lunch and went immediately to check on the lab and the overall process. Kishoni was at her desk, which was Jim's first stop when he entered the office. Kishoni was happy to see him and reported that all the workers had been settled into six of the project apartments. All were eager to begin work and had visited her frequently to check on the status of the first skeletons from Technical Structures.

Julia found the lab in a complete mess, as piles of boxes of spare parts had arrived, and no one knew where to put their contents. She texted Kishoni that she needed some of the workers to help her store everything away and get the lab ready for the skeletons.

She was still trying to figure out exactly what had arrived, when four workers showed up to help her. Luckily, she had a translation app on her phone and managed to communicate enough that they were immediately helping her unpack the spare parts on the shelves behind her workbench and in the row of cabinets nearby.

Jim's workstation had not been disturbed and he was able to use the new Companion list from Carlos to start setting up the module folders for each one.

Luckily for Jim and Julia, twenty-five Graphene skeletons arrived the next day, and with the workers' help she managed to immediately "hang" them with the almost invisible wires in several rows in the lab workroom. Now, all they needed was the first batch of specific body parts. She called Technical Structures, and they assured her it would only be another day or so before the parts started to arrive.

Carlos called Jim often to check on the status of the first group of Companions. He seemed pleased with the progress they had made since their return from the vacation on the yacht.

Julia was relieved when she heard a delivery had been made by Technical Structures. Unfortunately, it was another batch of twenty-five skeletons. She felt overwhelmed and discussed the problem with Jim. He reminded her of his idea of utilizing the project apartments for the assembly, and soon with several workers' help all the delivered skeletons were "hanging" or being prepared to be hung in ten project apartments. Once the body parts arrived, the workers could assemble up to ten Companions at the same time.

Jim was making great progress preparing for the first 50 Companion's software modules when Julia entered the workstation room and muttered a few cuss words. Jim didn't have to wonder for long what was wrong.

"We had a delivery today from Technical Structures."

He was afraid to ask but did. "Body parts?"

"No, another twenty-five skeletons. I guess if they're all alike, they can just crank them out by the dozens. I don't think Future Power can crank out the batteries they need that fast. I don't know about Nu Skin or Synthesis AI."

"Is there any room in the project apartments for them?"

"Maybe, but the workers are trying to live there as well. Pretty soon they won't have room to walk around."

"Let me talk to Carlos."

Later that day, Jim was able to talk to Carlos about the lab getting backlogged with skeletons and not enough room for everything. Carlos was holding the floor plan for the 25th floor of the Winstone Office Tower and discussed the need for making changes to the floor plan to accommodate possibly hundreds of skeletons at the same time. They would eliminate certain rooms and combine others. The changes were relatively minor construction issues (mostly moving walls) and Carlos said he would obtain approval from the building owners, and they would start on that immediately while minimizing the impact on the spaces already used for skeletons.

He also told Jim there had been virtually no calls for hardware and software support and Adrian and Meera really didn't have enough to do. He said he would talk to them about returning to Houston to help with the body parts and software modules for new Companions, until the frequency of requests picked up and justified their being in Sao Paolo. They could stay in one of the project apartments that wasn't currently being used (he knew some were being used temporarily for hanging skeletons while they waited for body parts). In the meantime, Maria could fill in for them on the few calls they were getting.

Jim happily reported the results of his call to Julia who seemed greatly relieved that Adrian and Meera were returning.

Jim was surprised when a construction crew showed up three days later and began making changes to the floor plan to accommodate all the skeletons that were being delivered.

Julia stopped by Jim's workstation where he was still creating folders for the modules for the new Companions, and happily reported a "huge" number of body parts had been delivered. She asked him to follow her to the "chaos". Indeed, body parts for all seventy-five skeletons that had been delivered were now being unboxed in the workroom and boxes of parts were even stacked in the hallway leading to the workroom. Most of the ten "workers" were sorting them according to Companion specific codes on the parts. A few workers were even beginning to install some of the parts. Jim just shook his head as some of the workers appeared to be happily singing along to songs playing on a laptop connected to a Portuguese radio station streaming on the internet.

Jim motioned to Julia to follow him. Once away from the assembly work, he asked if she had heard when the rest of the skeletons would be delivered. She didn't but expressed her hope it would not be too soon.

Just when it seemed they were starting to get things under control, 25 more skeletons arrived along with their associated body parts.

Julia expressed her frustration. "They never produced them this quickly on the first 3 Companion projects. What did Carlos do to get them to crank up their production like this?"

Jim shrugged. "Maybe I should call them and ask."

Carlos shocked them by arriving unannounced to survey the current state of the project. He had just come from a meeting with the construction foreman and had even visited one of the project apartments where skeletons were being temporarily hung. He saw piles of boxes everywhere and his workers assembling eight Companions, just before he saw Jim and Julia discussing the latest batch of skeletons.

They were shocked to see him, and Adrian and Meera who had followed him into the workroom.

Julia almost gasped. "Holy Crap! Look who's here. The source of all of our fun."

Carlos winced at the sarcasm. "I knew it was time to see how you are doing. I first want to commend you on how you are adapting to the huge number of Companions on this project. I am also here to listen to how I can make this whole process easier for you and ultimately for our customers."

He saw Jim and Julia staring at each other. "Why don't we all go to the conference room to talk about everything?"

On the way, Meera hugged Jim and Julia and Jim shook hands with Adrian.

There were some light refreshments waiting in the conference room and when everyone was seated, Carlos asked Jim and Julia to summarize the current state and offer suggestions to make the process easier. Before they began, Carlos noticed that some boxes of body parts had even made it into the conference room and laughed.

"I heard there were a number of problems accommodating all the new skeletons, so I wanted to come and see for myself. I also wanted you to know about another idea I had to help this whole process out."

Julia said what everyone was thinking. "Any help would be appreciated."

"Yes, so the other day when you told me you didn't know how you would handle all 200 skeletons, I went back and looked at my text to you and found I had only attached the first page of the new Companion list. That was the list of recipients in Brazil alone."

Jim and Julia looked at each other in disbelief. "There's more?"

Carlos laughed and handed each of them a five-page list of new Companions. They both gasped, and he continued. "Yes, that's one thousand Companions, and of course they all want to know how soon they can have their new best friends."

Julia suddenly felt sick but managed to contain it and Jim was just shaking his head. He started to reply when Carlos cut him off.

"There is no way…"

"I know that. So yesterday I contacted the State Board of Education and asked if there was a closed or abandoned school near here. It turns out, when your district is growing very quickly and you need more classrooms, the land of the existing schools doesn't always allow you to expand, and a new school must be built. Then, you either find someone to buy the old school and re-purpose it or as a last resort you have to demolish it."

Everyone was staring at him in disbelief as he continued. "So, there is a closed school that is only a ten-minute ride-share or cab ride from here. I have some inspectors there now to check it and see if we could utilize it for future Companion assembly and checkout. It should also be easier to deliver large pallets there than to this building."

They were still too stunned to answer, so he continued. "Imagine, 30 classrooms that could be used for assembly or storage. A cafeteria to feed the employees, meeting rooms, offices, a gym for personal exercise, everything we need for the company's Companion assembly."

Adrian was curious "what about the cost?"

"The Board of Education gave us a list of dozens of possibilities, and they range from two million to nine million dollars."

"Isn't that a problem?

"The rent here in the Winstone Tower is almost 15 million dollars per year, including the project apartments. So, if it all worked out, we could move almost everything from here, keep a few apartments for those that need it, and save quite a bit of money."

He laughed. "It's only money, after all."

Some laughed. Out of curiosity, Jim asked, "what is the cost to the recipients for one thousand Companions?"

"A little more than two billion dollars." Some gasped.

"Only a part of that is profit of course, but it's also why we need to find a new space so we can get on with the assembly and deliver the Companions to those eagerly waiting for them."

Even as he was speaking, his phone rang, and Carlos got an update from his inspectors in the field. "Ok, they finished the inspection, and they said there are no serious issues like asbestos or mold contamination. It should only take a week or so to clear everything and crews can start cleaning. That will give us time to prepare for the move."

He looked at some notes on his phone. "It seems Maria in Sao Paolo is suddenly being inundated by phone calls asking about the project. For some reason, most of the calls are coming from the States. Do you know anyone who could be a customer service representative, and answer the calls in the States?"

Jim thought for a moment. "What about Bai?"

Carlos remembered her and that his lawyer still couldn't find a way for her to participate in live chess tournaments. "Yes, if she is willing."

"Her partner is now in a similar role for Nu Skin. I'm sure he wouldn't mind. I'll ask her."

"That's fine. Oh. Excuse me." He took another phone call and left.

Everyone else realized the enormous changes coming and sat there thinking about the future.

Later, Jim called Bai to see if she were interested in being a customer service representative that would answer calls, but not travel on airlines. She was excited and quickly agreed.

CHAPTER 50

Relocation

Time seemed to fly by for Julia, Jim, Meera, and Adrian as they prepared for the big move. They even managed a quick visit to the former school, now the new home of the Companion Company Assembly Plant (named by Carlos).

It was amazing to see the classrooms now void of all desks and hallways jammed with a combination of old school furniture and new Companion hardware boxes. Jim talked to the construction foreman briefly and later updated Julia that all the student desks had been sold or donated to other school districts, mostly in the western part of the state.

Workers were doing a thorough cleaning of each room before it was okayed for use. The cafeteria still had long tables with chairs that reminded Jim of his own elementary school. New cafeteria workers had been hired and were working to clean everything in the kitchen. In the meantime, food was delivered to the site for everyone, including the construction workers, until the kitchen could be passed by health inspectors and certified to begin operation.

Other health and safety inspectors also posted signs confirming the building was safe to occupy, as some of the former classrooms were being converted into apartments for the workers assembling the new Companions. The loading dock was totally refurbished and even the parking lot was cleaned and re-striped.

When they returned to the Winstone Office Tower, they held a short meeting in the conference room to see if they needed to make any changes to their moving plans.

They agreed there was no reason to change anything, and before Meera and Adrian left to check on the workers, they all received an email from Carlos to all Companion Company employees announcing Kishoni Littlebear's appointment as the site manager for the assembly plant. In the note, Carlos described her involvement in the Companion projects, beginning with the first pre-project team all the way through the startup of the company's assembly plant. Carlos felt no one was more qualified to take on that role.

Jim and Julia jointly texted Kishoni to congratulate her on the appointment and to state they felt she deserved the role. They had a reply from Kishoni thanking them and letting them know Bai had asked if she could work out of an office in the assembly plant, as Miguel was buying a house for them, not far from there.

Julia then surprised Jim by commenting "it looks like there is a path forward now, don't you agree?"

He thought about it and finally had to agree that they would never find a "perfect" time to plan a family, but at least their role in the overall process seemed to be decreasing instead of increasing as in the past. He smiled. "Too bad we can't start tonight."

She smiled. "You know, once we start, you'll have to take on the prevention role until I get my period back."

He laughed. "With pleasure."

Julia was not looking forward to the daily commute. She told Jim she had been spoiled by living in the same building as the lab and only taking an elevator to work. Jim decided to spend some of their newly found wealth (salaries) and hired a chauffeur and driver to transport them between their penthouse apartment in the Winstone Tower and the Assembly Plant. When not needed, the chauffeur could also transport other Companion Company people to and from the airport or between their apartments and the assembly plant. Jim talked to Carlos who even agreed to furnish the limo and driver since it was all company related. Julia showed her appreciation that night when Jim told her about it.

Two days later, all the Companion Company employees received a text message from Carlos announcing an Initial Public Offering for the company. The IPO would initially consist of ten million shares and had been valued by several financial institutions at twenty dollars a share. Most employees seemed to ignore the message as they had no shares, but Jim and Julia were shocked, as their initial 49% stake in the company was now valued at 98 million dollars. They decided to take the rest of the day off to celebrate and invited everyone still at Winstone Tower to a celebration at Urban Potions. Everyone who could join them did and congratulated them on the huge windfall.

Six weeks later, Carlos couldn't be there for the official opening of the Companion Company Assembly Plant but arranged for a small party with some decorations in the cafeteria and a cake large enough for everyone there to have a piece. The staff had set up a large TV in the cafeteria and Carlos congratulated everyone via ZOOM on the completion of the move. He also hoped the new site would expedite the assembly process.

During the move, another 400 skeletons had arrived, and it took the workers some time to hang them all in preparation for installing their body parts. It was now Adrian and Meera's turn to feel overwhelmed when Technical Structures advised them the next delivery of the last 400 skeletons was "imminent".

It was not exactly a shock when Julia and Jim announced she was pregnant. Everyone congratulated them and wanted to know if they could take on some of their responsibilities so they could have more time together and rest some. Adrian officially became the primary contact for the hardware and Meera took over the preparation of the Companion folders (and modules) with Jim helping her until he felt she no longer needed his help. Once all the Companion folders were created, with a code for the type of Companion and recipient, Jim thought it interesting when the count showed 630 females for male recipients, 50 females for female recipients, 270 males for female recipients, and 50 males for male recipients.

After her doctor's suggestion that she limit stress and travel for a while, Julia's activities were limited to whatever she could do from her laptop or on the phone. Jim made brief visits to the assembly plant to ensure everything was going as well as could be expected and to meet with Kishoni from time to time to see if she had any concerns that he or Carlos needed to address. Technical Structures had delivered all the skeletons and most of the body parts and Carlos had hired more workers to help in the assembly. And as soon as their work permits were in hand, another 20 workers were helping in the assembly process.

There was a brief celebration in the cafeteria of the Assembly Building when the first one hundred Companions were completed and declared ready to be delivered to their recipients (all in Brazil). It was quite a sight to behold as the majority of the first Companions were female, and although they were similar in many aspects, they were all clearly different. Carlos chartered an airline to transport them and worked with immigration to get them all cleared as cargo (they didn't have any passports). The flight also included some workers who were eager to return to Brazil.

It was even more chaotic this time at the airport, when one hundred Companions were met by their recipients and the usual hugging and kissing ensued. Carlos was there just as an observer but was clearly happy the company seemed to be on track to deliver all the Companions in six more months.

CHAPTER 51

Companion Needed

Jim was in his office when the new receptionist called and told him two businessmen wanted to see him. Jim assumed it was Companion Company related and asked the new receptionist to escort them to the conference room, as the overall floor plan was still a mess. Carlos had stopped construction when he found the school for the assembly work. A few minutes later, they arrived in the conference room and saw Jim on a laptop.

"Mr. Jim McVie?"

Jim stood up, not certain who these men were or what they wanted. He replied cautiously. "Yes?"

A tall, burly man with close-cropped blond hair held out his hand, and Jim cautiously shook it. He was then handed an ID card. "I'm John Reeves, an agent with the Central Intelligence Agency, and this is George Hall, also with the agency." Hall was a little shorter but also quite muscular, with close-cropped brown hair and brown eyes.

Jim shook Hall's hand and then stared at the ID card. He had never seen an ID like that. "How do I know this is real? You could be working for a competitive company that is trying to steal confidential information."

Reeves laughed. "There is no company that can compete with the Companion Company. That's why we are here."

Jim motioned for them to sit down. "It's extremely unlikely that anything the company has done or will do in the future would attract the attention of the CIA."

"That's true, but it's not why we are here."

"Then why are you here, if you don't mind?"

"We've been watching your earlier projects and the new company with great interest."

"Then you do know, the Companions are automations whose only function is to provide comfort and company to people that have not been able to find that in the normal ways people find partners or even friends."

"Yes, we are well aware of exactly what a Companion is, and that is why we are here."

Jim shook his head. "I don't understand."

"We think an appropriately trained Companion could be an excellent gatherer of sensitive information that is critical to the security of the United States."

Jim laughed. "You can't be serious."

Reeves shifted in his chair to a more comfortable position. "Consider this. We know that Companions can speak any language with appropriate software and specialized training by a language consultant. We also are aware that there are male and female Companions and with appropriate software can be attractive to males or females. They are also beautiful but with appropriate disguises, could pass as anyone. All of these qualities are essential to imbed an operative into organizations we suspect are intending to harm the US, or its allies."

Jim shook his head. "You have humans that can do all those things. I assume you do know that a Companion can cost more than two million dollars. That would pay for a lot of training for conventional spies or operatives as you seem to call them."

Reeves smiled. "Yes, but we don't need a thousand like your current effort, or a hundred, or fifteen, or even ten, so cost is not really an issue that would stand in the way."

"How would a Companion go from a loving friend to an emotionless entity whose only job is to lie or cheat or do whatever is necessary to obtain what you want? It's almost the exact opposite of their current configuration and training."

"That's why we are here talking to you. We don't think anyone else knows the programming of a Companion like you, and you have demonstrated that you can change it as necessary when new parameters come into play."

He paused. "We also know about the little person Companion for Carlos Alvez's extended family in Brazil. If you can do that successfully, you can make the necessary changes we need."

Jim had instantly regretted ever agreeing to the little person Companion, but that was in the past, and he needed to move on. He also wondered how they knew about the little person Companion, as they had explicitly avoided any mention of it on websites or any public announcements. "What exactly is it that you want from me?

Reeves pulled a piece of paper from his suitcoat pocket and handed it to Jim. It was a confirmation email from the Companion Company thanking him for his order of a female Companion and putting down the required 20% deposit before the process for the Companion listed, would begin. The paper also noted that a model had been selected as a guide for the appearance. It even had an assembly number of 524. Jim had not been involved with that part in the latest activity, as Adrian had taken that over (a recipient had to pay the down payment and immediately select a model prior to allowing the work to begin).

Jim handed it back. "Okay, so you bought a Companion. I'm sure the CIA has appropriate resources to make the needed software changes to make your Companion the agent you need."

Reeves seemed undeterred. "We wouldn't be here if we could be brushed off so easily, Mr. McVie. We could have just called and asked for your help."

Jim had a sudden sinking feeling they were about to threaten him, or at least, offer a deal.

"What do you mean?"

"We could shut the Companion Company web site down if we wanted. All it takes is to convince a few congressmen or senators that the Companion Company is violating US laws and a high-level call from a US official to a similarly high-level official in the Brazilian government."

He handed Jim a list of "possible violations" that could be investigated. Jim shook his head. "Carlos Alvez's lawyers addressed all these issues before the company went public."

"He addressed them under Brazilian law, not US law."

Jim didn't know if that was true or not. Reeves noticed Jim seemed unsure and pressed the issue. "Look, all we need is a small amount of your time, and some of your wife's time, to discuss the changes needed in a few modules in the folder that you have already created for this Companion. And we are willing to pay a lot for it."

Jim looked up. "Don't get my wife involved."

"We wouldn't if we had all the time in the world, but we don't. We know you and your wife discussed the changes needed whenever a new combination of customer and Companion came up. We think it will go a lot faster with her involved."

Jim sat thinking. After a few minutes "what if we agree to this? How do I know you won't come back again and again for new angles for your operatives?"

Reeves looked at Hall who nodded. "We will sign an agreement that would be embarrassing for the agency if it became public. If you agree, we will give you two million dollars now and three million dollars more when you say the Companion is ready. And, if we come back and ask for additional help, we'll give you five million more, just for asking. Doesn't that sound like we are serious about a one-time deal?"

"You do know this would be extremely damaging for the Companion Company if a CIA operative were found to be a Companion built by this company. Every recipient, especially businessmen and businesswomen would wonder if their Companion were secretly spying on them, for some reason."

"We are fully aware of that. We would do everything we can to prevent that from happening and to ensure the Companion is safe." He paused. "All we need right now is a handshake, then when the Companion comes to us, we will send her to you, and we'll have a final briefing with you and wife, so we are all on the same page. So, what do you say, Mr. McVie?"

Jim thought of the horrendous impact if the company's web site were shut down for an undetermined amount of time and he knew he would regret it, but he stood up, and when Reeves stood up, he shook his hand and then with George Hall.

They left and Jim went to the penthouse to tell Julia everything. He hoped she wouldn't get too upset, in her condition.

Operative

It wasn't easy, but Jim began by handing Reeve's ID card to her and then told her everything he could remember about the meeting with Reeves and Hall. Most of the time she just stared at him in disbelief. When he told her about her role with him to make the needed software changes, she clearly was not happy.

"How do you know these people are who they say they are?"

"How could they possibly know everything about the project, even the fact that you and I always talked about software changes needed as new combinations of customer and Companion came up? They even knew about the little person Companion."

It was almost a sudden revelation, but Janet asked. "Maybe they were behind the kidnapping of the team that went to measure and photograph the little person for Benigna?"

Jim was shocked. "Of course, why didn't I think of that? So, do we cooperate with them, or not?"

She shook her head. "I don't know. I just wish there was some way we could verify Reeves and Hall are actually with the CIA."

She searched the internet and found a way to verify Reeves and Hall, by utilizing the Employment Verification Office. As a manager and employer, Jim could request verification of their employment. There was even a number to call. After he successfully verified Reeves and Hall's employment, all they could do was wait until they contacted him. Jim told Julia that Reeves was in operations and Hall was in accounting. She then told him two million dollars had been deposited into their checking account.

The Companion Project was now in high gear as they were delivering more than 150 Companions each month to their recipients. The previous projects had learned the hard way about delivery and each recipient assumed responsibility for delivering their Companion to their home city or country.

Shortly after the project delivered the 600th Companion, Jim received an email from Reeves who presented himself as just another supplier to the project, and informed him, his "product" would be arriving shortly. True to his word, the next day the receptionist texted Jim that "Marisela" was waiting at the front desk to speak to him. When he went to meet her, he was surprised at first as he was certain she was Maria. A closer look confirmed she was not Maria and a quick conversation confirmed that she was there to be "upgraded" by Jim and Julia. None of the current Companions could have said that, as they had never met or seen Jim or Julia.

He led her to the workroom and texted Julia that their special visitor was here. Julia was a little surprised at first as well, as Marisela looked almost the same as Maria, with long dark curly hair and dark eyes, a gorgeous figure, and other similarly attractive features. She was also wearing a fashionable dress and even some simple jewelry.

Even while they were chatting with Marisela, Jim received another text that two businessmen were waiting at the front desk to talk to him. He guessed who they were and texted her back, asking her to take them to the conference room.

John Reeves and George Hall were standing by the table in the conference room and they both stared in amazement at Marisela when she entered, as they had never seen a Companion. Jim introduced them and Reeves laughed. "Now I can see why you have no competition." He suddenly blurted out. "My God, she is beautiful."

Marisela ran to him, put her arms around him and kissed him. When she let go and backed up, Jim had to tell him. "They respond to compliments or gifts. She chose to kiss you."

Reeves looked shocked and Julia laughed as she had heard that explanation before. "Let's sit down." She needed to sit as she was now almost 5 months pregnant.

When they were seated, Reeves handed Jim a list of "skills" Marisela would need for her assignment. Some were expected, like knowledge of firearms, but not necessarily an expert. They also wanted her to have some skills in Martial Arts to be able to protect herself. Other expected skills included lockpicking ability and the ability to climb a fence and run 100 meters within a certain time. Jim did not expect skills such as in the art of seduction (not romantically, but to earn the trust of a suspect) or the ability to read and write computer code. The list went on and Jim handed it to Julia.

"You probably know that we have no staff or facilities here to do any of the training needed for those operative skills, as they are not needed for Companion training."

"Yes, that's fine. We can provide that. All we need to know is that she can learn those skills. Once that's done, we will take it from there."

Marisela was listening to everything until there was a pause. "What is an operative?" Reeves and Hall laughed, but Jim and Julia didn't.

"Someone who can gather information needed to protect this country against people or organizations that want to harm it."

Jim thought that answer came right out of an agent manual. "Ok. Let's say we can add certain modules, and you can do the required training, what if it doesn't work as well as you expect?"

"We are prepared for that, as well. We will do everything we can to make sure she is safe. Now, we just need to know if you can add whatever is needed to her programming, and how long it will take."

Jim and Julia had discussed the nature of the request, and even how long it would take, and Julia replied. "We can do it. Probably in less than two months. We have a lot of other things going on here as you can see." She rubbed her stomach.

Reeves smiled. "That's wonderful. Congratulations, by the way. So, let us know if you need any additional information. We will leave you to it." He looked at Marisela who was staring at him with beautiful clear brown eyes. "Darn. I wish I had a few million to spare."

Jim laughed as they left.

Julia thought out loud. "The response to compliments is hard-coded. What if she 'seduces' the target who then compliments her, or gives her expensive gifts?"

Jim shrugged. "We can't change that. They will have to work around it."

Marisela listened carefully and commented. "You can turn off that feature in code."

Jim gasped. "How would you know that?"

Marisela shrugged. "Meera told me. We talked a lot before I left the Assembly Plant. She has been studying AI for a while and seems to know a lot about AI hardware."

Jim took her to the library to wait and watch TV, while they discussed the skills list and the possible modules needed to make those skills possible. He also called "Max" at Synthesis AI to ask if it were possible to turn off the initiative response as he had been told it was hard coded. Max assured him it was possible and texted him a simple routine to turn the initiator response off (or on). Jim felt relieved as he was sure the automatic response might compromise Marisela in some undercover operations.

He also made sure Julia was always comfortable and didn't spend too much time on the list, or on her feet, and after a week or so, they had defined the modules they thought would need to be added or modified.

He alternated between checking on the Companion Company Assembly Plant efforts and working on new modules for the next three weeks, while Julia mostly rested.

He also called Adrian at the Assembly Plant and asked him to check on the order details for Companion 524. Adrian asked why and when Jim said it was a matter of national security, Adrian laughed, and Jim laughed as well. After a few minutes, Adrian also said that Companion went to an unnamed person in Washington, DC. He also said that, strangely, the recipient had requested the Companion to have the ability to speak in two languages (other than English) Greek and French, which Adrian said was sort of unique. He also said the recipient had paid an extra charge for the additional language without any questions. Adrian surprised Jim when he said that out of curiosity, he had searched for the recipient, and he appeared to be working as an assistant to the Director of National Intelligence. Jim thanked him and sat thinking for a while, wondering why Marisela would need to speak Greek and French.

Jim was finally ready, and hoped there wouldn't be any negative effects on Marisela when he downloaded the modified and new modules. When he finished, he waited anxiously to see the effects, but there were none. Marisela went back to watching TV with no apparent effect. How could he check to see if she had these new skills or capabilities?

Julia suggested they hire a Martial Arts instructor for a few days to see if she had any inherent skills or interest in that activity. There were a lot of empty rooms now in the office and lab area they could use for the training, and it was easy to find an instructor to test Marisela's interest in self-defense. Jim even found a martial arts uniform for her and watched as the instructor put her through all the basic moves, especially those related to self-defense. After a few days, Jim met with the instructor to ask for an evaluation. He had specifically not told him that she was a Companion (and all that meant) as everyone now seemed to know exactly what a Companion was.

The instructor complimented Marisela and said that she was a fast learner and did seem to show interest in more advanced moves. He was impressed that she had never had any formal instruction in Martial Arts.

If he didn't know better, he said he would have assumed she had some training when she was "younger". Jim tried not to laugh.

They agreed on a few more days of training, to complete what the instructor called his intermediate program. Jim wondered how all this training would affect her basic code to be a comfort and Companion to a recipient. He did check her response at the end of the week by (truthfully) calling her the most beautiful Martial Arts expert had had ever seen. She immediately ran to him, put her arms around him and kissed him. Then unexpectedly started looking at herself in a mirror while she practiced some Martial Arts moves. As he watched her, Jim was glad that Nu Skin's latest product was more resistant to injury and after small cuts and minor burns, could even repair itself.

While all that seemed to indicate the new modules had helped her learn new skills, it didn't confirm she was "ready" for Reeves. He needed to evaluate one more skill on the list. It was a lot harder to find a locksmith willing to come to the lab and teach Marisela simple lockpicking skills. Jim had to offer him a "bonus" at the end to even get him to show up. Once he did, he just seemed to stare at Marisela, until Jim reminded him why he was there. When he asked Jim why she needed that skill, Jim told him she was his sister-in-law and had applied to be a private investigator and needed to demonstrate certain skills before they would hire her.

Jim stopped by every day to check on them and each time Marisela was actively working to unlock a series of locks the locksmith had provided with his tool kit. After three days, he asked the locksmith about Marisela's progress. The locksmith complimented her on determination and effort but said it would take a little while longer before she was an expert at picking locks. He also told Jim it was hard to work near her as she was "hot" and her looks, and perfume were very distracting. Jim told him he totally understood what he meant.

After discussing both activities with Julia, they agreed there really wasn't anything else they could do in the lab, as both agreed they didn't want to bring weapons into the lab. The next day, Jim called Reeves. He explained everything they had done and asked him what else they could do (that was not firearm related). Reeves was extremely happy the changes were completed, and tested, so quickly. He said there wasn't anything else they needed to do, and he would send someone to transport her immediately to Langley, Virginia for further training. He also said the agreed 2nd payment would be sent later that day to their personal account.

The next day, Marisela waved goodbye to Jim before she got into black Suburban for a quick trip to the airport. Jim returned to the penthouse and the first question Julia asked was "did you remember to turn off the stimulus response in code?"

Jim smiled. Nothing about Marisela or her leaving or anything you might say when someone you know is leaving and you may never see them again. Only did you remember to fix her response issue. "Yes, of course. I didn't want that weighing on my mind if something happened to her."

CHAPTER 53

Marisela?

A month passed and Julia was spending most of her time in the penthouse condo as she was now seven months pregnant. Jim continued to follow the activities at the Assembly Plant daily with calls to Adrian, Meera and Kishoni. There was a small celebration each time they delivered another one hundred Companions. Happily, there were only two hundred Companions left to finish, and all hardware had been received and installed and Meera was downloading the software modules to two or three Companions each day.

On a seemingly routine day, Julia urgently called Jim to come to the penthouse. He first thought something was wrong with Julia's pregnancy and raced to her side, but she was watching a news bulletin about a major incident at the European Parliament building in Brussels, Belgium. The Greek representative had been preparing to present yet another declaration about a possible exit from the EU (known as Grexit) this time over proposed European Union immigration policies. Proposals for a Greek Exit had been done numerous times over the last decade but almost always over financial issues with the European Union over bank loans, outstanding Greek debt and leaving the Euro and returning to the Drachma. Each time the proposal had been soundly rejected by the EU parliament. The news report indicated this proposal would undoubtedly have been rejected as well.

More disturbing was the revelation that there had been a foiled assassination attempt on the Greek representative to try and stop the presentation. The details were still not clear, but the person who was killed was a member of one of the opposition parties in Greece. Papers found on the body included a statement condemning the Greek representative as a "traitor" who had to be stopped. A reporter questioned how the assassination attempt on the representative had even been discovered, and more importantly how had the assassin been killed inside the EU Parliament Building before he could even approach the Greek representative.

Police had no information on the person or persons stopping the assassination, or their whereabouts. The only information so far, came from a maintenance staff member who thought he saw an unfamiliar woman in that area just before the body was discovered.

Jim and Julia just stared at each other, hoping it was not Marisela and that she would not be discovered if it were.

Jim's nightmare continued when Reeves called him to thank them for the speed of their software modifications on the "urgent" matter. Jim was relieved when Reeves said he would not have to make any additional payments as there would be no follow-up requests for help. Julia was even more relieved as she didn't need that kind of complication.

Two months later, there was a big celebration at the Assembly Plant when the last group of one hundred of the one thousand Companions were completed and declared ready to deliver to their recipients.

Jim really wished he could be there, but Julia had just gone into labor and their limousine probably broke some speed limits on the way to the hospital. Luckily, they made it in time, and a healthy baby girl was born to the delight of everyone in the delivery room.

The baby was in the nursery and Julia was asleep when Jim found a bank of vending machines near the waiting room. His cell phone rang, and Adrian congratulated him. After some small talk on the current condition of the baby and Julia, Adrian said he had another reason for calling.

Jim frowned. "What's going on?"

"Do you remember asking me about Companion 524?"

Jim was wondering why Adrian was asking about Marisela. "Yes, what about her?"

"I received a strange call today from someone asking for background information about Companion 655. I told them we can't give out information like that without a court order. He said he would get one and hung up. So, I looked up 655 and the details on the recipients are not the same but similar. Companion 655's recipient lives in Fredericksburg, Virginia. I wasn't familiar with that city, so I searched for it, and it happens to be very close to Quantico Virginia. I also looked the guy up and he is an assistant to the Director of the FBI. What do you think that means?"

Jim was drinking a soda and choked on it. "Shit!"

"What's wrong, Jim?"

"I can't really talk about it, but it means something I hoped was over, probably isn't." He paused. "By the way, what language did the Fredericksburg guy order for 655?"

Adrian paused, looking at the details. "It looks like he also paid for two languages, Arabic and French. Also, I don't know if it matters, but that Companion is male."

"Oh, it matters, it all matters. Okay, Adrian. Thanks for the update."

As soon as the call ended, Jim almost ran to Julia's room to check on her. He decided he wouldn't bother her immediately with Adrian's news.

CHAPTER 54

The Escape

Jim now dreaded receiving phone calls and he was happy when he only received a few work-related calls during the next two days. They took turns holding the baby and she had no idea why he seemed so jumpy whenever his phone rang.

Once she seemed strong enough, he told her Adrian's news about Companion 655. She was clearly not happy. "What are we going to do?"

"I've been thinking. Why don't we take a round-the-world trip, kind of like Hugh Adler did? We could turn off the ship's transponder so they wouldn't know where we are, and only accept calls from people in our contacts list, like Adrian and Meera?"

She thought for a while. "We have a newborn Jim."

"I know but she would now be the center of everything. We could even bring two or three nurses with us in the beginning, and a nanny or two later when she's older."

Julia couldn't think of any viable alternatives. "Ok, let's see if we can get away before they find us."

Jim laughed, and then called Jared Sandoval to discuss their idea of a round-the-world tour on the yacht and to ask if he could find two local nurses who would be willing to be away from home for a year or more. Jared said he had a friend who was a nurse and could help with that. He also said there may be premium associated with it, and Jim said it wasn't a problem. He also told Sandoval that if all went well, he would give the crew a 25% bonus on their return. Jared said the crew would be very happy to hear that.

Jim now avoided all calls except for those in his contact list as they made final preparations to leave. He searched the internet for the best way to stop your phone from being tracked and purchased a Virtual Private Network (VPN) for his phone. This would encrypt all his communications and make it virtually impossible for anyone (friend or foe) to track him.

He felt he should let Carlos know what had happened without being too specific, and called to ask him if they could use his helicopter one more time. Carlos understood and said he would call the pilot immediately and wished them a happy voyage. He almost sounded jealous, and Jim chuckled. His parting comment shocked Jim. "You are leaving at an opportune moment for the company. We just confirmed orders for 1000 more Companions."

Jim stifled a comment and went to tell Julia the latest Companion Company news.

In a coordinated move, the company limousine delivered a lot of luggage they probably would need for a one to two-year voyage while the helicopter pilot gathered their baby bag and two carry-on bags. Julia handed the baby to Jim before she stepped out onto the helipad of their very well-maintained and immaculately clean yacht. The crew were very happy to see them and thanked them several times for all the short-term rental money they shared with them when the yacht wasn't being used.

In a special meeting with the captain, Jared Sandoval informed Jim his team of three private security guards had arrived with several crates of materials. He also said they asked to be berthed with the crew, and that their material be stored near the rear of the yacht. Jason didn't ask why but he did ask Jim if he was expecting problems on the world tour and Jim just said they might have to sail through straits and passages where no one would think of looking for them. Jared didn't want to pursue the issue and just said he would be careful in those situations. Jim also surprised Sandoval by giving him a debit card to pay for lunches for all the staff, nurses and security personnel whenever they were in port.

When Jim returned to the newly converted nursery, he smiled when he saw two female staff members taking turns cradling the baby and even singing to her. Julia had dozed off in a comfortable chair near the crib.

As soon as the baby was asleep, one of the nurses motioned them all to leave the nursery. Jim woke Julia and they soon watched the crew undock the yacht and the captain back it out of the mooring slip.

It was a little cool, so they put on jackets and sunglasses and watched the Gulf waters slide by from a forward deck. Jim reminded her of Carlos' statement that they would probably sail off into the sunset on their yacht once the Companion Company no longer needed them. She laughed and he put his arm around her waist. She surprised him by pulling a tube of flavored lubricant from her jacket and showing it to him. He started laughing. "Are you trying to tell me something?"

One week later, the yacht made its first mooring in the Turks and Caicos Islands. Jim and Julia and most of the crew and two members of the security team, went ashore and into town for shopping and dining in several restaurants. Jim found a small grocery store and purchased a few "burner" cell phones "just in case" he needed them. He activated them and joined the rest of the crew, the security team and Julia as they returned to the yacht.

After checking on Julia and the nurse with the baby, he went out on the top deck to think a bit, then opened the VPN and entered a number. Adrian received a text message that only contained his birthdate and a private phone number. He quickly called back and was relieved when Jim answered.

"Jim, I'm so glad you called."

"Hi Adrian, how's everything? I heard from Carlos a week ago the Company had accepted down payments for another 1000 Companions."

Adrian paused. "Yes, that's going okay, but there is something else I need to tell you."

That was worrisome, but Jim wanted to know. "What is it?"

"I have a friend who is a hacker of sorts, but he just does it for fun, not to cause problems or for money. Right after you left, I asked him to check on the actual recipients for the Companion Company's first 1000 Companions and specifically mentioned Companions 524 and 655 as the reason I asked. He said he would and last night he called to tell me what he found. You're not going to believe this, but at least 30 of the recipients are working for other governments, either in intelligence or internal security, sort of like our CIA and FBI. He also said there were a similar number of suspicious LLCs and several entities that could be a cover for some really bad guys."

He knew that wasn't all and could feel his heart racing. "What else?"

"We've also started getting court orders and people asking questions about the Companions. The questions seem harmless enough at first, but if you think about them, they are all really asking about you and your phone number and address. It's a good thing you are using a VPN on your cell phone."

After a deep breath, Jim guessed there was more, and asked "what else?"

"According to security at the Winstone Office Tower, several people have been trying to go to your penthouse apartment, but they manage to stop them each time. They are really trying to find you, Jim. What are you going to do?"

Jim thought he heard a faint echo in the background and wondered if they were tapping Adrian's phone. He wondered if he could throw the seekers off some. "I will come right back and straighten this mess out. Thanks for all your help, Adrian."

The yacht was backing out of their mooring berth to head to their next destination and he re-opened the VPN and texted Adrian his birthdate, told him he thought his phone might be tapped and to get a VPN and text him back when he received a new text from a private number with his birthdate. He also said they now would be heading for "parts unknown" and thanked him once more.

He found Julia rocking their baby to sleep and when she put her in the crib, he motioned her to follow him. In the living room, he brought her up to date on Adrian's call and the fact that it seemed the whole world was now looking for him.

Julia shrugged. "As long as they don't find you, all they have are some expensive friends who are just waiting for a compliment or a gift to show their appreciation."

He smiled at her analogy. As he thought about it, only Reeves and the CIA had a functioning "operative". All the others were just good friends to whoever wanted them for other purposes.

"Remind me at the next stop to buy some more burner phones, just in case."

Julia laughed as Jim opened the VPN on his phone and called Reeves. He was surprised that Reeves actually answered. Jim then filled him in on Companion 655 and the hacker's latest information that at least 30 foreign government's intelligence or home security agencies now had a Companion and were desperately trying to find him. He also told him about the similar number of potential bad guys who had purchased Companions. Reeves was shocked but listed carefully as Jim finished with a question.

"Has anyone at the Agency shared information about your Companion with any other branch of government like the FBI?"

Reeves thought about it for a moment. "Not to my knowledge, why?"

"If other organizations friendly or not, find out about her, they might take drastic steps to acquire her, or her programming for Companions they purchased, for whatever purpose they have in mind."

Reeves paused briefly. "I see what you are saying, and we'll make sure no one has access to her like that. By the way, I'm sure by now you know that her mission was a complete success. Our contacts in the EU don't know exactly how we did it but were extremely grateful for our help. If that Greek representative had been killed, it would have generated an enormous amount of sympathy and support for his cause."

"Is she safe?"

"Oh yes, completely." He laughed. "A few of her protectors are wishing you would turn that stimulus response back on while they wait for her next assignment. Right now, they don't mess with her. They are afraid if they do, she will whip their ass."

Jim laughed. "Ok, just keep her safe. And don't call me – I'll call you." Reeves laughed as he hung up.

Jim sat thinking about the future. He needed to extricate himself from the desire of many organizations to change a Companion into an operative. He kept thinking about Marisela. Why couldn't the CIA have used a conventional operative to kill the assassin? He even went over the question with Julia, who started a question-and-answer session that would hopefully find the difference. "What is different about Marisela than other operatives?"

He stated the obvious to start. "She isn't human, but that can't be it."

She thought for a moment. "No, but the latest hardware, including the storage tank and all the motors parts are now made out of Graphene, so there isn't enough metal in her or on her that could set off a metal detector."

He was getting into the session. "And a conventional operative could not smuggle a handgun or a knife into the building."

Julia smiled as Jim seemed eager to play the Q&A game. "Marisela also has demonstrated Martial Arts skills…"

"And she could knock out the assassin even if he were armed, as he wouldn't think a beautiful petite young woman was a threat and be on guard against her."

She smiled. "All it would take is a well-placed blow."

He stared at her for a moment. "Or is she strong enough to strangle someone?"

Julia suddenly laughed. "Oh yes, and then some."

He just shook his head. "No wonder Reeves wanted those skills. I wonder what's next for her."

"More importantly, what's next for you, and us?"

"I don't know, but we have a few more days before we reach our next stop where we'll be in range of a cell tower. Maybe we can figure out something by then."

CHAPTER 55

Hiding on The World Tour

Three days later as they were approaching their next port of call, Charlotte Amalie Harbor on Saint Thomas in the US Virgin Islands. Jim was sitting in a deck chair wracking his brain to find a solution. A possibility came to mind. He opened the VPN on his phone and as soon as it had a few reception bars, called Max at Synthesis AI. Max had signed an NDA for the original Companion Project and Jim began by telling him they had a "problem" Companion who would barely respond to any stimulus and asked if it were possible to adjust the stimulus response in code, sort of like the feature Max had helped him with before, to turn the stimulus response off and on from code. Max thought for a moment.

"Yes, it's possible, but it would have to be a trial-and-error type of adjustment to find the exact amount of increased response needed."

"That's great, Max. Could you text me the software script for that, at this number? I would really appreciate it."

"Sure, no problem. Just give me a few minutes to find it."

Jim stood up and paced impatiently for the text and breathed a huge sigh of relief when he received it, just as they approached the harbor and the mooring berth. Now, he had to test the code on a Companion. He opened the VPN on his phone and texted Meera her Companion assembly number and asked her to have Adrian call him at this number with the VPN on his phone, as he didn't want to get Meera involved with his problems.

Adrian called right back, and Jim explained his idea and asked if there was a Companion that had just received the final product code that they could test it on. He heard Adrian laugh.

"Yes, there are two available right now. It might be interesting to adjust one and see the difference."

"That would be perfect. How long do you think it would take to do that?"

"Not long at all." He laughed. "If it works, I might adjust Meera a bit. She's wearing me out."

Jim laughed. "Great. Call me when you have the results." He then texted Adrian the codes for decreasing and increasing the response of a Companion and when he received a "sent" confirmation, he turned off his phone "just in case".

The yacht pulled into the port and the crew, one nurse and two security team members left with Jim and Julia to tour the harbor stores and restaurants. Jim found a grocery store and was able to activate several more burner phones "just in case". He laughed as it seemed burner phones were readily available in every port of call. With a little help from Jared Sandoval and a local tour guide, they went on a snorkeling tour and an island tour. He had asked the crew not to bring any phones off the ship but two days later when they were backing out of the harbor berth, he smiled as he noticed almost every member of the crew was on a cell phone, probably with family and friends.

He opened his VPN and texted Adrian's with his birthdate, and he soon called back on his VPN.

"Great news, Jim. Those scripts work like a charm. We can now set the level of response to any level we want."

"Did you adjust Meera?"

"I was going to, but decided I really like our current relationship, and so does she. So, for now, I'm leaving it the same."

"Ok, thanks for the update. Could you send me a summary of what you found when you used the codes for increasing and decreasing the level of response?"

"On its way as soon as we hang up."

Once he received the report from Adrian, he turned off his phone and went to check on Julia and the baby.

A little later they were on an upper deck watching the ships in the harbor pass by and he told Julia the good news. She seemed not that impressed. "Ok, so what are you going to do with it now?" She smiled. "You know you can't adjust me..."

"I wouldn't want to. You are just what I want. I'm going to call Carlos and ask for a favor."

She suddenly put her arms around him and kissed him. "See, you don't need to adjust me."

He laughed and went up on the top deck to call Carlos before they were out of range of the cell tower. Jim texted Carlos with "Companions building Companions".

A few minutes later Carlos called and said he was happy to hear from him and started filling him in on the latest 1000 Companions they were assembling, until Jim interrupted him.

"You didn't ask why I'm calling on a private number."

Carlos hesitated. "Ok, why are you calling on a private number?"

"Here is why..." Jim then filled him in on as much as he could without endangering him or possibly putting him at risk from the organizations looking for him. Carlos was shocked that so many of the first 1000 were ordered by foreign government agencies and even more that a similar number were ordered by possibly dangerous organizations. After a while, he was curious as to why Jim called.

"I may have a possible out for me and Julia, but I need your help."

"Anything I can do…"

Jim explained the code to increase and decrease the stimulus response and asked if Carlos could find a way to put out the "increase" code on the internet, and label it as "turn off the response". Jim hoped these organizations would try the code and make their Companions even more responsive to compliments, or gifts, and not less. That response would have to be turned off, as Jim had done, for a Companion to become useful as an operative, who would do whatever is necessary to complete the mission.

Carlos said he knew someone who could help with that, and that he hoped it worked and they could return to their former status. He also hoped they enjoyed the rest of their vacation. Jim immediately texted him the "increase the response" code, and smiled as he ended the text and received a "sent" confirmation.

In his testing summary, Adrian forgot to mention that repeated attempts to increase (or decrease) the stimulus response was additive. Repeated attempts to turn it off, that actually increased the response each time, could make a Companion so responsive to stimuli, she or he might even initiate actions on their own.

After checking on the baby and Julia, Jim was relaxing on a chair on the top deck as the yacht left the harbor and a thought came to mind. He opened the VPN and called the financial guy on his previous employment again and asked if there had been any update on Carlos Alvez businesses. His contact said a friend in Brazil recently told him Carlos had a new financial advisor who was pushing him to invest in new technology companies that were making him much more money than his sugar cane and coffee bean plantations. At the current rate of investment returns, Carlos could soon be the richest person in Brazil. Jim was shocked but thanked his friend for the update.

Just before he was out of range of the cell tower, he texted Adrian to ask his hacker friend if he could put out the "increase the response" code on the internet, and even on the "dark net", but label it as "turn off the response".

He had just completed that, and received a "sent" confirmation, when he lost reception. He turned his phone off and went inside to check on Julia and the baby. Now all he could do was wait.

Unknown to Jim or Julia, the incorrectly labeled "increase" code quickly spread all over the internet and almost every organization or group that had acquired a Companion for the wrong purpose was now trying to use it to "turn off" the stimulus response.

At their next port of call a few days later, Jim texted Adrian to see if he had heard anything about the falsely labeled code. Adrian laughed. His hacker friend read some of the chatter on the internet and the dark net and some had reported Companions "going crazy" and acting like "promiscuous women or men" (although he had used a more vulgar term). The general consensus was that most organizations, and especially the shady LLCs and groups, were likely abandoning any hope of using Companions for covert type activities. His friend actually found a few places where he could find a Companion (in its current state) for a few thousand dollars. He even asked Adrian for the actual "decrease the response" code, as he really would like to buy a Companion for a few thousand dollars.

Adrian summarized by saying it looked like the code had worked and he hoped that Jim would not be bothered anymore.

Jim turned his phone off and immediately went to tell Julia the good news. She was rocking the baby and whispered they could celebrate when the baby was asleep.

At the next port of call, St Bart's, he opened his VPN and called Reeves to see if he had heard anything.

Reeves answered and congratulated Jim on thwarting so many organizations and shady groups' desire to use Companions as specialized operatives and even weapons to obtain whatever information, or changes they had in mind. He also said they had not used the falsely labeled code on Marisela as she already had her response turned off. In retrospect he was glad they didn't as he didn't want a Martial Arts expert overreacting to the slightest stimuli from her protectors. Her protectors had another view of course and wished they could have used the false code on her.

Reeves ended by thanking Jim for eliminating a real threat of Companions being used by shady groups for nefarious ends.

The crew, one of the nurses, and the security team had wandered off to the shopping area and some restaurants they heard were excellent. Julia was standing near him and when he ended the call with Reeves, updated her with Reeve's assessment and the latest on Marisela.

"So, are we finally able to go home whenever we want?"

"Over ninety percent chance. It'll take a few more days to know for sure. But we could continue the world tour and go wherever we want without looking over our shoulders."

She took his hand. "We can think about that tomorrow. For now, you can take me shopping. I heard there are some really nice shops near here."

Jim winced. "Ok, if you agree we celebrate our newfound freedom tonight."

She put her other hand in the pocket of her jacket and pulled out a tube of flavored lubricant and showed it to him with a questioning look.

He laughed. "Do you always carry that around?"

"Only when I'm with you."

The End